A BEAUTY QUEEN'S GUIDE TO MURDER AND MAYHEM

KRISTEN BIRD

Storm

PUBLISHING

Ebook ISBN: 978-1-80508-896-7
Paperback ISBN: 978-1-80508-898-1

Cover design: Lisa Horton
Cover images: Shutterstock

Published by Storm Publishing.
For further information, visit:
www.stormpublishing.co

ALSO BY KRISTEN BIRD

Dakota Green

A Beauty Queen's Guide to Murder and Mayhem

An Heiress's Guide to Death and Diamonds

A Bride's Guide to Happiness and Homicide

The Night She Went Missing

I Love It When You Lie

Watch It Burn

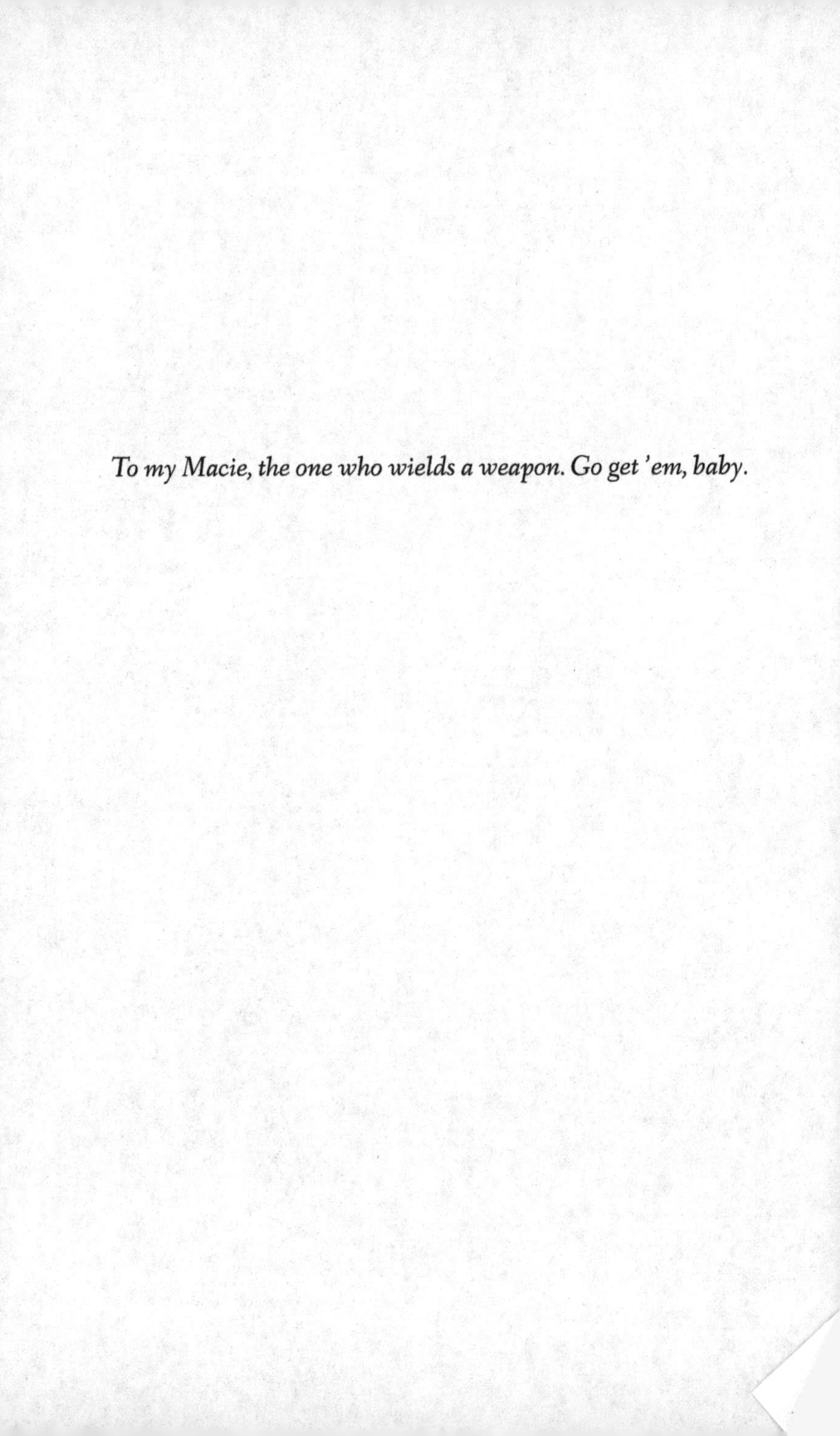

To my Macie, the one who wields a weapon. Go get 'em, baby.

MONDAY
MOMMA'S LETTER, MONTH ELEVEN

Dakota,

It's been eleven months since you buried me. Grab a pint of butter pecan and curl up on the sofa with Bucket. Play Dolly's "Mama" and keep a box of tissues nearby. Go ahead, sweetheart.

I'm serious.

I'll wait.

Now then, once you're settled, let's begin.

When I found out I was having a daughter on my own at forty, I swore two things: First, that I'd still hold my head high at First Baptist every Sunday, and second, that you would never doubt that I was your partner in crime. Me, you, and your aunt: the Green Girls. I never planned for you to be the one taking care of me, and I never wanted to leave you like this. For goodness' sake, now I'm mostly bald and worn slap-out even on my good days.

I trust you've done each of the ten assignments in my previous letters, but those—the starlit campout with Lacy, the fancy dinner with Aunt DeeDee, the ride through the mountains with Bella—those were a nice way to remember your roots. Call upon those good moments, savor them, cause you're not going to like this month's request. (But none of this coming to my graveside and cursing me out, you hear?)

Look, I know that by now, financially, things are tight. I'd like to think you've gone back to school, but even then, you won't be able to cover your student loans or those credit card bills you hid from me. If the debt collectors haven't started calling yet, they'll be on you soon.

So, here goes. Deep breath—you, not me (sorry, I can't help myself).

In just a few days, I need you to compete in the Rose Palace Pageant.

I know, I know, but it's the closest and fastest way for you to get the money you need. With less than a week of effort, you can win enough to keep the house and pay off those pesky student loans and that pile of bills. Then, you can start that new life that I wish for you.

I'm sure this isn't what you expected me to ask. I know you've heard the stories of the disappearing pageant queen, and I realize you've never been a fan of that great big house on the edge of town—the turrets and towers have always given me the spooks too. But I went round and round with your Aunt DeeDee about this idea, and she swears on my grave that competing in the pageant is the best way for you to get money fast (unless you want to rob the bank downtown). She also promises that she can turn you into a winner.

Inside this envelope you'll find the completed registration and all fees paid for competition in the Centennial Rose Palace Pageant, and at the top of that form, you'll see your name.

So, no. This is not a joke. I know it's been a hard year, but I promise this: All will be well. Especially if you obey your mother. Remember, family matters most.

All my love,
Momma

ONE

One of the best things about working with animals is that they aren't people. I don't care who you are, deep down you know people are overrated and not worth all that emotional energy. I bet if you'd asked Mother Teresa—basically the best person ever —whether she'd rather spend a day with a mare or one of those ladies from *Real Housewives*, she would've chosen the horse.

That's what I was telling Bella, a brown and white American Paint, before almost turning her around and taking her back out to ride. I'd noticed a pair of arms resting on the side of the corral, and even though I didn't feel like chatting with another human, those brown arms and that dark head of spiraling curls were as familiar as my own reflection. If any person can be tolerated, I suppose it's Lacy.

We'd bonded in kindergarten when I got my first pet, a cat that had belonged to one of Momma's hospice patients. When I'd told the other kids its morbid origins, half my classmates made faces and the other half stopped talking to me. Except for Lacy. She asked what the kitty looked like and how old did I think it was and what had I named it. *Bucket, as in "kicked the —"* I'd said with a grin. Lacy and I had been best friends ever since, and on this particular day, I knew she had something for me.

"Hey, I brought your next letter," Lacy called, as I hopped down and closed the gate. Because it was a sunny day with only the slightest breeze, dust and dirt floated up, threatening to coat us both.

I gave her a curt nod, acting like I wasn't craving the words inside the envelope in her hand. "I've still got another hour here."

Lacy tried to stomp off her Jimmy Choos—I only know the brand because she refers to her shoes like they're people. We are very different.

"You can spare five minutes," Lacy drawled, as she examined her heels. "They barely pay you a living wage."

Circling the paddock, I began Bella's cool-down and ignored the comment. "What's the letter say this time?" I called over my shoulder.

Lacy's mouth hung in faux appall. "How dare you insinuate that I would open something addressed to you."

I circled back, and she handed over the parcel. My mother's distinctive scrawl brought a fresh wave of grief, but I blinked against tears and attempted levity. "I'm not insinuating. I'm saying that I know you read them."

Lacy's eyes were playful. "Just because the letters from your dead mother have already been opened and retaped when you get them, doesn't mean I'm a snoop."

"Uh-huh." I leaned against the galvanized bars of the corral. Bella nuzzled my shoulder as if she wanted to read the contents.

It was the eleventh such letter I'd received in as many months. Momma knew that if she'd given me all twelve—one for each month after her death—I would've read them in one sitting and then stayed in bed for weeks. This way, I could wean myself off her voice.

"You know I only read them because she told me to," Lacy

said, as I slid my sun-kissed finger underneath the lip of the envelope. "She said at least one person needed to know what she was asking you to do, to make sure you didn't become a complete hermit. I think you should read this one sitting down."

So I did. I plopped my butt onto the hard earth as Bella huffed out a breath, blowing my long brown ponytail.

"Not what I meant." Lacy squatted next to me.

My eyes scanned the contents like someone dying of thirst after a day in three-digit heat seeing an oasis.

Dakota,

Huh. Momma usually called me "Honeybee" because I'd overcome my fear of them—and because from the time I could walk, I loved helping her in our back garden, filled with vegetables, peach trees, blueberry bushes, and wildflowers. *Dakota* meant that this one must be serious.

It's been eleven months since you buried me. Grab a pint of butter pecan and curl up on the sofa with Bucket.

The corner of my mouth lifted. I could almost see the look on Momma's face—the pert nose, the dimple in her left cheek that I'd inherited, the thin lips turned into a nearly constant smile—as she wrote the words.

After I finished reading, I gave back the letter to Lacy and stood, reaching out a hand to stroke the white on the bridge of Bella's nose, acting as if Momma hadn't just asked me to do something utterly ridiculous.

Lacy watched me with a practiced eye. Like most people in our tiny hamlet she viewed the Rose Palace Pageant as a harmless pastime. She'd never competed, said she refused to be the token Black girl in the show's PR pics, but this year she'd been contracted to be the event coordinator. She suddenly cared about the show because she was kind of in charge of it.

In similar fashion, Momma had raised me to view the pageant as a necessary evil for our small town's economy. She would explain away Aunt DeeDee's involvement every year with a wave of her hand: *It's just a job.* We both knew that wasn't true. My aunt lived and breathed all things pageant.

"You okay?" Lacy asked.

"Fine," I answered, even though my heart beat against my ribcage like a hummingbird flapping its wings. I think I sensed even then how all of this would end, how I'd be forced to do something that would upend my predictable existence.

"No, you're not," Lacy insisted, folding her arms across her chest as she studied me.

"I'm fine," I insisted, guiding Bella into the stable. "Because I won't do it. I will never compete in that awful show."

Lacy knew that I'd already humored Momma when she'd asked me to have a picnic at her graveside behind First Baptist at month four, and I'd reluctantly agreed when she'd encouraged me to try a couple of blind dates at the Spoonful Diner, which Lacy had arranged in month nine. But this? Compete in the Rose Palace Pageant? I hadn't thought that the chemo had damaged my mother's brain cells, but maybe I was wrong. Either way, she could haunt me all she wanted. I'd actually prefer that. I could tell her little orb what I thought of her absurd request.

"There is no way I'm dressing up and prancing around in high heels for money," I said, hoping Momma could hear me from the Great Beyond as I led Bella into her stall.

"Even third place comes with cash," Lacy said. "We both know you need money."

I unbuckled the saddle and raised an eyebrow. "I'm not going to win any place because I'm not competing. The Rose Palace is a"—I tried to find the words—"danger to thinking women everywhere."

"It's a pageant," Lacy said, rolling her eyes. "Not the annual Hunger Games."

"What about that winner who disappeared when we were

kids?" I hated my condescending tone but couldn't keep it out of my voice.

Lacy's mouth screwed up in thought. "Do you remember when we were in high school, and we did that big project about the town's history for Mrs. Ember's class?"

My brow furrowed at the change of subject, but I answered anyway. "Sure. I wrote about the first hospital."

"Right. And I tried to write about the missing pageant winner. True crime before true crime was a thing."

I listened, not actually recalling much of this.

"I had to change topics," Lacy said. "Couldn't even find the woman's name in the newspaper archives. Like it had been scrubbed clean."

"This isn't helping your argument that I should compete."

"What I'm saying is that we can't base what we do on things that happened more than two decades ago. If we did that, no one would drive down Hickory Lane after that terrible car accident. Or attend the Peach Festival because of those out-of-towners who threw fruit at the mayor a few years ago." Lacy gave a shrug and her face relaxed back into a smile. "Anyway, the pageant's not like that now—women, including your aunt, mostly run everything. We gotta let the past lie."

Famous last words, I wanted to say. Instead, I pulled off Bella's saddle, hung it on the wall, and tried a different tactic. "You've heard Aunt DeeDee's stories about other pageants. You remember that one lady who slept with every judge in the state of California in order to secure her win? Or the mother who threatened to 'cut' the coordinator at Florida's Little Miss Pageant if her daughter didn't win? That world is vicious."

"For the kind of money they're offering this year, I'd think about competing myself if I wasn't helping run the show." Lacy looked up at the fluffy white clouds and reframed her argument as I started brushing Bella. "Look, I get it, I really do. I mean, it's not like your mother had the forethought to sign you up for an event that might help you earn the money you desperately need and force you to leave your house for more than"—she looked at her feet and wrinkled her nose—"for more than literal horse shit."

"I can get money other ways."

"Oh yeah?" Lacy raised her eyebrows. "Have you started turning tricks instead of just teaching them to Bella?"

"Ha-ha." I put a hand on Bella's rump to let her know I was behind her before moving to the other side as I batted my eyes at my oldest friend. "Lacy, dearest, I'm not a slut like you."

"More like a cloistered nun." Lacy glanced at my lady regions with a look of pity. "How long has it been for the old girl?"

I gave her a bland smile. "I'm saving myself for marriage."

"Right. Just don't let her dry up. It's easy to get parched in this summer sun. Seriously though..." She tilted her head and gave me a half-smile as she gestured to the mountains in the distance. "You used to hike those ridges from dawn to dusk. You were the one taking names and getting shit done. By the time you were thirty, you were going to open your own practice and heal all the animals within a hundred-mile radius, remember?"

Once upon a time, sure, I'd been salutatorian of my high school, class president of my undergrad, a top pick with a full ride in the veterinary program at Cornell. But I was no longer those things.

"This could be a chance for you to get back out there. To reconnect with... you know, actual people... to start acting like yourself again." Lacy knew where my mind was at. "You've grieved for almost a year, and it's been a long one. Will you at least try?"

I didn't answer, busying myself with Bella's final preparations for the evening.

I might not have been a beauty queen, but I was a fab stable hand. Bella's stall was pristine enough for a human to sleep inside each night. Thankfully, I hadn't yet had to stoop that low, but with the late notices coming from the mortgage company every month, the clock was ticking.

"I'll pick you up Wednesday," Lacy said matter-of-factly, as if the question was settled. "Oh... and your aunt will be at your house tonight to start preparations."

"Preparations?" It sounded like Aunt DeeDee would be readying me for sacrifice.

Lacy turned to leave, calling back over her shoulder, "You're about to find out the kind of work it takes to look this good."

TWO

Aubergine—yes, like the purplish eggplant color—in Virginia just happens to be the capital of the oldest beauty pageant in U.S. history.

We're nestled in the Blue Ridge Mountains, named for a compound that conifers release, scattering blue light across the hazy ridges. Because we're at the tip-top of Virginia, only a four-hour train ride from Manhattan, we've got the reputation of having more... we'll call it *je ne sais quoi* than other run-of-the-mill small towns. Still, we offer the delightful oddities expected of a Southern hamlet of fewer than three thousand residents, and whose economy thrives off of women in flouncy dresses. If you take a stroll past the red-brick buildings on Main Street, you'll not only find Morning Brew, a coffee shop that sells lattes *and* potions to help contestants win, but also Fixin' To, a mechanic shop that features a sewing machine and doubles as a quickie alterations depot for all emergency pageant wardrobe needs.

The Rose Palace Pageant pulls from residents of the Eastern Seaboard and acts as a stepping stone for Miss Universe, Miss America, and Miss Whatever the Hell Else Is

Out There. Plus, as I soon discovered, our town's show offers one of the biggest cash prizes in the pageant world.

I know the one-hundred-year-old history well because, regardless of how you personally feel about the pageant, if you live in Aubergine, the show is in your blood. You're either related to a former contestant, you've been a former contestant, or a former contestant has bullied you. My great-grandmother—a woman I've never met—won the damn thing in 1928. All that to say that for one week a year, our town exists for the sole purpose of showcasing sparkling tiaras and choreographed dances and women strutting around in high heels. The rest of the year, it eagerly awaits for that week to arrive again.

What the annual beauty pageant worshippers don't realize when they flock to Aubergine on their pilgrimage is that we also know all the pageant secrets—or we make guesses and spread rumors, which is about the same thing. Even though Momma kept me out of that scene, as a child I heard stories of the missing winner, Miss 2001. The fact of her disappearance has become local lore, whispered about every year though no one has any new information.

The first time Momma took me to the pageant was the very same year, and it didn't go well. I was four years old and running around in the dressing room when I accidentally knocked into a contestant who was in the middle of putting on her makeup. That lady toppled, creating a domino of half-dressed contestants who eventually got to their feet with smeared lipstick, boobs spilling out of duct tape push-up bras, and a murderous look in their sparkling eyes. Suffice to say, we didn't go backstage after that, but each year I did get roped into folding pageant programs or organizing contestant applications for Aunt DeeDee—and of course, I attended each grand finale. I still remembered my favorite talent: Miss 2007 kickboxing a man in a padded uniform. That memory alone made me think that perhaps I could win—or at least place.

After I told Bella and the other seven horses in my care good night, I drove my beat-up '99 Honda hatchback to the two-story, four-bay-window house on the edge of town, the place where I'd grown up with two of the best women in the world: Momma and Aunt DeeDee. Both never married, both part of every good memory I had.

Not that Aunt DeeDee lived with us—she had her own little loft above the shops on Main Street so she could entertain when she felt the urge—but while I was growing up, she was there every afternoon with a plate of snickerdoodles. Even after I was old enough to be on my own until Momma finished her shift at the hospital, she would stop by to drop off a pie, to tend to her corner of the garden, to give me advice about the goings-on at Aubergine High. Still, Aunt DeeDee, for all her home cooking and good intentions, wasn't Momma.

As I pulled into the driveway, the sun was setting behind the mountains, the orange-pink light casting a serene hue on the robin's-egg blue of the hand-split weatherboard. At first glance, you wouldn't notice the treehouse Momma had built me or the nails where we hung multicolored Christmas lights the day after Thanksgiving. You might also miss the rotted boards at the base of the house, the clogged gutters, and the dangerously outdated electrical wiring that could set the house aflame at any moment. A couple of years ago, Momma and I had walked the property and made a list of all the things we'd fix on this hundred-year-old house as soon as I finished school and started my own practice. Then she got sick, and any dreams of repairs or money—or a real life—vanished.

Our last happy memory is from the day before she died, when she'd had a few conscious hours and asked me to open the curtains in her room so she could count the bluebirds and warblers at the feeder I'd made in sixth grade. Her cheeks, long pale, had pinkened as the two of us communed with nature one last time, and I'd understood why I loved the outdoors and animals. It was because of Momma, because she'd encouraged me to observe and explore, to take a chance and have an adventure.

I blinked back tears and peered into my rearview mirror to see Aunt DeeDee emerging from her Cadillac. My first instinct, I'm ashamed to say, was to crouch low in my seat to hide from her. Aunt DeeDee can be... *a lot*, and I didn't feel like talking about the one thing I knew she'd want to address: me competing in the pageant.

Before I could duck, she knocked on my driver's side window with her elbow.

Unlike Momma, who mostly dressed in scrubs or comfy jeans, Aunt DeeDee always dressed to kill. Tonight she wore a tailored lavender dress suit with matching pumps, and in her hands was a casserole dish.

"Hey, Aunt DeeDee." I crawled out of the front seat and, like a good niece, took the oven mitts and hot dish from her. She slid them off, and I could see that she'd painted her long nails fuchsia and added tiny diamonds to her pointers.

"Hello, doll," she said, planting a quick kiss on my cheek and speaking in that half-pitying, half-concerned tone she used. I loved her for it, and it drove me crazy. "How you doing?"

I shrugged, avoiding the question and hoping she wouldn't comment on my muddy jeans or the pieces of hay inevitably caught in my hair.

"It's a chicken and rice casserole," Aunt DeeDee said, patting me on the shoulder. "I know you might be counting calories with the pageant coming up, so I brought margarine instead of butter for the rolls and I used skinless chicken breasts."

We both knew that I'd never counted a calorie a day in my life, but sure. Maybe it was her assumption that I would compete or maybe it was a twinge of rebellion that I'd never acted on, but I felt my back stiffen, pulling me to my full five-foot-seven height.

"I need to talk to you about something, Aunt DeeDee," I said, as I watched her find her key to the front door.

"Yes, darling. What is it?"

"I know you mean well, and I'm sure Momma wasn't thinking straight, but I just... I can't believe the two of you would come up with a plan to..." My cheeks grew hot and I took a breath, trying to steady myself. "It's just... I can't believe that y'all would sign me up for the pageant without telling me."

"Now, Dakota. It's not that—"

"No, it's too late." I cut her off as I walked through the front door and living room before setting the casserole on the kitchen counter. "The pageant starts in two days, and even if I wanted to compete, I'm not any kind of show-ready. I haven't had a haircut in a year, and there's literally dirt under my fingernails. Besides, that is not my crowd, and I don't have time to learn how to charm and flatter my way into the top tier of superficial contestants. Y'all waited too late to tell me, so that's that."

"Excuse me, princess." Aunt DeeDee followed me inside, putting a hand on her hip. "But you need to stop acting like you're too good for this pageant right this minute."

I hadn't heard that tone since I was sixteen and tried to convince her to sign off on me skipping school to drive out to the rodeo by myself for the day.

"You know that you and I don't have any other chance of making the kind of money that this pageant throws at the winners each year," Aunt DeeDee continued. She was right. Working twenty hours a week for $12.50 an hour as a stable hand wasn't cutting it. "If I could steal it for you, I would, but I've never been great at thieving, so that option's out unless you have some breaking and entering skills I don't know about."

I wasn't amused.

Aunt DeeDee gave me a long look as if to say she was disappointed in me. "You used to be up for any adventure, ready to conquer any fear." She sounded like Lacy as she put her hands on my shoulders and stared into my eyes, searching for my can-do spirit. She'd have to search long and hard. We both knew that when I'd failed at the most important task of my life, it had knocked the wind out of me. I hadn't quite gotten my breath back since then.

I thought of the stories of how my great-grandfather had worked in the Virginia coal mines, trying to earn enough to make a decent life in this home for his wife and children. He died well before I was born, but in the few photos I'd seen of him, black streaks always coated his hands. The Greens had never lived in high cotton, but we'd always been proud of what we had. Except... now, I might lose the home he'd built, the backdrop of my first-day-of-school pictures and the place where Momma had taken her last breath. Granted, I stood by my decision to max out several credit cards and take out two mortgages to pay for Momma's experimental treatment, but I hadn't considered how I'd live after treatment failed and she was gone. That alternative had never been an option.

"Your momma knew this was the best bet to get your hands on money so you won't lose the house. If you haven't noticed, there's not much in the way of business opportunities around these parts. So, doll baby, this is your chance." Aunt DeeDee attempted an encouraging grin. "But don't you worry: I'll get you fixed right up."

Fixed right up... as if I was broken.

I watched her while she pulled plates out of the cupboard as if the issue was settled. Feeling a pout inch its way into my bottom lip, I stepped onto the back porch lined with bird's foot violets and Virginia bluebells. In the corner was where I'd constructed a fairy garden when I was eight, and there was the pecan tree that I would climb every day after school with *Black Beauty*. I'd dog-eared the corners of my copy, reading it in the rain and sunshine so that almost every page was somehow stained. *Well loved*, Momma had called it when I'd refused Aunt DeeDee's offer to buy me a new one.

"It's not even safe," I said, grasping for another excuse as I walked back inside.

Aunt DeeDee held a spatula in mid-air and scrunched her nose. "Safe? What in tarnation are you talking about?"

"The missing pageant queen?" I reminded her.

"Hogwash." She waved the spatula. "That's all stuff and nonsense."

I took a few heavy steps into the center of the kitchen, painted in soft yellows and greens, and I distracted myself by pouring food into Bucket's bowl before slouching into a chair.

"It's not nonsense for that Miss 2001," I muttered.

"She's fine." Aunt DeeDee tasted the tiniest piece of chicken and added salt to the entire dish. "Just couldn't take the spotlight."

"And you know that because...?"

"Because I was at that very pageant, and no one ever found any evidence to the contrary," Aunt DeeDee said. "Let's not talk about the missing queen at the actual pageant, okay?"

I didn't make any promises, but she didn't really seem to be asking a question.

Aunt DeeDee sighed when she noticed my crossed arms. "Trust me, Dakota. I would never send you into something dangerous. You know that, don't you?"

I knew that Aunt DeeDee loved me like her daughter, would protect me with the same fierceness that Momma had possessed—and perhaps a little sparkle– but I didn't feel like admitting it.

"All righty then, let's turn you into royalty." Aunt DeeDee clasped her hands and practically bounced with excitement. "Getting pageant-ready is a bit like ripping off a Band-Aid..." She paused and closed one eye. "Or perhaps getting a Pap smear. Grit your teeth through the discomfort, and soon you'll be all done, pulling up your panties, and getting on with your life."

I was horrified by the imagery, but when I caught the reflection of my gaunt grimace in the oven door, I realized that she had a massive job to do.

"Listen, sugar, beauty is pain. But don't worry: it won't kill you."

Unless it did.

Aunt DeeDee turned to the big bag she'd brought inside and pulled some kind of wand-shaped torture-device from it.

"What is that?" I asked, eyeing the metal and plastic contraption.

"It's a microdermabrasion kit."

"You just happened to bring that with you?"

"Let's just say that I knew how this conversation would go." She took out bottles of goop and placed them in a Tetris-like row across the kitchen counter. "How long since you had a facial?"

I shook my head at her.

"Since you did a face mask?"

More shaking of the head.

"Oh dear." She sighed. "I guess tonight's the night."

Over the next twenty minutes I watched her set up several stations. There was a rainbow of nail polish, a steaming bowl of wax, an orange container of highlights, and more creams and metal wands than I'd ever imagined.

Aunt DeeDee ushered me toward the couch and continued her commands, dropping glops of hot wax on my calves as soon as I was lying before her. As I watched her move around the living room, I had no trouble believing my aunt had been Miss 1990 back in the day. Her erect posture, her long legs, and her perfectly symmetrical face practically guaranteed it.

She attached strips of paper to my legs. "Now, take a deep breath."

I did as commanded, but I couldn't help howling as she ripped the hair out at the roots.

"Oh, sweetheart, this is nothing. Wait till I get to your nether regions."

Tears sprang to my eyes, and I brushed them away.

After a few more minutes of waxing and yelping, Aunt DeeDee rubbed oil into my red legs before splattering on talcum powder for good measure. Then, she took off a plastic glove and rubbed the frown out of my brow. "Listen, hon, your fees are paid, and I've ordered all of your gowns and costumes in colors that will bring out the green in your eyes and help restore that peaches-and-cream complexion. All you need to do is show up, smile pretty, and follow the schedule. I helped your mother arrange everything." Aunt DeeDee cleared her throat. She tapped her pointer finger on her chin and studied me. "Now, dear, what do you know about the pageant?"

My eyebrows stayed knitted this time. "I know that the entire show is a tool of the patriarchy and dependent entirely upon the toxic male gaze."

"With an answer like that, you're a shoo-in for the grand prize," Aunt DeeDee tisked. "Please don't forget that your feminist aunt, namely *me*, helps run that 'tool of the patriarchy,' and you know I carried signs alongside you at the Women's March a few years ago."

I eyed her, reluctant to concede the point. She'd passed out cookies and worn a sign that said, *Treat Us the Same as the Menfolk*. Not exactly activism at its finest. Still, she'd shown up for me.

"Sometimes it's easier to infiltrate something that's outdated in order to change things." Aunt DeeDee ran a hand down the front of her perfectly ironed skirt. "Listen, I was almost your age when I won first place. I'd been through an awful breakup, and my own mother thought it might be a good experience for me. And it was. The winnings gave me enough money to buy my own little apartment in town and to start my clothing line. The prestige gave me recognition and a way to network. This show can give you the push—and the resources—you need to keep our family home, to go back to school, to start your own practice, to do"—she waved a hand in the air as if dreaming big—"whatever you want to do. That's about the most feminist thing you can do."

I turned on my side, resting my head in my hand. "You don't even know if I can win."

"With a little help from me, you're golden." Aunt DeeDee straightened her shoulders. "Good. Now then, there are three things you absolutely need to know: First, the judges watch you all four days, not just on the night of the grand finale. They're assessing the Four Cs: confidence, comportment, conversation, and costumes."

"Costumes?"

"Attire and talent, but that doesn't start with a C."

"If I think all of this is *Crap*, may I be excused?"

"Funny, as always," Aunt DeeDee said without laughing. "Secondly, since this year is the centennial, there are more prizes"—she gave me a pointed look—"which means more *money* than any other year. First place is three hundred thousand dollars. Second place is two hundred thousand dollars. Third place is a hundred thousand dollars and a tractor, which is a bit odd, I realize, but a donation's a donation. And then there's the Miss Rosie prize, which is based on likability and popularity and comes with—" Aunt DeeDee noticed my expression, which Lacy called my Resting Horse Face because it was long and blank. "Maybe..." Aunt DeeDee wrinkled her nose. "Maybe we should skip Miss Rosie and aim to place, yeah?"

"Okay." I sighed. "What's the third thing?"

"I told you I'll protect you, but in order to do that…" Aunt DeeDee took a long inhale. "I need you to stay away from Dr. Bellingham."

"Who's Dr. Bellingham?"

"The only male judge—and plastic surgeon to half of the ladies there."

"I'm not sure how to avoid him if I'm competing."

"You don't have to ignore him, just don't be alone with him. He's a longtime friend of the pageant, but he's… unsettling. He'll tell you how much he admires you. Then, he'll tell you everything that's wrong with the way you look before he makes a pass at you." Aunt DeeDee must've seen the ickiness on my face. "I've learned how to manage him after all these years, but you, you steer clear." Something specific must've come to mind because she shuddered as she added, almost as an afterthought, "That man should've been castrated decades ago."

"This is sounding better and better."

Aunt DeeDee plastered on her smile again. "You'll be fine. Just stick with the other contestants. Make friends. Safety in numbers."

"Okay, but I'm not wearing the hats. That's where I draw the line."

Aunt DeeDee pursed her lips as if to communicate that we would see about that.

"I'm not," I repeated. "Unless my old Stetson's allowed?"

"No!" Aunt DeeDee practically yelled. "That thing is disgusting."

Perhaps we'd reached an impasse, which was fine by me.

A nearby meow startled me, and I looked around for my sweet, ancient kitty, who was walking slowly toward me, stretching as she went. I sat up and ran my hand along Bucket's fur before spotting the mail that had been dropped through the slot at the front door. One was a hot-pink envelope and, even without opening it, I knew the contents: Notice of Foreclosure. Shoot.

Every takeout meal, every full-bellied laugh, every game of Phase 10 flashed in my mind. This house was the only piece of my life with Momma I had left, and if that letter was like the last one, it meant I had less than a month to get my hands on a lot of money.

"Listen, dear." Aunt DeeDee licked her lips and looked down at her hands as if she needed to confess something. "The money could really help... both of us. Your mother's treatment... she wasn't always able to... cover everything."

"That's why I took out the credit cards," I said, thinking of the numerous voicemails from debt collectors that I'd received today.

Aunt DeeDee continued, averting her gaze. "But the travel, dear, and that specialist she saw in Houston. All of that cost even more."

My mouth went dry. "Momma said she'd found the money."

"Yes, well." Aunt DeeDee looked me in the eye. "I told her that *I'd* found the money, but in actuality I took out a line of credit on the business."

A lie inside a lie. This family had once been transparent, open, honest, but now it seemed we were so busy trying to take care of each other that we'd neglected one thing: the truth.

"How much do you owe?"

"Forty grand, give or take, and I could really use it by the end of summer," Aunt DeeDee answered. "So, you can see how important it is that you compete, and not only compete. Compete to win."

WEDNESDAY
THE ROSE PALACE PAGEANT SCHEDULE:
DAY 1

CHECK IN: 3 to 5 p.m. Please arrive on time as failure to do so may affect your ability to enter the gates. Because of the prestigious reputation of the pageant, as well as the fact that we are celebrating the one hundredth anniversary, security has been increased exponentially to enter the grounds. Once you arrive, you'll settle into your comfortable quarters and won't even notice the extra measures taken to ensure the safety of our contestants, our judges, our staff, and our visitors.

MEET & GREET: 6.30 to 8 p.m. We invite all contestants to join us in the Main Ballroom for an opportunity to mingle and bond with the other participants in this year's pageant. You'll see former winners, meet the judges, and perhaps even make a new best friend. Be sure to follow tradition by wearing your most fabulous hat for our first evening together!

ALL THAT GLITTERS... JEWELS & GEMS PARTY: 9 p.m. to midnight. We are excited to welcome you into the Primrose Ballroom for the All That Glitters... Jewels & Gems party, where a light dinner, drinks, and dancing will be in order.

After the party, be sure to get your beauty rest because we'll have a packed few days of fun and festivities ahead as we prepare to welcome thousands of visitors to the Rose Palace at the Through the Decades Centennial Show this weekend.

Dakota's To-Do List:

1. Win. Ha.

THREE

True-blue pageant contestants everywhere would kill to have all of their entry fees covered for an event like the Rose Palace Pageant so, really, I should've been grateful when Lacy picked me up for the Aubergine event of the year.

As I packed my overnight bag, tossing in hair ties, extra socks, and a tattered notebook where I sometimes scribbled, my eyes landed on the stack of books that were in the corner of my bedroom, gathering dust. Despite my best efforts to ignore the Laboratory Procedures textbook and the Merck Veterinary Manual, my mind ticked off the months since I'd left my program: fifteen. That's how long it'd been since I notified Cornell's registrar's office about a leave of absence to come home and care for Momma—despite her protests. I'd planned to go back, but it hadn't happened, and now, if I was lucky, I was about to replace what could've been a doctoral degree with a crown. I'd never expected my life to go in this direction.

Finally, I threw a dress and a hairbrush into my bag before plopping onto the front porch in my red pearl-snap, button-down and stained jeans to wait for Lacy.

When she pulled up in front of the house a minute later, I threw my bag in the back seat.

Lacy's mouth dropped open and she got out of the car to gawk at me. "Are those highlights? And did DeeDee pluck your eyebrows?"

I didn't answer, even though I was slightly pleased by her reaction. Maybe my aunt's efforts had worked.

She got back into the car and eyed my bag. "You look amazing, but..." She nodded at my overnight bag. "That's all you brought?"

"I packed a dress for socializing, and Aunt DeeDee said she's taking care of the rest."

Lacy squinted. "What dress qualifies in your mind as fit for 'socializing'?" A second later her eyes widened as realization struck. "Not the crumpled, polka-dotted green thing you wore out to dinner last month? When I invited that guy you barely said a word to?"

I looked at her but didn't answer. I didn't need to further shame myself.

"And where's your hat?" Lacy asked.

I crossed my arms. "I'm not wearing a hat."

"Not even a cute little cowgirl thing? That would be adorable."

"I do not have a *cute little cowgirl thing*," I reminded her. "I have a real cowboy hat, but apparently, that is unacceptable."

She let the matter drop—at least for now. "Be glad Aunt DeeDee is on the job," Lacy mumbled as she shifted her car into gear.

Despite my reluctance about this entire endeavor, I was beginning to feel grateful for my makeover, particularly since nerves were already settling in. At least I wouldn't look too much the fool, even if I felt like one.

I changed the radio station every minute or two to distract myself until we drove under a tall, arched metal sign that read,

The Rose Palace, Home of the World's Longest-Running Beauty Pageant, where a guard stopped us.

"Hey, Lace," said the man wearing a shirt that read *Security*. I recognized him just like I did almost everyone else in town, but we'd actually graduated together, even dated for an entire three weeks of our junior year.

I looked over the dashboard and saw spikes on the asphalt and some sort of laser system to keep out unwanted vehicles.

"Hey, Joe." Lacy showed an official-looking badge and handed him my driver's license. "Is the rooster in the hen house?"

"Affirmative," Joe Larson answered with a smile, as he walked around to my side of the car and leaned into the window. "How you doing, Miss Green?"

"I'm thriving," I said dryly. "Can't you tell?"

He laughed and took my hand in his, pretending like he was going to kiss it before I yanked it out of his grasp. He chuckled and extended a scanner. I hesitated only a moment before pressing my finger onto it.

"Just need to upload your print to the system," he said. "Be back in a flash. Don't miss me too much."

"What was that about?" I asked Lacy as he sauntered back to his booth.

"Increased security. Mr. Finch has all of these ridiculous code words that we had to memorize in case someone is listening over the comms. His wife is 'the diamond,' and his daughter is 'the rose.' He's 'the rooster,' and 'the hen house' is this place."

"Which means we're 'the hens.'" I wrinkled my nose. "How does Savilla feel about that?"

Lacy shook her head at the mention of Mr. Finch's daughter, a girl who'd been with us all through the innocent primary years, the pimply middle-school stage, and the finding-ourselves high school era. Savilla's family was royalty around here, and like so many royals, it was complicated: Her biological mother had fled the scene shortly after her birth, and her father had married one of the pageant winners a few years later. From what I understood, Savilla had been living—and likely partying—in the family penthouse in New York, so I hadn't heard from her in half a decade.

"No idea," Lacy said. "I haven't seen her yet."

After two scans, a brief call, and a few overly serious glances, Joe came back to my side of the car and handed me my ID, as he addressed both of us. "There's been a disturbance already up at the big house. A bunch of police cars went through here a half-hour ago."

"Maybe it's the security team?" Lacy asked.

Joe shook his head. "Something went missing. Keep an eye out for anything suspicious."

"Will do," Lacy said, sounding official again.

"All clear," he said as he tapped the roof of the car, lowered the spikes in the ground, and sent us through the gates.

I turned to look behind us as Lacy's car bumped along. "What do you think was stolen?"

"There's a lot of valuable items on display: jewels, crowns, some high-value artwork. The Rose Palace has changed since we toured it as kids. Less homey now. More like a museum."

"Security Guard Joe takes his job very seriously," I mused. "I thought he might make me sign away my firstborn or insert a tracker under my skin."

"They do that while you're sleeping." Lacy steered past a peach orchard. "Supposedly, they've installed a top-notch system with an invisible laser all around the perimeter."

"Why? What are they trying to keep out?"

Lacy gave me a knowing look. "Better question: What are they trying to keep in?"

We drove down the tree-lined lane toward the estate, and despite my mixed feelings about the pageant, I couldn't help but admire the front of the building as we pulled up to the château-esque structure.

Built of weathered white stone, the palace stretched four stories high to a pitched roof. Grotesques and gargoyles lined the house, and spires rose above the ornamented stone, promising mysterious passageways and grand promenades to those who dared cross the threshold. Low clouds hung in the early evening twilight, giving the architecture an ethereal grandeur, but the silhouette of the blue-tinged peaks still dwarfed the man-made structure, as spectacular as it might be. The top-most part of the building reminded me of Rapunzel's tower, and I suddenly wondered if someone—a wicked queen, perhaps—might be watching me.

This house had been part of my Aubergine education for most of my life. According to the tour I'd taken of it as part of my fifth grade studies, it's approximately one hundred thousand square feet and a quintessential representation of the Gilded Age. Savilla Finch had been bored throughout the entire tour: she'd kept running off to the kitchen to grab a piece of string cheese or a bag of Cheetos, before finally sneaking up to her room. Lacy and I hadn't been sure if she'd been showing off that she actually lived on such an amazing estate, or if she'd really thought her home was nothing special. Probably the latter.

Built in 1896 by the diamond-mining Finch family of New York, the Rose Palace was so named because of the swamp rose bushes that had grown prolifically on the land before development. The nineteenth-century Finches had chosen to build in Aubergine for its charm and because they'd wanted to compete with the glory of the Biltmore Estate in North Carolina, which had been christened a year earlier. The home had been a gift for the then-Mr. Finch's wife, and she'd in turn hosted the first-ever Rose Palace Pageant on the grounds in 1925. She had been seventy-two years old by that point but, according to photographs, she'd dressed in frills and lace just like the contestants. The home had stayed in the Finch family all this time, hosting weddings and funerals and always—every year without fail, even through the Great Depression, World War II, Vietnam, and the 2008 Recession—the Rose Palace Pageant.

Lacy dropped me at the front, where, sure enough, a line of police cars were in a row. Before she left to park, she placed a hand on my forearm. "Hey, one more thing. There's a guy here I want you to meet."

I rolled my eyes. "If he's anything like 'Mister-I-Collect-Anime-Figurines,' then no thanks."

Lacy chuckled. "I set you up on one bad date, and I never hear the end of it."

"What about 'Mister-I-Match-My-Shoes-With-My-Underwear'?"

"I still think he could've been a fun time." Lacy batted away my concerns. "But this isn't a setup, just someone I think you might want to keep an eye out for. Did you vote in the last county election?"

I squinted one eye, thinking. I'd always been a fan of doing one's civic duty, but I had no clue how this related to her train of thought. "Uh... are you trying to get me to run for office?"

"The new sheriff is here this weekend, volunteering with security, and girl, that man is fit. If you don't win a prize, maybe you can at least bring him home as a consolation."

"Who'd he run against?" I asked, thinking it might jog my memory.

"Joe," she answered.

"Joe Larson? Security Guard Joe?" I asked.

Lacy shrugged. No wonder this guy had won. Joe Larson could barely tie his shoes when we'd graduated and, as far as I knew, he'd done odd jobs ever since. Still, Aubergine was a tight-knit community, loyal to its own.

"The sheriff lives two towns over in Mount Cedar, so it was a close race," Lacy said. "I think he's trying to get to know people, make friends in Aubergine, try to convince them he'll do a good job."

"Sounds like a lot of work," I said. Regardless, I couldn't imagine being smitten with any man at this point in my life. "You sure you don't want to have at him? I'm sure your boyfriend would understand."

Lacy had started a long-distance relationship with a guy she'd met at a conference a couple years ago. She'd decided to open her new business, so she'd wanted to get all of the contacts and networking and resources that she could find to give herself the best start possible. Lacy had arrived home with all of those things, but also with the phone number of one of the waiters who'd accidentally served her the vegetarian plate instead of the steak she'd requested. Within months, Anton had left his extensive family in Texas and moved to Virginia, continuing to work odd jobs, just to be near her. They'd been living together for the past six months, and I expected him to propose any day now.

"I'm taken, not blind. Just try to chat him up if you two meet. He's worth your attention, and by the end of the pageant, who knows? You two may be having sleepovers and licking whipped cream off of one another."

"You're funny," I said, exiting the passenger side. "You should do stand-up. Really."

"Get checked in. I'll see you at the meet and greet in a couple hours." Lacy pointed me toward the grand entrance and then she drove away.

FOUR

You can do this.

You will do this.

You were made to do this.

Okay, the last line wasn't at all true, but those were the words I thought to myself as I stood at the massive door of the Rose Palace and looked around for my aunt. Behind me was a manicured landscape of rainbow-colored flowers that could rival the finest European lawns, and in front of me, through this giant, wood-paneled door, was quite possibly my future.

Aunt DeeDee had told me she would be at the front steps to greet me and to calm my nerves, but here I waited and she was nowhere in sight. I checked my phone. No missed calls or texts. I dialed her number, but it went straight to voicemail.

Fantastic. The one person who knew this place from floor to ceiling, hidden passageways and all, had abandoned me.

But... that wasn't like Aunt DeeDee, the rule-following, always-early-just-in-case woman who'd helped raise me.

I steeled myself with a long inhale and gripped my pitiful overnight bag as I pressed my fingers into the brass door handle and stepped onto a white marbled floor. My hand went to my chest in fright as I took in the rows of women—or rather life-size, cardboard cutouts of women—lining the long entryway. I'd known this event would be strange, but I hadn't expected greeting-by-cardboard-cutout strange. Only in Aubergine.

The cathedral ceiling towered above me, and I had to pull my eyes away from the crisscrossing beams as I stepped forward, passing a five-foot-tall black-and-white image of a woman wearing a long strand of pearls and a sleeveless dress that hit her mid-calf. The spindly crown on her head was tall and ostentatious, and the girl's smile proved she was thrilled to have won. At her feet was written in large numbers the very first year of the pageant.

My fingers trailed along the whitewashed stone walls before I began weaving through the other women. I was both impressed by the attention to detail and appalled at how these women had been captured forever in the glare of a camera flash. I marveled at the idea that with my now soft curls and newly buffed skin, I could actually join their ranks.

As I neared the end of the long hall that would take me to the center of activity, I spotted Miss 1999, Miss 2000, Miss 2002... I paused and backed up, sure I must've missed one.

But no. I retraced my steps.

Miss 1999.

Miss 2000.

Miss 2002.

Miss 2003... and on the years continued. Just like the story of the actual missing beauty queen, Miss 2001's cutout had vanished or been ignored—and only those who cared were likely to notice.

A shiver ran up my spine and goosebumps sprang up on my forearms. For a fleeting second, I considered leaving. I could recross that threshold, step back outside into the late-afternoon sunshine, and let the pageant do its thing without my involvement.

But then the call I'd received from the mortgage company that morning came to mind. The man, though real, sounded robotic as he informed me of my situation and options, which basically amounted to catching up on seven months of payments on two different notes or being evicted in twenty-seven days.

If I left the pageant, then I'd have no chance to save Momma's house, to pay back Aunt DeeDee, or to restart my life. I felt strangely guilty that my aunt had taken on debt when it was my mother who'd been ill.

I propelled myself forward and into the open lobby, where modern circular chandeliers belied hundred-year-old rose patterns carved into textured limestone. A two-sided fireplace stood giant and unlit, and beveled windowpanes looked out on a lush lawn. A garden with a hedge maze stretched back to a fountain.

A man in uniform almost bumped into me as he spoke into a walkie-talkie. Women in fantastic hats of every shade—but particularly blues, reds, and yellows—occasionally stopped to give air-kisses or a quick hug. My heart palpitated. The uniformed officer wouldn't have bumped into these ladies. He would have seen them—or at least their hats—coming from a mile away.

I knew about the hat tradition, mainly because every year my aunt bought what seemed gaudier and more outlandish headwear. "Every contestant—current and former—wears them on the first night," Aunt DeeDee had once explained. "At the end of that night we symbolically remove them to make room for the crown."

I squared my shoulders, stretched my neck as far as it would reach and reminded myself of Aunt DeeDee's words as she'd plucked, powdered, and painted me.

"You'll be a breath of fresh air," Aunt DeeDee had said to our reflections in the mirror when she'd finished transforming me. After her work, we looked more alike than I'd ever noticed with our long eyelashes and high cheekbones. The worry lines hadn't vanished, but she *had* brought out the green in my eyes. It was nothing short of miraculous, I'd had to admit. "It's been almost a hundred years of the same kind of winner. Time for something new."

I could do this, hat or no hat, tradition be damned.

The front desk looked like one I would imagine at a five-star hotel, the granite countertops gleaming and glistening. Even the floors sparkled in the afternoon sunlight streaming through tall windows that showcased the majestic blue mountains watching over all of the nonsense. Staff members came and went, many of whom I recognized. It was as bustling as the hotel might've been almost three decades ago before Mr. Finch had shuttered it to all guests, with the exception of pageant week.

As I surveyed the open space, I couldn't help but admire the jewels that shone from behind polished glass cases. Lacy was right. Notwithstanding the creepy cutouts in the front hall, this place gave off definite museum vibes. Dozens of crowns, each gleaming underneath track lighting, broke into prisms of rainbow refractions sparkling against the walls.

I walked over to read the typed labels in front of the crowns.

1931, Bonny Brock

1932, Kathleen Daugette

1933, Sarah Applegate

Even with my hesitancy to step foot onto this estate, I had to admit that those shimmering objects were quite a sight.

I must've looked out of place because two guards—one of whom I recognized as the son of Aubergine's mayor, and the other a deacon at First Methodist—checked the badge hanging from the lanyard Lacy had strung around my neck.

"Good to see you, Dakota," the mayor's son said, tipping his head.

"My condolences," said the deacon.

I gave them a half-smile, surprisingly grateful that the town remembered. Maybe I could get pity votes if nothing else.

Half a dozen women, their eyes shaded and their lips pouty, passed me without a word, click-clacking their way across the marble floors of the lobby. I didn't recognize these ladies, which was to be expected. One or two women from Aubergine might compete any given year, but for the most part the contestants were from moderate-to-obscenely wealthy families up and down the East Coast.

Women who don't need the money half as much as I do, I thought, before a pang of guilt bit at me. How was I to know who needed the money or why? Perhaps one of these ladies was a daughter competing to earn money for a parent's medical treatment. Or maybe another gal was in this thing to bring home enough money to pay off a mountain of student loan debt.

There had to be other people here in need, I tried to tell myself as a woman dressed to the nines strode up to me.

What Aunt DeeDee would call a "tasteful" navy fascinator sat across her forehead, and she rolled a Louis Vuitton case behind her. The badge around her neck read Jemma Jenkins.

"Where's the nearest restroom?" Jemma asked.

I looked behind me, wondering if she was addressing someone over my shoulder.

"The restroom?" she asked again. A nervous energy exuded from her. The woman's fingers and wrists were laced with jewels, and her outfit was modest but fashionable, her heels making her legs appear ever more slender.

"Oh... uh... I don't know. I just got here."

"You don't work here?" Jemma frowned as if this were some kind of prank, and I might be the prankster.

"Perhaps someday, but only if I'm lucky." If every contestant was as intense and condescending as Jemma Jenkins, this was bound to be a delight.

"Oh, well, you look like the help," she said, dismissing me as quickly as she'd demanded information.

I was fairly confident that wasn't true, but if it was, I needed Aunt DeeDee more than ever. As I spun in a half circle, desperate to find her, a flash clicked only a couple of feet from my face.

FIVE

"Dakota?" It was Savilla Finch, my old classmate whose father owned—and reigned over—the Rose Palace. She'd cut her teeth on society events both in New York and our little town, and she stood before me now in a flowing mint-green dress, thick-rimmed rectangular glasses, and an old-fashioned pillbox hat with a swath of netting hanging over one eye. She held an old-fashioned-looking camera in her hand.

"Savilla?"

She stared at me, her smile fixed, her eyes unblinking. We'd been in school together, but education, learning, books had never really been her *thing*. "Gosh... you look... different," Savilla said, tilting her head as she took me in.

I felt like a specimen being observed under a microscope. "*Good* different? Or *bad* different?"

She pursed her lips as she considered. "Good, very good," she decided. "You learned how to use makeup, and you're thinner."

Oh, yay. A thirty-minute tutorial and a year of picking at Aunt DeeDee's food while grieving had done wonders.

"Nice... shoes," I said. I hadn't looked at her shoes, but she didn't seem to notice as she kicked up a gold six-inch heel covered in rhinestones... or actual diamonds?

"Do you think so?" She leaned toward me conspiratorially and put a finger over her mouth. "I stole them from Mommy's closet. She doesn't even know they're gone. Gosh, it's been..."

"A while," I said, tucking my hands in my pockets. "You're a photographer now?"

"An *artiste*," she corrected, pronouncing the word with an *ee* where the *i* should've been. "What are you doing? And *here?* I thought you, like, broke back horses." She drew out the words for a beat too long as she narrowed her eyes with a questioning, and perhaps even suspicious, look.

Um, that's not a thing, I wanted to say. I eyed the row of crowns behind her. "I've come to case the joint."

Savilla stared at me and then broke into a grin as if she realized I was joking. "You're funnier than you used to be."

"I'm actually..." I had to make myself say the words. "I'm a contestant."

"Oh, goody!" she exclaimed, her voice pitching up an octave in excitement. Pageants she understood. "I'm a contestant too." Savilla carefully brushed a finger under her eye as if wiping away a speck of dust. "Well, not really. I'm an 'honorary attendee,' but I can't, like, win because my family runs things. You know, it's a contest of interestings."

I squinted, trying to understand her meaning. Savilla had always spoken her own kind of language that the rest of us had to interpret if we wanted to converse with her. "You mean a conflict of interest?"

"No," she frowned, like I was slow on the uptake. "*Contests of interestings.* The most fascinating women from the East Coast descend on The Rose once a year, and this year I'm planning to capture it all." Savilla held up the camera and wiggled it in midair before lowering her voice in a breathless and conspiratorial whisper. "Oh my goodness. Did you see the police here already? A missing crown, if you can believe it!"

A missing pageant queen decades ago and now a missing crown. How exciting! I could almost see the headlines, the swirling rumors, the speculations like thought bubbles above the heads of eager pageant fans: *What else might soon disappear from The Rose?*

I started to ask when exactly the crown had gone missing, but a woman who must've been in her mid-forties yet somehow had nary a wrinkle on her forehead walked up to Savilla and whispered something in her ear. A much older man, slightly stooped but still surprisingly spry, followed behind the woman at a distance, stopping to nod at the workers and contestants streaming past him, their arms filled with organza and chiffon.

I would know this couple anywhere. This was *the* Mr. and Mrs. Finch, Savilla's father and stepmother, the two people most responsible for the Rose Palace Centennial, an event projected to bring more than ten thousand people through their gates that weekend.

Their expressions were strained, likely from the police presence at their event, but at the sight of Savilla, Mr. Finch visibly relaxed.

As Mrs. Finch briefly admired her rail-thin reflection in a nearby mirror, one of the passing contestants beamed at Mr. Finch. He was obviously a favorite.

"StepMommy and Daddy, this is Dakota Green," Savilla said. "You remember her?"

The woman's eyebrows attempted to turn down, to no avail. "Oh, yes. You poor dear." Mrs. Finch spoke in one of those northeastern accents that had gone the way of Katharine Hepburn films. "We attended your mother's funeral, isn't that right? Or, perhaps, we sent flowers?"

"That's right," I said, actually having no idea.

"Some kind of tragic accident, wasn't it?" she asked.

"Um... cancer," I answered.

"Yes, of course. Terrible." Mrs. Finch's gaze followed a young woman who held boxes stacked atop one another. She didn't say a word and instead snapped her fingers at the girl, who froze and turned around to head back from whence she came.

"Pretty... you know, deadly," I said, bringing Mrs. Finch's attention back to me.

She acknowledged my snide comment with a faux grin. "So glad you could make it, though I don't remember your application. Fred, dear, do you remember a Dakota Green?"

I didn't mention that Aunt DeeDee had told me she'd slipped it in last minute.

"Not that I recall, but I'm a forgetful old man these days." Frederick Finch's eyes flickered to me and he offered a charismatic smile that featured even, white teeth. "But the name Dakota Green. Yes, I certainly remember you and your family. Your aunt is DeeDee Green, isn't that right?" He tilted his head in a mannerism similar to his daughter and took my hand in his own.

At seventy-five, Mr. Finch was no longer handsome like he'd once been, but I could see how his eyes could've turned heads a couple of decades ago. They were the color of forget-me-nots, a flower that grew in the hills nearby. It was an open secret that he'd had many love interests over the years, that he was a philanderer, but neither he nor Mrs. Finch seemed to let it affect their union.

Perhaps that's because Mr. Finch was rich. Very rich. Like, rich enough to buy up Aubergine and most of Virginia if he so chose. He didn't though. Instead, he gave generously to annual town events like the Peach Festival and the Rose Palace Derby, to the subpar school system that educated a thousand or so kids every year, and of course to the annual pageant in his ancestral home that brought in a steady stream of tourism.

"Dakota is a contestant this year," Savilla told her father, beaming as if I was her new pet project.

"Ah. Yes, perfect. A breath of fresh air." The comment startled me, made me wonder if Aunt DeeDee had been talking me up, planting the idea of needed change in the minds of these pageant people. "Well, my dear," Mr. Finch continued, "you have a startling resemblance to your aunt, our very own Miss 1990, though perhaps you shouldn't mention her this week. Some of the judges might not be on the best terms with her."

I tried to keep my expression neutral as I recalled the male judge she'd told me to avoid.

Mr. Finch studied me longer this time, and I had the sudden urge to hide in the curtains or blend into the wallpaper, even though his expression was neither judgmental nor predatory. Just curious—delighted, even. I made myself arch my shoulders and stand up straight like the queen I needed to become. I met his gaze until my eyes caught the jewelry on his right hand.

He wore a pinky ring with the Rose Palace insignia: a crown with a rose springing up from the center.

"Do you like it?" he asked, holding his hand up for me to admire. "It's my personal design."

I fidgeted with my polished nails. "Lovely," I said, in a voice that hardly sounded like my own.

Mr. Finch changed the subject. "I hope you'll take this opportunity to network with other young women across the East Coast. Now that we've met, I believe that your aunt mentioned you're in need of a full-time job? You know, we've been discussing putting an actual museum on the back side of the property in the original house that my great-grandfather built. Perhaps your aunt could take you back there sometime this week, talk to you about joining us here?"

"Sure," I answered. "The pageant has always fascinated me." I smiled, wondering at my new ability to lie, to turn on the charm so easily. Perhaps Aunt DeeDee was right. Maybe this show was in my blood.

"Or... perhaps Savilla could take you instead. She's helping out this year." He signaled proudly to his daughter. "She had the brilliant idea to offer a little teamwork exercise during our opening ceremony this evening, a bit of a twist on our first-day hat tradition. I know she'll do great things when she takes over all of this someday."

At the mention of the tradition, I felt all three pairs of the Finches' eyes on my bare head, and I silently—and unfairly—cursed Aunt DeeDee for not making me adhere to this one thing.

Savilla wagged a playful finger at him. "But not too soon, Daddy." She took her stepmother's arm. "The two of us wouldn't know what to do without you."

Mrs. Finch's eyes continued to wander. She didn't seem interested in agreeing with Savilla's sentiment.

"I'm certain that you'll find this week to be an enlightening and beneficial experience, and afterward, I'd love to hear what you think of our efforts here," Mr. Finch added. "Good luck this week."

"Daddy, I wonder if we could think of some things Dakota might enjoy when she isn't busy with pageant duties..." Savilla thought aloud as she glanced at the long registration desk. "Aren't you, like, really into animals? Didn't you do that Future Farmers program?"

"Yes," I said, ready to end this conversation and get to my room for a few minutes of silence. I was no longer accustomed to small talk. Bella and Bucket—and even Lacy and Aunt DeeDee—didn't require much of me these days.

"Wonderful! We have a lovely apiary where we produce our own honey, and"—Mr. Finch proudly turned to his wife and chuckled—"we have a beautiful equestrian center with a dozen horses. You know, Gigi was once quite the cowgirl. She can tame the wildest beast." He wiggled his eyebrows in a playful innuendo.

Funny stuff since word around town was that Mrs. Finch was a farm girl from the backwoods of Appalachia, a gold-digger with one hand on the plow and the other reaching for diamonds. They'd been married more than two decades, but small towns don't forget.

He touched his wife's lower back, and she jerked away from him as if he'd scalded her. Interesting. Maybe his charms no longer worked on Mrs. Finch.

"We have some of the finest stables behind the guest cottages as well as a fabulous collection of personalized saddles," he continued. "In fact, I'm sure that Savilla or my wife could show you if you're—"

"Yes, yes, they're lovely," Mrs. Finch cut in. "But perhaps later, Fred. I have no idea the state of the stables with us so rarely on site. Besides, we mustn't waste this young lady's time any longer, and we need to get you back upstairs for your evening pills." Mrs. Finch pinched an invisible thread on his suit collar and dropped it to the floor. "You know how your heart palpitates if you don't take them on time."

Was it my imagination, or did this final sentiment send a little thrill into Mrs. Finch's tone?

"Don't let me keep you," I said all too willingly, but before I could make a clean getaway, Savilla reached out a hand, touching the base of my jaw with her knuckles and tilting my face toward the track lighting.

"StepMommy, look at her," Savilla breathed. "I would kill for those cheekbones."

For the first time, Mrs. Finch leaned in, assessing and pleased. "Sharp, like cut glass. Stunning."

"Do you mind if I take a quick pic?" Savilla asked me. "To show Dr. Bellingham? He does the best work. Gave me a whole new nose last year."

That name set off an alarm in my brain. That was the man Aunt DeeDee had warned me about.

"Oh, um... maybe tonight after I've had a bit of time to properly prepare them?"

Oh my God. I'd rather my cheekbones not hang in some plastic surgeon's office, the envy of Manhattan socialites. There had to be some circle of hell reserved for individuals who offered up their body parts as exemplars for the rich and famous.

"I guess you're right. A bit more blush will bring them out spectacularly." Savilla sighed enviously and then seemed to remember something. "You need to get settled in, and here we are talking your ear off. Registration is right over there. I'm sure DeeDee set up everything for you, but if you have any questions... well, don't ask me because I probably won't know the answer." She giggled. "But there are plenty of people in black shirts to help direct you."

Black shirts? I was in my Western wear, which meant Jemma Jenkins definitely hadn't mistaken me for the staff and simply wanted to put me in my place. But... that would mean she felt threatened by me, which could not actually be a thing, could it?

"Our staff is phenomenal," Mr. Finch said with an appreciative nod. "They'll get you all sorted."

My eyes bounced around the room to them. The staff, many of whom I recognized from church, school days, or running errands around town, seemed to be side-eyeing us, presumably holding their breath until the three Finches—or perhaps only the indomitable Mrs. Finch—exited.

Savilla pursed her lips and studied my forehead for a moment too long as if considering another photo op. "See you soon, que-een," she said, drawing out the last word playfully.

SIX

In the pages of the program, row after row of toothy women smiled, all of them wearing a rose somewhere on their person: woven into their hair, behind an ear, on a wrist corsage, or—and this was my favorite—in their mouths. Props to that lady, I decided, glancing down at her bio. *Tina Kline likes to bake dairy-free, gluten-free cheesecake in her free time.* Yuck, never mind.

In my other hand I held a bag containing the welcome packet, an itinerary, and a tiny jar of honey with a label featuring a purple bee. *Rose Palace Honey*, the words across the front read. *Hand-harvested by Mr. Frederick Finch.* Perhaps he was trying to seem like an approachable everyman rather than a millionaire who invited dozens of gorgeous women into his home once a year. I wasn't sure that this jar could accomplish that.

Aunt DeeDee still hadn't appeared or answered my calls or texts. I'd officially checked in, and though my room wasn't ready yet, staff would be delivering my bag to my tiny cottage somewhere on the grounds. According to the itinerary, I was scheduled to appear in the Main Ballroom in less than an hour. In the

47

meantime, I'd settled into a chair in the expansive lobby and was flipping through the pageant program that the lady at the front desk—who'd also been my driver's ed instructor—had handed me, along with an electronic key and a pitying smile.

"Good luck, sweetheart," she'd said, patting my hand. How had I gone from the top ten percent of Aubergine High's senior class to... I don't know... Most Likely to Evoke Pitying Glances?

On the front of the glossy program, published by our very own Aubergine Press, Savilla Finch stood in front of a wreath of pink and white roses, a crown featuring a multitude of gems on her head, and "Page 7" written next to her name. I flipped to it and found a double spread featuring the First Daughter of the Rose Palace Pageant.

Savilla Finch hails from Aubergine, Virginia. She's been an honorary contestant every year since her twenty-second birthday, and before that, she acted as pageant mascot. As seen in last year's talent show, Savilla can shoot archery, but that's only one of her impressive accomplishments. After graduating from Sarah Lawrence—

After Daddy bought a building, I added mentally.

—with a degree in Art History, she returned home for a week each summer to help her family run the show. Though the Finches now spend most of the year in New York, Savilla helps with planning in and out of season.

Strange that Aunt DeeDee and Lacy had never mentioned Savilla's involvement.

Just like bees drawn to roses, every attendee and contestant is drawn to our very own First Daughter of the Rose Palace Pageant. Congratulations!

I read that final word a couple of times. What exactly was this writer congratulating Savilla for? Her birth into this family? Then I spotted the author name at the top of the article. Ah. It was Savilla, congratulating herself. That checked out.

I leaned my head against the soft chair and closed my eyes,

thinking of the heiress of this estate and the flawless contestants I'd seen checking in. I thought of Momma writing the letter shortly before she died, filling out the application on my behalf, deciding I could be one of them. My chest ached with longing to see her again.

I must've dozed off because I startled a few minutes later when a gentle chime sounded above and around me. Next, my aunt's voice—prerecorded, it seemed—came across the sound system, reminding contestants that their presence was required in the ballroom.

"The festivities are about to begin!" Aunt DeeDee's drawling timbre proclaimed from a discreet speaker hidden behind numerous plants in the corner.

I stood and ran my fingers through my hair, taking a deep breath as I tucked the pageant program under my arm. The first C was confidence, so I tried to gather my courage and ready myself for whatever came next.

When I arrived on the second floor for the meet and greet, I walked past another long gallery where gems were displayed along the wall, lights shining on the topaz and jade, opals and quartz, emeralds and aquamarines. Some of the jewels had been grafted into patterns fitted into necklaces and crowns, labeled with the year of the pageant in which they'd been worn, but others stood uncut as giant, glittering wonders.

I passed a case with a massive rock that had been sliced open, showing off sparkling purple and white stones, in front of a sign for *The Rose Palace Pageant Color Gallery*. I knew from Aubergine lore that this was how the Finches had continued to make money: finding, excavating, buying, and trading precious —and perhaps illegally obtained—gems, which they then turned into exquisite jewelry, a tiny percentage of which the pageant winners wore. The slogan, placed strategically at every

Aubergine event they sponsored, read, *Finch Gems for the Jewel in Your Life.*

Police officers milled around one empty case, devoid of treasure, along the periphery of the hall, which was probably larger than the entirety of Momma's house. One policeman was dusting for fingerprints, another stood watch, and a third jotted notes in a handheld spiral notebook.

My eyes were drawn to the case like a homing beacon, maybe because of the police presence or maybe because it was on the outskirts, like I wanted to be. The light still shone on the empty black velvet that had once held a crown from... *Miss 2001.*

My breath caught. The year of the missing pageant queen—and the missing cardboard cutout. What was it with that year's winner? Had she suddenly resurfaced to reclaim her crown? Was someone trying to remind us contestants what might happen to us if we won?

I stepped into the ballroom, where banners featuring the names of the winners hung around the room. I tried to recall what I knew about 2001's winner as my eyes scanned the names until I landed on *Glenda Finch*, Savilla's beloved "Step-Mommy." But I knew—everyone knew—that Glenda hadn't been the actual winner that year. That title had gone to the disappearing queen, and Glenda had merely stepped in and taken the crown second-hand. Runner-up turned royalty.

At least two dozen contestants, giggling and hugging one another as if they were old friends, were already swarming around me. Each of them wore not only a symbolic and colorful hat atop their head, but also had a refined beauty that no amount of Aunt DeeDee's ministrations could impart to me: the swoosh of hair, the soft laugh, the swanlike movements of hands and arms and feet. These women looked like they belonged in this ballroom awash with banners and glinting gold fixtures and shimmering chandeliers, but as I walked through them, parting the crowd, all eyes turned to me.

Confidence, comportment, conversation... I chanted in my mind, forgetting the stupid last C. *Calm? Cheerful? Clean?* Dammit. My stomach roiled, but I planted my feet and thought of the prize money and my family's financial situation. I needed to place this weekend. I didn't have to win, but I needed to appear in the top three. I pasted on a smile, hoping to *compensate*.

It must've done the trick because they looked away and resumed their chatter.

Savilla shrieked as she ran over to me and grabbed my arm, her fingers digging into my skin.

"I think I'll just watch from the corner," I said, motioning with my head as I tried to yank my arm from her grasp.

"Don't be silly," she insisted, as she pulled me back to the women with whom she'd been speaking.

I considered running in the opposite direction but noticed the other ladies watching with curiosity. I wondered if they knew I was DeeDee's niece, if they were judging me as much as I was trying not to judge them. Regardless, it seemed that if I was friendly with Savilla then they wanted to know me. The connection alone could serve me well this week.

"Ladies, this is Dakota Green," Savilla said, showing me off. "She's a top contestant this year, comes from a geriatrical line of queens. Her great-grandmother and aunt were winners."

"I think you mean *matriarchal*," I said quietly, so as not to embarrass her.

"You're hilarious," Savilla said in response. "But those winners... they are old now, aren't they?" She blinked innocently enough.

I supposed she was right: Aunt DeeDee was in her sixties and my great-grandmother would have been close to a hundred and thirty now. Touché.

The first woman, Jemma Jenkins, smoothed her platinum-blond hair and looked me up and down with her steely blue eyes as if sizing up the competition. She didn't seem to recognize me from earlier, even though I must have still looked like the help in her eyes.

"Dakota Green, this is Jemma Jenkins. She's an aspiring actress, lives in New York," Savilla continued. "She's been in two off-Broadway shows and is trying out for a much-anticipated musical in a few weeks. It's *Hamilton* meets *Cats*. Very nouveau art."

Very.

"Charmed, I'm sure." Jemma put out a hand and offered a strained smile.

"And this is Summer Patel," Savilla said, motioning to a woman with dark brown hair, cut and highlighted to perfectly frame her face. Her hat was red and wide-brimmed with a giant bow stuck on the back. "She's a kindergarten teacher, and this is her third year competing."

A kindergarten teacher was a surprising occupation for this crew, who I'd assumed either had pretend jobs—artiste, actor, writer—or lived off of family money. But going to work every day surrounded by little people with sticky hands and runny noses was real work. I was impressed.

"You have no idea how long I've wanted to meet you," Summer said. There was a sweetness in her manner that I hadn't expected from a pageant contestant. She pulled me into a big hug and I could smell hints of vanilla and cinnamon on her, as if she'd just stepped away from baking cookies. I could easily imagine this lady in Circle Time surrounded by adoring five-year-olds. "You look so much like DeeDee that I would know you anywhere. She's my unofficial mentor, the person I want to be when I grow up."

Wow. That was some adoration. I knew Aunt DeeDee had made a name for herself in Aubergine, but I had no idea that contestants from all over the Eastern Seaboard were so bewitched by her.

"Please let me know if you need anything. I've done a dozen pageants. I can give you tips or help you with your look or... whatever!" Summer practically squealed this last sentence before adding, "I have peppermint tea bags in my room."

"Thanks?" I responded, wondering why she was inviting me for a tea party.

Jemma enlightened me with a smirk. "For the bags under your eyes."

I rubbed at the corner of my eye. Who knew so many things could be wrong with a face?

"You should really try a darker shade of lipstick too," Summer suggested, so kindly that I couldn't be offended. "It will make your mouth appear fuller."

I didn't mention that I wasn't wearing any and instead forced the corners of my mouth into my best imitation of excitement to be there.

Jemma frowned. "Is your mouth okay?"

That's what I got for trying.

"Ladies, ladies," a familiar voice echoed from the stage. I turned to see Lacy speaking into a microphone, her voice and posture authoritative. She'd changed into her navy blue Dior suit and five-inch pointed heels. "You all look fabulous."

The ladies trilled.

"One quick note: We can't seem to locate our MC for all things pageant, so if you see her, direct her to me. I'm sure we'll find her soon." She tapped the microphone. "DeeDee... Deanna Green, if you can hear me, please report to the ballroom." Lacy's eyes landed on me as if she thought I would know where my aunt might be.

I waved my phone to signal that she wasn't answering my calls.

"I saw her leaving the Color Gallery with a bag when I first arrived," Jemma said, leaning toward me just enough to plant a question in my mind. "Dr. Bellingham was with her, and he didn't seem happy."

I tried to ignore her.

Lacy spoke into the mic again. "Regardless, it's good to see all of you in your finest regalia at this hundredth year of the pageant." She spoke with ease, smoothing away any awkwardness created by the absence of the official master of ceremonies and the intrusion of a police presence.

Whoops and cheers went up around the room, and Lacy smiled without her usual smirk.

"I hate to get down to logistics right away—and I promise a fun bonding activity, courtesy of Savilla Finch, is coming soon—but our first order of business is announcements, before we put everyone in proper order and run through the choreography for our pageant song that we'll perform on this very stage Saturday night. Hopefully you all received the choreography in your welcome packet via email two months ago."

Nope. Thanks for telling me about this new humiliation, Aunt DeeDee. Irritation followed by mounting concern at her absence pricked at me.

Lacy mouthed, *Sorry,* at me before turning back to the microphone.

"Our first announcement is just a reminder to everyone that each minute of the next seventy-two hours is considered applicable to the final score. Consider yourself watched and evaluated in every conversation, in every interaction, in every single step you take on these grounds. Understood?"

Heads nodded enthusiastically.

I straightened my shoulders in case any eyes happened to land on me. *You just need to place. You just need to place. You just need to place,* I chanted to myself over and over.

"The second announcement is that Jemma Jenkins has graciously volunteered to lead a Broadway Butt-Busting workout over the next three days." Jemma waved a hand and beamed as if she were the fearless leader of... *butt busting?* "Please feel free to join her near the fountain at seven each morning, and don't forget to let her know your favorite Broadway tune, so she can include it in her song selection."

Women either eyed Jemma as if they wished they'd thought to offer something so useful, or grinned as if they couldn't wait to get their butts into gear.

Lacy waited for the room to settle again and then continued. "If your last name begins with A through K, please step to this side of the stage and line up by height, and if your last name begins with L through Z, please move to the other side and do the same."

So it begins, I thought, before joining the others in ascending the stage. I was relieved to be next to Savilla so I could follow her lead.

Lacy, exhibiting talents I'd never known, led us through walking onto the stage with precise spacing. "Wait a moment," she would say, putting a hand out until the person in front had taken at least four paces. "And don't forget: shoulders back, chins ever so slightly downward. Your feet should walk in a line like you're on a tightrope."

All of the feet in front of and behind me were in heels at least three inches off the floor, but they were somehow more graceful than me in my nice boots, the only ones Aunt DeeDee had approved for this weekend. It also seemed that most of Lacy's instructions were for my benefit, and I appreciated the guidance.

After I relearned how to walk, Lacy stood in front of us, moving to a count of eight as she performed the choreography, which mostly consisted of waving one arm or the other in the air while we stepped to the right or to the left. If it hadn't been for my eye on the prize, I would've died laughing, especially because in order to remember the moves, I had to pretend to hold a lasso in my hand and envision that I was corralling a horse. It may have caused a few too many wrist flicks, but at least I didn't lag too far behind, and by the time the music played, I'd actually mastered the steps, which was good because an elderly woman in the back was watching me and taking notes.

Lacy cued the sound guy in the back, and music blasted through the speakers. Somehow all of us found the beat and proceeded to step in tandem. I did my best to mimic them, keeping a smile in place until the very last note.

"The official Rose Palace Pageant song," Savilla said, her eyes warm with nostalgia as a 1990s ballad, complete with soaring vocals, played. "I grew up listening to this song over and over while Mommy and I ran errands."

A childhood filled with pageant tunes. I couldn't begin to imagine.

Mrs. Glenda Finch stood on the floor in front of the stage, lightly swaying along to the beat. I could see her waltzing around this mansion, crown perched on top of her head as she recalled her glory days. A certain gleam in her eyes gave away her longing to be up there with us.

Before the song finished ringing through the venue, though, I noticed her check her watch a couple of times, tapping a hand against her leg impatiently as if deciding whether or not she should stay. I almost felt sorry for her, the former beauty queen now a bit aimless in her husband's show, but then her gaze fell on me and she gave the slightest shake of her head. What was that look? Perhaps she was blaming me for my aunt's absence. Or perhaps she didn't want me here at all.

I swallowed, trying to relax my tight muscles.

She checked her watch one more time and hurried toward the door. Then she was gone.

At the end of the song, we fanned both arms in front of us and took one step forward. Savilla gave me an approving nod, and a surprising flush of accomplishment washed over me. Okay. That wasn't as bad as I'd expected, not that I would choose this as a pastime of my own volition, but after three or four more run-throughs, we had it down, and I was strangely proud of us—well, of me mostly. I could now appreciate some of the challenges of the pageant world. It wasn't all about a pretty face and a nice smile. A bit of coordination was necessary as well.

"See. It's fun, right?" Savilla asked.

"Let's not get carried away," I answered, hoping it sounded like teasing.

Savilla tilted back her head and laughed a tinkling sound.

I'd never been a sorority girl, but I'd had a tight group of girlfriends in college and a handful of friends in my vet program —none of whom I'd spoken to or texted or emailed in months. I'd stayed at home on my own a lot the past year, hunkering down in my sadness—*wallowing*, as Momma so eloquently put it.

Though it wasn't a conscious thought, as I danced across the stage with these women I realized how certain I'd become after Momma died that if I moved on with my life, even an inch, it would mean losing my connection to the one person who'd known and understood me the best.

Aunt DeeDee had built a relationship with me over the years, of course, but it didn't come naturally like it'd been with me and Momma. When all dolled up, I might favor Aunt DeeDee on the outside, but my insides—my love of hiking and horses, my preference for sweet iced tea instead of coffee, my disdain for all things showy and pageant-like—that was all Momma. She'd been the mirror I'd held up to myself for my entire life, and without her, I barely knew who I was.

Now, I was being forced out into the open like a sitting duck by that very person, and somehow it wasn't killing me. Yet.

SEVEN

After we proved that we could manage the moves to the opening song, Lacy gave us a few minutes to grab sparkling water and mingle before our "bonding" got underway. A couple of days ago, I would've guffawed at the ridiculous waste of time that the choreography had been, but I'd enjoyed being a part of something bigger than myself as I'd waved my arms and swayed from side to side. I'd missed that kind of connection, and I wondered if perhaps that feeling of community was what these contestants were actually chasing. That and a lot of money.

Lacy came down from the stage and pulled me to a corner of the ballroom while other women chatted and air-kissed. One even slid off her heels and hat for a moment and began doing jumping jacks. With such a spectacle, I could barely focus on Lacy.

"Where is DeeDee?" Lacy asked.

"No idea. I haven't seen her since I got here." I bit my lip. "I talked to her last night. Do you think she's okay?"

Lacy's eyes scanned the room. "She's fine. She must be."

"I'll go and find out which room she's in," I offered.

Lacy checked the schedule. "No, don't go. The judges are

already watching from that corner." She nodded to three people on the periphery of the room, one of whom was the elderly woman who'd been taking note of me. "I'll ask someone on security detail to find her."

"Okay..." I hesitated, torn between my role as a contestant and my concern for my aunt. "But let me know as soon as you hear anything."

I told myself not to worry, but it wasn't like her to disappear, especially not when ladies in poufy dresses needed her help. Not that we were poufed yet, but we would be soon enough.

Just then another man in uniform entered the door to the ballroom, and I froze for a second. He was one of the finest men I'd ever laid eyes on. He was solid without being entirely made of muscle, like a sexy, impenetrable wall. He had a cleft chin covered in day-old stubble, a uniform that hugged him in all the right places, and he'd nestled a hat beneath his arm. But it wasn't just his appearance that drew my eyes. He had a quiet intensity about him, as if his real strength resided deep inside a place that he rarely revealed.

"We can ask the sheriff if he's seen DeeDee," Lacy said, pointing in the man's direction.

I closed my lips and forced my eyes to the floor. I hadn't had this kind of reaction to a man in... *ever*. I couldn't start now.

"What?" Lacy noticed my weirdness. "Oh, so you *do* like the look of him?"

I ignored her and forced myself to take the necessary steps toward him as if his presence didn't bother me.

"Hi, hello, um, sir," I started, almost tripping over those simple words. I swallowed and started again. "We're... we are looking for the MC who's supposed to be running this event. Her name is Deanna—DeeDee—Green. Have you or your... your officers spoken with her this evening?"

The man's face barely moved as his eyes scanned the assembled crowd, practically ignoring my presence. "Quite the coincidence. I'm looking for the same person."

The response was not what I'd expected. My mouth went dry, and Lacy had to step in front of me. "Why are you trying to find DeeDee?"

The man didn't turn to either of us as he answered, "That information is classified."

I decided to start again, putting on my brave face. "I'm Dakota Green."

His eyes flickered to me, widening a fraction before he extended his hand.

I reached out to find a surprisingly soft one that swallowed mine. I thought of what Lacy always said: *Soft hands, hard—*

"Charlie. Charlie Strong."

"You are," I breathed, before I could stop myself.

The faintest hint of a smile played about his lips. A tuft of hair emerged from the collar of his shirt in a David-Harbour-minus-the-mustache, aka Hopper of *Stranger Things*, kind of way. I'd always envisioned sheriffs as... well, old. If they were young, then they were trim, close-shaved men who wore polos and loafers when they were off duty.

One of his men approached and addressed him. "Fingerprinting is finished, sir. We got what we needed, including one witness who says she saw an older woman fleeing the scene at about the right time."

At the officer's words, a few disparate pieces fell into place. "Wait. Does Aunt DeeDee... Are you thinking that she has something to do with the missing crown?"

The sheriff looked at me—really looked at me—for the first time, and something sparked between us. It almost felt like attraction, but was more likely animosity.

"You might be able to answer that question better than I can," he said.

I took a step forward, planning to say something super witty like, *Now you wait a minute there, partner*, when I tripped, stumbling into him chest-first.

Great, Mr. Sexy-Deep-Well-of-Emotion officially knew I was only a B cup.

He righted me, practically with his pinky, and I attempted to reclaim some of my dignity. "My aunt and I... we... neither of us would ever have anything to do with steal—"

Lacy must've sensed that I was moving toward the shaky ground of suspicion if I hadn't already reached that destination because she tugged at my arm. "Dakota is a contestant—only arrived around, what?" Lacy looked at me. "Four o'clock or so?"

I kept my head held high and nodded.

"The Green Girls aren't thieves," I said.

He frowned. "Shouldn't it be the 'Green Women'?" he asked, catching me off guard with his apparent feminism.

"Yes, well. It's just that my mom, she was alive and then... so now she's dead..." Oh God. This was coming out all wrong.

"I'm sorry for your loss," he hurried to say. Those dark eyes seemed to really mean it. "She called you three the Green Girls?"

I nodded again.

He studied me and ran a hand through his dark hair. It was just long enough to curl slightly at the ends. "Sometimes I say things without thinking."

I knew the feeling.

"But to answer your question, yes, your aunt may be involved." His hands fell to his side, and an invisible shield moved across his expression. His jaw clenched in a way that showed he meant business, and I sensed that he struggled to live in two worlds: whether to be official or personable. He'd chosen official. I didn't like it.

I was about to try to find the words to tell him what he could do with his speculations when Lacy checked her Fitbit.

"Oh, shoot." Lacy began to pull me away. "Looks like it's time to bond. We'll see you soon, Sheriff."

When we were out of earshot, I scowled in the man's direction. "That's the guy you wanted me to keep an eye out for?"

Lacy raised her eyes to the ceiling. "He's nicer when he's not investigating a crime."

"A crime?"

"The missing crown."

"Right. Well, he's a real gem, a peach—a catch and a half."

"He certainly isn't at his best." Lacy hit her hand rhythmically against her side as she considered what to do next. "Okay, so we have to do this bonding thing."

"And then we're finding Aunt DeeDee," I finished for her.

Lacy gave a curt nod before she took to the stage, put on her best smile, and tapped a finger against the microphone at the podium. "Before we continue, I'd like to officially introduce our judges. Would the three of you please come to the stage?"

Women issued excited gasps as the trio waved from the edge of the room and began to make their way to the dais. A middle-aged man and two women—one rather round and nearing fifty; the other willowy and slightly stooped and well into her eighties—climbed the steps.

Lacy put on her best smile for them and signaled first to the man with the handsome face and head of salt-and-pepper hair who stood in the center. He waved and let his eyes settle on each contestant as if readying for a feast. When he reached me, he paused for a brief moment, and I could almost see him quarrelling with my aunt.

Ew. This was the man that Aunt DeeDee had warned me about.

"Many of you know the renowned Dr. Bellingham as a New York plastic surgeon," Lacy said as if the judge wasn't giving off creep vibes. "He's won numerous awards for his medical work with women all across the pageant scene. This is his fourth consecutive year acting as a judge, though we could count this as his seventh year since he served a three-year stint dating back to 1999. All that to say, he knows this pageant inside and out."

He'd served as a judge back in 1999 and then left the pageant for more than two decades. Why such a lengthy hiatus? I eyed him more closely.

"You can call me Jimmy," the man said, taking over the podium as if he was about to mansplain his own name. "I've been lifelong friends with Mr. Finch, who"—he paused and scanned the room—"must be overseeing final details for the party this evening." He stopped and breathed in the aroma of the women surrounding him. "Can I just say I'm delighted to be back at The Rose among the most beautiful women on the East Coast? I'm also excited to offer a twenty-five percent discount on all procedures scheduled by contestants by the end of the calendar year."

Those two statements sounded contradictory to me, but the other women didn't seem to notice as they pinched eyebrows with pointer fingers and rubbed at noses with pinkies, considering possibilities.

This man had to be the one doing important work like butt lifts and cheekbone implants on Savilla and her ilk. Dr. Bellingham turned his head to Lacy in thanks for the introduction. He placed a hand on her shoulder and slid it down to the small of her back. She inched away.

"Next we have Ms. Katie Gilman," Lacy said after scooting out of Dr. Bellingham's reach, "who proudly worked her way up from housekeeper to nanny to business owner to pageant judge. Welcome, Ms. Gilman!"

Elegant and classy, Katie Gilman wore platform heels and had her hair pulled into a tight bun. Her premier women's boutique in town—Beauty & Baubles—carried many of my aunt's signature designs and was known for inclusive sizing, boasting that they could fit anyone from size two, like Aunt DeeDee, to twenty-two, like Ms. Gilman, and beyond.

Savilla beamed and waved at Nanny Kate—as I'd grown up knowing her. Not for the first time did I wonder if Savilla had been a pleasure or a pain to raise. She hadn't been a bully or a mean girl, but she had been a ringleader, popular for her family's wealth and influence.

"Katie has been a specialty boutique owner for the past ten years in our very own Aubergine, and she says that the purpose of her business is to make women feel good about their bodies with the bespoke clothing and accessories she carries in her stores. She's happy to be serving as judge for her ninth year."

Most of the women at this pageant—contestants and staff alike—were thin, some almost waif-like, but Katie Gilman had a full figure, a buxom chest, and heavy hips. Although she hadn't been born in Aubergine, she'd invested enough time and energy into the pageant, the town, and the Finches that she was more than welcome as a judge.

Katie, wearing a tailored, peach-colored maxi dress with a three-quarter-length white shrug, curtsied.

"And finally," Lacy said, motioning to the elderly woman onstage, "we have the winner of the 1962 Rose Palace Pageant, Doris Davis. She's been working with the show in some capacity since she won decades ago, but we're so happy to have her with us this year as a judge, because the centennial is all about remembering the past as we look to the future."

Miss 1962, wrinkled and stooped, was the woman who'd been watching me. She wore an expression that said she could take any of us any day, her thin lips only faintly smiling.

As I watched the three judges watch us, I was reminded of the incestuous nature of this pageant. The Finches kept their judges close to home: an old friend, a previous employee, and a former queen. I just had to convince them that I belonged there.

EIGHT

As the judges went back to their spot in the corner and the staff began preparing for Savilla's bonding brainchild, Lacy told us to get into groups of three and four.

A frantic sort of energy hummed. It was obvious that many of these contestants had already been assessing alliances. I assumed everyone would want to be with Savilla, but before anyone else had the chance, she pulled me into a tight cohort with her, Jemma, and Summer. Relief at being included in their little circle of frivolity washed over me—not that I would choose to be there, but when at The Rose...

I kept my face in what I hoped was an open and welcoming expression.

"Along the walls are stations stocked with flowers and feathers and ribbons," Lacy informed us. "You'll have everything you need to make a floral headpiece that you and your team will model for the judges in a half-hour."

A headpiece? The first thing that came to mind was Halloween at seven years old when Aunt DeeDee had dressed me as a daisy, my face in the center surrounded by huge white petals bursting out of my head and my body covered in green spandex. Momma had got home from work at the last second, shocked. Still, she hadn't contradicted Aunt DeeDee's declaration that I was *the cutest thing since spring chicks.* After the fifth house at which I refused to lift my head and let anyone see my face, they finally took pity and let me run home and change into the cowgirl hat, chaps, and red boots I adored.

Surely *that* was not the kind of headpiece they had in mind.

"This may seem easy for those who are crafty and love to dress for all kinds of occasions, but here's the twist..." Lacy paused for dramatic effect. "Let's see what you can do while blindfolded."

Giggles issued from the women even as a competitive edge, almost as tangible as a knife's blade, inserted itself into the room. These women reminded me of mute swans: gorgeous creatures that will peck you bloody if you step foot in their territory.

"The staff will come around with bandanas, and all but one person in each group should blindfold themselves. No peeking." Lacy playfully waved a finger in the air. Some kind of pageant professional had temporarily taken residence in my friend's body. "Whoever isn't wearing the bandana will be the instruction-giver, and the other team members can't make a move without your say-so."

"You'll be our eyes," Savilla told me as she took the cloth and tied it around her own head.

"No, really." I tried a smile even as panic bubbled to the surface and the bandana lady moved on to the next group. "I have no idea what a headdress should look like."

"It's a head*piece*," Summer gently corrected.

"Exactly. I don't even know what it's called." I glanced at the rows of ribbons and fluff that a staff member was setting on a table near us.

"You'll be great," Jemma huffed, her words sarcastic.

Summer kept grinning, and I wondered if her cheeks ever ached.

It was too late to protest. Within a minute, we were standing in front of our craft station.

"On your marks. Get set. Go!" Lacy shouted from the front as she clicked an oversized timer on the podium.

Suddenly, I was blurting out instructions to Savilla, Jemma, and Summer.

Grab the flower. No, the other one. Pick up the glue. That's the glitter bottle!

I had no idea what I was doing as I tried to guide these three women to construct something that resembled a floral arrangement for someone to wear atop their head. It was giving Queen Charlotte in *Bridgerton*, and I wondered over and over why this was still a thing.

I stumbled over my words and wiped sweaty palms against my jeans. As my team felt around the table, Summer laughed as if this were great fun while Jemma and Savilla worked so well together that I wondered if they could actually see what they were doing. Meanwhile, I practically shouted at them to add more... *Feathers! Glitter! Gauzy stuff!*

Minutes crawled past until Lacy called time and everyone removed their blindfolds.

Behold what I hath wrought, I wanted to proclaim. It was a haphazard mess of blue silk roses covered in bright green glitter and neon pink sequins, black and pink feathers jutting out at all angles.

"It kind of looks like a bird's nest," Summer said, tilting her head and trying to see the good.

"More like a glitter sparkle bird that exploded," Jemma clarified.

I followed Savilla's eyes around the room to the other teams and the headpieces they'd created. Each was tasteful; some were downright gorgeous, like something you'd see on the cover of a bridal magazine.

"They cheated, of course," Savilla said, waving away the other designs. "It's fine. The important thing is that we bonded. Right, ladies?"

Summer nodded, happy to be there. Jemma rolled her eyes.

"In just a moment I'd like to invite the team member who wasn't blindfolded to the front to model your group's unique fashion piece. And remember, ladies..." Lacy's eyes darted to me. "Our three judges are watching! The centennial is a special contest this year, and the Four Cs are the pillars of this pageant."

Lacy held up one finger at a time as voices swelled in the room.

"Confidence!"

"Comportment!"

"Conversation!"

Lacy held up three fingers and spoke before the crowd could name the final C. "We all know the last C is 'costumes', and now you have these fabulous headpieces to show off as part of your attire. So, without delay, I'd like to invite our models to the stage to show off your teams' designs," she exclaimed.

Enthusiastic applause swept across the ballroom.

I tried to keep my voice low as I pleaded with my group. "I can't go up there."

What I didn't add was this: People—complete strangers— would be looking at me. Only me. And I wouldn't be doing anything worthwhile like barrel racing or even cantering. I'd be standing there, wearing a monstrosity. Oh God. My tongue was parched, and a tickle had begun on the back of my tongue.

"But ours looks so good," Jemma said, pouting her lips like she actually believed the lie.

"You're fine." Savilla gave me an encouraging push forward. "You better get used to it if you want first place."

"No, really," I nearly cried, my hands growing clammy. "I just couldn't possibly..." I turned toward Summer. "Please. Would you do the honors?"

"You'll be perfect," Summer told me, the words so lilting and musical that I would've believed her if my cheeks weren't already hot. "And anyway, now you have a hat—kind of."

Savilla plopped the creation on top of my head and pushed me toward the stage. Somehow my legs carried me. I swallowed back my fear. All I needed to do was walk across the stage. It would be good practice for the real deal in three days' time.

I waited in line, watching women glide down the runway. They were poised and beautiful and graceful while I was... something else.

When Lacy called my name, I could sense apprehension in her tone.

I reminded myself that I needed to do my duty for Momma, for my future, for the money, and even for the one or two allies I'd already made. I held my head high, put one foot in front of the other, and fixed my eyes on a point at the back door, my only means of escape. This was almost over, and I hadn't yet tripped or collapsed or humiliated myself.

As I reached the end of the stage, a familiar figure slipped into the ballroom: Glenda Finch, blanched white, her eyes as round as saucers and her mouth downturned. She looked in my direction but she didn't really see me this time, as if a hazy veil had been lowered across her brow. No one else seemed to notice her presence, but her cloudy expression concerned me.

When I stopped midstride, everyone's eyes followed mine to where she stood. Savilla's stepmother and wife to the owner of the Rose Palace Pageant walked into the center of the room, issued a small cry, and fainted dead away.

Savilla rushed to kneel beside her as I spotted a disheveled Aunt DeeDee hurrying into the ballroom, followed by Sheriff Strong. The expressions on both of their faces told me that something was very wrong.

The arrangement on my head fell and splattered onto the stage.

NINE

"Forgive my crumpled state," Aunt DeeDee said as she found me in the glittering lights of the ballroom. She slid a hand across her periwinkle pants suit, the wrinkles very out of place in this grand setting. Then she took my arm and pulled me into a hug. "You, though, look fabulous despite the jeans."

"Where have you been?" I asked, both relieved to see she hadn't lost her normal focus and frustrated that she'd gone AWOL.

"I was out at the back of the property, getting something for the tent displays, and then I was in my office when the police arrived and…" She shook off the question. "I lost track of time. It doesn't matter."

"One of the contestants said she saw you arguing with Dr. Bellingham and holding a black bag."

Aunt DeeDee narrowed her eyes and studied me. "That was two hours ago, and I was carrying my makeup bag. I needed a touch-up."

I didn't doubt her for a moment. "What were you two fighting about?"

"He wanted me to introduce you to him. A one-on-one. I

told him over my dead body—not in those exact words, but he didn't like that I encouraged him to meet you with the others at the tea tomorrow morning like everyone." Aunt DeeDee's cheeks reddened in her frustration. "He's either looking for a good time or a new patient, and you'll be neither, not for all the money in Aubergine." She lowered her voice to keep from listening ears. "Sweetheart, the police are searching my room. They got an anonymous tip... something has gone missing..."

"Miss 2001's crown?"

Aunt DeeDee assessed me as if trying to read my thoughts. "Yes, that, and... well, never mind. For now I need to go with them, answer a few questions. I should be back later tonight for the Jewels and Gems party, but if I'm not, I had all of your makeup and hair products sent to your cottage. Listen: you'll want to use the curling iron to make soft tresses, and your outfit is—"

"Stop." I cut her off, hardly believing that my aunt was trying to give me advice on how to wear my hair this evening. "Why would anyone need to question you about the missing crown?"

She gave me a knowing look and whispered in my ear, "Dr. Bellingham."

The judge's face sprang into my mind, and Aunt DeeDee could see that I was hearing her message loud and clear.

This man was framing my aunt.

Before she could say more, whispers arose from the middle of the room as Savilla helped her now conscious step-mother to her feet. The woman leaned against Savilla for support while contestants watched with concern etching their foreheads.

The three judges—Miss 1962, Katie Gilman, and Dr. Bellingham—made a sort of blockade around Savilla and Glenda Finch, and for a moment I was distracted from my aunt's dilemma.

"My husband has disappeared," Mrs. Finch said, her voice shaky and her face gaunt.

A murmur went up: concern for Mr. Finch no doubt, but also fear that the pageant might be cancelled.

I side-eyed Aunt DeeDee, who didn't seem as worried as she should be at this announcement.

What was happening at the Rose Palace? What exactly had I stepped into? I'd arrived with my own concerns about a vanished pageant queen from two decades earlier. Now, in less than a handful of hours, I could add the following:

1. A missing crown
2. A fainting Mrs. Finch
3. A disappearing owner
4. My aunt, suspected of theft

I'd come for a pageant, but this was quickly becoming a different kind of show, and each of us contestants, a new kind of participant.

"I know all of you likely saw my husband earlier this afternoon as you arrived," Mrs. Finch said, pulling a piece of paper from the pocket of her Gucci bag. "I thought he'd gone to lie down to rest before the party this evening." Her voice trembled with emotion. "If I'd known that he might... I would never have left him in our apartment, drinking a glass of whiskey and..." She trailed off and held the back of her hand to her mouth as if she couldn't go on.

Savilla took the page from her stepmother and read the contents to herself. From my vantage point, I was close enough to see the handwriting: a distinctive slant with occasional looping letters.

"Read it out loud, will you, darling?" Mrs. Finch stammered, tears forming.

Savilla, familiar with the spotlight, didn't seem to revel in delivering these words, but she swallowed hard and began reading.

"'I regret what I did to Miss 2001. I'm only getting what I deserve from the one who took her crown. To the real jewels of my life: Go on without me. Frederick Finch.'"

At the words, Aunt DeeDee took my hand and squeezed it hard enough for me to wince. A realization was dawning on her, one I couldn't yet comprehend.

Mrs. Finch let out a huff of air as if on the verge of another fainting spell, and the contestants pulsed forward as a unit. One of the judge's hands—that of Dr. Bellingham—extended as if to steady her.

The entire crowd of women as well as the sheriff, who'd recently entered the ballroom, seemed to be processing this missive, a brief one filled with regret and admonition.

I regret what I did to Miss 2001. Was this a confession? A suicide note? Had Mr. Finch known something or someone was coming for him?

Go on without me. The command, if interpreted one way, could sound like someone's last words, but the same words could also signal that he'd gone out for a walk and thought it best that his wife go about her evening without expecting his return—though why Mr. Finch would disappear on opening night, when he was "the rooster" and we were his "hens," I couldn't quite understand. He certainly hadn't seemed like a person contemplating the end during our brief encounter.

As Momma would've said, *Something's not setting right here.*

Savilla swallowed back emotion. "He's only been gone a couple of hours, StepMommy. You haven't had time to search the property, much less talk to the judges or the staff or"—here, her eyes landed on Sheriff Strong—"security."

"Oh, dearest," Mrs. Finch sighed. "You know how unhappy your father has been."

I thought of his wide smile that afternoon—not that people couldn't mask things, but still.

"Your father never goes out on his own these days, and he doesn't speak to the help."

That surprised me. Though Mr. Finch was obviously in his seventies, he'd seemed as cognizant and capable as anyone here —and eager to talk to any passerby.

"His phone and keys were left next to the note," Mrs. Finch added, watching our reactions as if to ensure we believed her story.

I couldn't help but notice that this woman seemed eager to jump to the worst possible outcome. But why? What did she— or anyone—stand to gain from her husband's disappearance? And a very public one at that...

My eyes went to the chandelier of cut glass and glimmering lights, and I knew my answer. The palace. The pageant. That's what she undoubtedly stood to gain.

"I've already checked his favorite spots myself, and I've asked members of staff to scour the property for him. I'm sure we'll find him soon, although..."

Although what? He'd likely be dead? That's what her free-flowing tears seemed to imply.

Savilla gently touched her stepmother's shoulder. "Doesn't all of this concern seem a bit pre-unsure?"

I studied Savilla, trying to decipher her particular misuse of language.

"Premature?" one girl offered from the back.

"No," Savilla said, turning to face the crowd again. "*Pre-unsure*. It's too early to be certain of anything." She looked back at her stepmother. "We're acting like Daddy is never coming back when he could just be out at the stables or even at the back of—"

Mrs. Finch threw up a hand, halting her stepdaughter's

musings. "Dearest, let's try not to assume the best. It can lead to so much unnecessary disappointment."

I almost laughed unceremoniously before realizing that Mrs. Finch was serious. The image of her jerking away from her husband's touch earlier in the lobby came to mind.

"However," she said, addressing the room, "the disappearance of my dear husband will not stop the good and important work we are doing here."

Work. Good. Important. None of these seemed fitting descriptors, unless someone like Summer won.

Mrs. Finch took a step forward. "For now, all of you, please continue as usual. I know this is a daunting ask, but I'm confident that my husband, who adored this pageant and all of you, would want nothing less. Besides"—here she extended a hand toward the sheriff—"law enforcement is already on the scene, and we may find Mr. Finch sooner than later. For now, if you know anything of my husband or of the missing crown, please come forward immediately."

For the briefest moment, I thought I saw the woman's eyes flicker to my aunt, but I must've been wrong. Aunt DeeDee could never be involved in something so... sinister, so... tawdry.

As I debated the reason for the flash in Mrs. Finch's eyes, I realized that, as selfish as it might be, I didn't want the pageant to be postponed or cancelled. I'd allowed Aunt DeeDee to wax and loofa me. I'd already accepted the fact that I would likely be watching TikTok eye makeup tutorials and caking my face with an inordinate number of products this weekend. Perhaps most importantly, I'd already started spending the winnings in my mind. I would save Momma's house. I would pay off the debt collectors. I would help Aunt DeeDee's business recover financially. I might go back to school. We would have a future again. My mantra ran through my mind: *You just need to place.* But I couldn't place unless there was a pageant in which to compete.

Plodding feet interrupted my thoughts as another man in

uniform stepped forward, holding a black velvet bag with sharp angles above his head and motioning to the sheriff.

Sheriff Strong stepped toward Aunt DeeDee, a look of resolution on his face. He took his handcuffs and held them at his side, and for a split second I thought he was coming for me.

Aunt DeeDee's eyes bored into mine. "Now, Dakota, don't believe a word they say, you understand?"

I found myself nodding, even though I had no idea what she meant.

Aunt DeeDee turned back to the sheriff, the hint of a pout around her lips, an expression I'd never seen her wear before. Sheriff Strong's gaze flickered to me, and I almost thought I caught an apology in his eyes.

As the sheriff pulled my aunt's hands behind her back and secured the handcuffs, I thought about how I hadn't been able to save Momma from what had come for her, but now Aunt DeeDee—the only parent I had left—was in a different kind of trouble, one that I might be able to fix if I could think straight and find a solution.

"Arresting me will take time away from you finding the actual culprit," Aunt DeeDee protested as shocked mouths fell open around us. "You know that."

The handcuffs clicked into place, and the sheriff turned DeeDee back around, scratching at his jaw. "Maybe. That's why I'm gonna take you in, get you settled, and hurry back as soon as I can." He took a deep breath and avoided eye contact with me. "For now, Deanna Green, you're under arrest for theft. You have the right to remain silent. Anything you say can and will be…"

As Sheriff Charlie Strong stoically read my aunt her Miranda rights, tears welled in her eyes, and my heart cracked at the edges.

The only time I'd seen Aunt DeeDee cry had been when I'd walked into Momma's room a week after her death, and she'd been lying in her sister's bed, holding one of Momma's ratty sweaters against her cheek, bawling her heart out. Even then, five minutes later, she'd collected herself, blotted her eyes with a tissue, and apologized for bothering me with all that noise.

Now Aunt DeeDee was sad and scared, and I didn't know how to help her. But I needed to try.

The contestants—their expressions frightened and intrigued despite their colorful hats, lined eyes, and glowing cheeks—parted like a curtain around Aunt DeeDee as the sheriff marched her out of the palace in handcuffs.

TEN

When I was little, Momma tried to make me fall in love with *Winnie the Pooh and the Honey Tree* because she'd loved the short film as a kid. We watched Pooh singing to the bees about being a storm cloud so he could steal their honey. For reasons only a good therapist could explain, this scene terrified four-year-old me, giving me nightmares about bees and trees and suffocating in honey. For years whenever so much as a fly buzzed past me on the playground at recess, I would fall to the ground, curl up in a ball, and wail until help arrived. So, Momma did what she always did: She made me face my fears.

By the time I was ten, she'd taught me how to find hives in the mountains. She'd taken me to visit a working honeybee farm where I learned to smoke bees to sleep. She'd encouraged me to climb every tall tree I could find. By my eleventh birthday, I was no longer afraid of bees.

All that to say, before the anger I'd experienced upon Momma's death, fear had always been my go-to emotion. No doctor had ever diagnosed me, but after taking my first psych class in college, the requisite 101, I figured that some kind of anxiety disorder—a hint of obsessive, a smidge of compulsive, and the smallest zest of depression—had coded its way into my neural pathways. Maybe that's why grief mowed me down like a Mack truck.

And maybe that's why time froze around me now. My aunt in handcuffs was a reality I couldn't comprehend. It made my knees weak and my heart thud in my chest. I stood still, immobilized by questions and that too-familiar fear.

I'd already lost my mother. I couldn't lose my aunt. I pulsed my fingers in and out, trying to remind my body to move again, trying to make my brain jump-start as I watched Savilla tend to her stepmother.

These two women, the two closest to Mr. Finch, had to know something they weren't saying—something about this palace, the pageant, or the people in it—and I needed information to help clear my aunt's name before I let them out of my sight.

I sidled up to Savilla, trying for a sweet tone that came out more eager than I intended. "Can I do anything?"

Savilla appeared relieved. "Thank you, Dakota. I need to take StepMommy back to her apartment. Can you help?" She addressed the person behind me as well. "Summer, you too... can you get her other side?"

I turned to see the petite contestant still hovering behind me. Summer's dark pink lips turned down in concern. "Of course."

I did as bid and offered my arm to Mrs. Finch while Summer hurried around to act as a kind of crutch on her opposite side. Mrs. Finch hesitated only a moment before deciding to allow both of us to give her aid while Savilla led the way to the Finches' personal residence. I caught Jemma watching us from beneath her hat, a hint of envy at our proximity to the Finches in her long-lashed eyes.

As the crowd dissipated, likely at a loss as to what to do with their unexpected free time, we slowly trekked past the library, down a long skylit hallway, past the lobby, around the edge of a solarium, and through a door camouflaged to look like part of the wall to a back flight of stairs ascending to the third floor. With all the twists and turns, I would never be able to find my way back to the ballroom, and I could only imagine what kind of montage we made: Savilla and Summer in their hats, me in my boots and jeans, and the glamorous Mrs. Finch sandwiched between us all.

As we strode through the halls of the palace, the light airiness of the public spaces gave way to a dimmed, yellow-tinged hue, and the fading wallpaper grew more ornate, less modern. A vine pattern on a dark blue backdrop meandered round and round the wall in endless figure eights, winding and threading into an infinity of intersecting lines. The Gilded Age influence was apparent and I realized that this must be the original décor. These were the rooms we hadn't toured back in middle school, the ones reserved for family and close friends.

The rooms in the residential wing were labeled with placards like *Anniversary Apartment, Queen Elizabeth Suite, The Remembrance Room*, and the shift in ambiance gave the sensation of stepping into a well-preserved version of the early 1900s. I wondered how many other secret doors fed off this hallway of suites.

I wasn't sure who else might be staying in the residential wing, but I guessed those closest to the Finches—perhaps the judges, maybe even Aunt DeeDee. I spotted two people trailing behind us, one rather quickly for her age. It was the female judges: Miss 1962, aka Doris Davis, and Katie Gilman.

"Have you checked the wine cellar?" Miss 1962 asked Mrs. Finch.

Of course there would be a wine cellar. I could almost see row after row of expensive labels, of corks being removed, of drinks toasting the woman of the year.

I turned to take a closer look at the elderly woman as she

theorized. Her blue hair had been cut close to her eyebrows and the edges of her mouth. "I know that Mr. Finch isn't typically a lush, but I've seen him imbibe a time or two, and those stairs are no joke for folks of our generation. Perhaps he poured himself a drink and got stuck down there. I'm not saying it's happened to me, but I'm also not saying it *hasn't* happened."

"Yes, Doris. We've done our due diligence," Mrs. Finch said vaguely as she continued to oscillate between leaning on my arm and Summer's shoulder, even though, as far as I could tell, nothing was actually wrong with her own two legs.

"Regardless, I'm sure it's nothing to worry your head about. He's bound to show up and surprise us all—a little pre-pageant fun," Miss 1962 continued as we reached the door to what I took to be the Finch apartment. "Maybe he's taking time to prepare a grand speech for the hundredth year. You know how he loves attention. He'll be delighted to get us all worried for nothing."

As Miss 1962 chattered on, I gave Mrs. Finch back to the care of Savilla, let the others step inside, and excused myself for a brief moment to text Lacy.

Can you come to the residential wing? We're somewhere in the third-floor hall. Near the Finch apartments

Can't come now—with security, organizing search and then need to check on setup in the decades tents, sorry!

When I looked up, Summer was in the hallway, watching me. "Who are you texting?" Her words sounded inquisitive rather than accusatory.

"Um... Lacy."

Summer studied me before glancing from side to side to ensure no one could overhear. "Do you think your aunt had something to do with... with Mr. Finch... with that note he left?"

I found myself appraising her tone and, instead of answering her question, I asked my own. "This is your third year competing now, right?"

Summer nodded.

"Do you know who might have access to every part of the estate?"

"With it being pageant week, I'd assume security staff and housekeeping." She considered. "But if you mean the entire estate, I guess that would be Mr. and Mrs. Finch, Savilla... DeeDee..." She scrunched her face in a way that let me know she was sorry to have to mention my aunt again.

I lowered my voice and moved toward Summer, encroaching on her personal space. "Listen, I know Aunt DeeDee had nothing to do with whatever's happened to Mr. Finch... but to confirm that, I need to take a quick peek in her room and I'd rather not go alone."

"Oh... well. Earlier when I said I would help you, I meant with makeup or... um... how to talk without being so nasally."

I furrowed my brow. I did not need pageant tips at this moment.

"I'm not sure if I should..." Summer trailed off, obviously torn.

Before she could answer, Miss 1962 appeared, peering around the doorway and calling out in a voice far too loud for her eighty-odd years, *"THEY'RE IN THE HALL!"* Then, she stomped back into the apartment.

The other judge, Katie Gilman, opened the door wider, her eyes darting from Summer to myself. "Are you two all right?"

"We're fine," I said.

Summer took two steps toward Katie. "Ms. Gilman, Dakota needs to get a couple of personal effects for her aunt to have in jail."

Okay, I was impressed. I loved Summer and her ability to lie when the moment required.

Katie narrowed her eyes. "What kind of personal effects?"

"Her makeup"—Summer was thinking on her feet—"and her wig."

I widened my eyes. Did my aunt even have a wig? I had no idea, but I didn't want to spoil whatever Summer was attempting to accomplish here.

"If she could just have five minutes in her room? To gather her... supplies?" Summer's voice was gaining authority. "You know what it's like without one's... one's creature comforts. Her eye mask, her powder, her perfume... It could make a world of difference for DeeDee."

I nearly balked at the fact that Summer was right: This was the exact list my aunt would likely request—minus perhaps the wig. I kept my thoughts hidden as best as I could.

Katie seemed to vacillate for a few seconds before she responded. "Give me a minute." When she re-emerged, she held a key card. "I need to bring this right back to Savilla, and I'm coming with both of you."

"I don't know which room she's staying in," I admitted.

Katie waved a hand as if it was no matter and led the way to the stairs and up one more floor. "Deanna is always in the same room, the one right next to mine. It's tradition."

As the three of us reached the fourth floor, Katie gestured toward her own room. "That's the old nursery suite where I lived for years as nanny. The Finches offered me and your aunt cottages, but it's a force of habit to stay up here. Every year, the same week, like clockwork. A family reunion of sorts."

"How wonderful," Summer said softly.

A sudden guilt pricked at me as I realized that I'd never even asked my aunt about her annual foray into the pageant world. I knew the basics—that Aunt DeeDee had won the crown thirty-odd years ago, that she got a job as coordinator and MC a few years later, that she came back here to stay every year like a pilgrim returning to a holy site. But beyond asking, *Did you have a good week?* I just hadn't bothered, and I certainly didn't care half as much about her role here as Summer did. The back of my throat clenched, and I wiped at one eye.

Katie opened the door to Aunt DeeDee's room and moved to let me and Summer step inside. It was obvious from the few beauty products and unmentionables scattered across the bed that the police had already been here, but I was determined to take a look for myself. The paisley carpet was thick beneath my feet, and a hunter-green wallpaper darkened the room. A gold-tinted comforter and rectangular pillows with dark blue cases sat atop the made bed. An unlit but gleaming fireplace with a tiny mantel sat at the back of the room, and paintings of crowns, scepters, and roses hung along the walls.

My eyes landed on my aunt's summertime purse—she preferred to change them with each season. Next to the mirror was her black makeup bag and on the bed was a garment bag with a Post-it reading, *For Dakota, All That Glitters... Jewels & Gems party. Trust me—Aunt D.* This must be the outfit that my aunt had selected for me to wear to the opening party this evening. She'd been thinking of me despite all of the drama.

Katie must've noticed the emotions rising in me as I stepped across the threshold because she reached out a comforting hand. "I'm sure she'll be fine."

"That's right," Summer added, already making a beeline for the bathroom, where my aunt's beauty supplies might be kept.

"They'll hold her for a few hours, realize they're barking up the wrong tree, and send her home," Katie added. "Nobody thinks your aunt stole a crown—or was involved in anything else."

I considered the "anything else"— Mr. Finch's disappearance and possible demise. I tried to believe her.

While Summer checked the bathroom, Katie scanned the room and I stood still, assessing the space. Aunt DeeDee's room appeared to be pretty standard with a sitting area and a queen-sized bed. I took in the neat row of perfume bottles on the desk and the line of dresses hanging inches apart in her open closet.

"I know this isn't about a wig, so what exactly are you looking for?" Katie asked. "I'm happy to help if I'm able."

"I have no idea, but I'll know when I find it," I told her as I got on my hands and knees and felt under the bed, which was spotlessly clean. Not a dust bunny in sight.

"Oh dear. I can't join you down there, but I'll check the..." She studied the cherry wood dresser at eye level. "Perhaps the drawers?"

"Sounds good," I said. I stood back up and rifled through the nightstand that held a stained glass lamp that looked like Mr. Tiffany himself might've made it. Inside, there sat a Bible and notepad and pen, but no notes scrawled across them.

"What's this?" Katie asked, holding up something she'd found while poking in my aunt's undergarments. Heat rushed to my cheeks as I thought about how much Aunt DeeDee would hate anyone searching through her things, but the police had already done as much. "I heard something rattle when I pulled open the drawer, and I found this wedged in the slides."

I took three steps forward so I could study the object Katie extended in an open palm. It was a ring, thick and sturdy, but small. Summer joined us from the bathroom, a makeup bag in one hand and, sure enough, a wig draped over her arm.

Katie placed the object in my hand, and all three of us formed a triangle, trying to understand what we were looking at.

"It's too small for a ring finger," Summer commented.

She was right.

I held the piece of jewelry up to the light and my stomach dropped.

ELEVEN

"Hello, Miss Green," Sheriff Strong said evenly as he entered Aunt DeeDee's room, where we stood staring at the ring.

Katie and Summer shrank back as if we were wayward children, and I could understand why. His intensity, along with his evergreen scent, filled the room.

"May I ask what you found?" He stepped beside me, taking in the object in question, and I hated the way that his nearness made my face flush. "Something shiny?"

"Something that's... that's none of your business," I stammered. I wanted to keep my cool with him this time. He was just a man after all, a man who was trying to prove my aunt guilty of who knew what. But still.

"My business is anything in this room," he said just as quickly.

I gripped my palm around the ring and slid it into my pocket as I glared at him. Momma's words from the past—*Family matters most*—and Aunt DeeDee's plea from earlier—*Don't believe a word they say*—rang at once in my mind.

He seemed content to wait for me to hand over the object as he folded his arms. "Did you know that the first-ever beauty pageant was staged by P.T. Barnum, the circus guy? He had all sorts of contests—the cutest babies, the finest flowers, the best chickens..."

"And the prettiest girls?" I asked. "How very progressive of him."

"You're the one competing," the sheriff said. I glared at him, and he was the one to backtrack this time.

"Not that you're not pretty... or that you shouldn't compete," he said, scanning my face.

I could almost swear he was embarrassed, and I had the urge to laugh.

He held out an open hand, waiting for me to deposit the ring. When I didn't move, he tapped at his badge. "Miss Green, please."

I didn't budge, and neither Summer nor Katie Gilman said a word. If this were a Western, we'd be in a good, old-fashioned stand-off.

"I'd rather not accuse you of withholding evidence. But if I must..."

"If you *must*? Surely you get to decide your own fate, Sheriff Strong."

"Not as an elected official, I don't." He reached out his hand again.

"Fine." I let out a heavy grunt and dropped the ring in his palm, refusing to touch his skin.

He moved his hand up and down as if feeling the weight of it. I could see the machine churning in his mind, coming to the same conclusion I'd reached. This was a man's ring, not one that belonged to Aunt DeeDee. I knew her jewelry. I didn't like most of it—too gawdy—but I knew it. This looked exactly like the ring that Mr. Finch had been wearing earlier. I hoped the sheriff hadn't made the same connection.

"I thought you were taking my aunt to jail," I said, attempting to distract him.

He reached into his jacket pocket, pulled out a small clear plastic bag, and dropped the ring inside before stepping back on his heel. "I sent one of my men with her. I had a feeling I should stick around. Now I know why." He glanced between me, Summer, and Katie. "My men already searched the room, so what exactly are the three of you doing in here?"

"I wanted to check out the curtains," I said with an innocent shrug. "See if I could make myself a nice dress."

"Frankly, my dear, I don't give a damn," the sheriff said without missing a beat.

Shoot. I hated that he could keep up with my classic film references.

"We plead the fifth," Summer said a moment too late as she straightened her back and looked the sheriff in the eye.

I wasn't sure if pleading the fifth even applied in a situation like ours, but sure. Crossing my arms, I took a long look at the sheriff, appraising him. "You arrested my aunt on theft charges, but I didn't see what was inside the black bag your man carried. What exactly did he find? A shade of blush that will work for him?"

I was pretty sure I already knew, since my first clue had been the empty spot in the case filled with crowns. Still, I wanted to see how the sheriff would answer. If he told me this was classified information, I would suspect him of trying to pin something on her, but if he was straight with me, then he might be someone with whom I could reason.

"We found the Miss 2001 crown among your aunt's things," Sheriff Strong answered. "That evidence, combined with the letter that Mr. Finch left behind, is concerning, to say the least."

Okay, fine. His response was reasonable, which I hated.

"You know my aunt only arrived this afternoon—"

"Yesterday," he corrected as he raised his eyebrows, highlighting how little I knew about my aunt's comings and goings. This wasn't a great start.

"Fine. Yesterday." I tightened my jaw. "My point is that someone could've easily removed the crown from the case before she arrived—or, even after—and planted it in her room."

"Except she's one of only four people with a key to the case." He began listing off the owners of said key, the same owners that Summer had mentioned: "Mr. and Mrs. Finch, Savilla, and your aunt."

"Anyone can make a key out of... I don't know... a paper clip." Now I was just saying random words to combat the sheriff's logic, logic that I didn't appreciate.

"This is a beauty pageant, not *MacGyver*," he said. "Regardless, do you know the significance of that particular crown, Miss Green?"

I didn't answer, so he turned to Katie Gilman, who stiffened before raising her hand as if answering a question on my behalf. "It belonged to the missing contestant. From 2001."

"Very good."

Summer seemed surprised by this information, and I realized that the story of that former winner's disappearance must not be a common conversation topic among current pageant participants. Perhaps only those who'd grown up in this town or been a part of it for decades knew anything about the mystery.

"Mrs. Finch was runner-up," Katie continued. "Miss 2001 disappeared and Glenda stepped in and took the crown."

Those last three words conjured Mr. Finch's note: *I'm only getting what I deserve from the one who took her crown.*

"So you're saying that in 2001 the actual winner disappeared, and all these years later her crown went missing from the display case?" Summer asked.

"Mr. Finch's note suggests that whoever stole that crown is enacting some kind of revenge on him for the disappearance of the original winner," the sheriff said.

"I love that you're relying on a letter Mrs. Finch could've written herself." A snort of derision escaped from me. "If he did write it, he could be saying that whoever originally took the crown from Miss 2001 is out to get him. That would be his wife."

Summer blinked and one of her eyelashes stuck to her cheek before coming off entirely. She yanked at the extension and stood there with one eye suddenly appearing smaller than the other as she considered the situation. "So, Sheriff, you believe DeeDee is involved because of that letter... and because the crown was in her room?"

"That seems circumstantial at best," I added.

The sheriff's expression was blank, which was maddening. "We are still gathering information at present, but from witness statements we do have probable cause to—"

"—to take my aunt into custody?" I met him eye to eye as much as his six inches on me would allow. We stared at one another for a beat too long, and my hands began to sweat again. I noticed the stubble running along his jawline, his matter-of-fact stoicism.

"For now, we're holding Deanna Green for the theft of the crown, but we'll be questioning all suspects as we search for Fred Finch." The sheriff took a deep breath as if weighing how best to proceed with three misbehaving women. When he began speaking again, his words slowed, as if we were children. I was not amused. "We had a tip from someone who said they saw a woman who looked like Deanna Green carrying a black bag and hurrying away from one of the ballrooms."

"Was it Jemma Jenkins?" I asked. "Or Dr. Bellingham?"

He paused and studied me. "Would you like to list everyone here this week?"

I did not appreciate his tone or the fact that he knew more than me. I would need to remedy that.

"Every woman here could look like Aunt DeeDee from a distance," I said. "What about Mrs. Finch?"

"The intel we received about DeeDee seems to check out.

Your aunt has been in this world for decades; you have no idea what she's seen or done."

"She would never take something that didn't belong to her." I answered without hesitation.

"If your aunt knows something, I hope she'll talk."

She wouldn't talk because she had nothing to say. That's what I wanted to scream at him. I wanted to shout, *There is no crime. There can't be! And you know how I know?* Because that was the woman who forced me to go to church, who taught Sunday School to obnoxious fourth graders every week, who tried to keep me from listening to anything other than gospel music for most of my childhood. More than that, she was the woman who returned to the register at a restaurant if she thought they hadn't charged her for a fountain drink. She was the woman who lived "Do unto others as you would have them do unto you," and up until this moment, I hadn't appreciated that moral compass like I should have.

TWELVE

When the sheriff didn't make a move to leave my aunt's room, I let him inspect the garment bag before I took Summer by the arm and carried my dress away. The two of us, heads held high like the queens we could become, made our grand exit into the darkly wallpapered hallway while Katie scurried back to the Finch residence.

The thing was, I had no idea where to start in order to prove my aunt's innocence or find Mr. Finch. I didn't know the extensive palace layout, much less where an old millionaire who'd left a cryptic note and then disappeared liked to spend his time on the estate.

"I'll see what Savilla and her stepmother are up to," I told Summer, pretending to know what I was doing.

"They may be getting ready for the party tonight."

I was taken aback by the suggestion. "But... Mr. Finch is... missing. You think they'll still attend the party tonight?"

Summer shrugged. "Mrs. Finch herself said that the show will go on, at least for now." She checked her watch. "And it starts in an hour and a half." She removed the eyelash extension from her other eye and wiped away streaks of mascara as if parts of her face falling off was all in a day's work. She looked down at the makeup and the wig that the sheriff had inspected before allowing her to remove it from my aunt's room. "I guess I should actually get these to DeeDee somehow?"

"If they'll let you." I wanted to be the one to go, but more than that I needed to stay here to clear her name.

"I'll at least try. It'll make her feel more like herself during… during all of this nonsense," Summer said. A rush of gratitude to have someone besides Lacy in my aunt's corner washed over me. "Then I'll hurry back and fix my face and change. I have some milk of magnesia if you want."

"For…?" I patted my stomach, assuming that she might be feeling queasy after all of this drama.

"Oh… sorry. No, although I do drink it after a long day with my students…" Summer laughed. "Milk of magnesia makes the best primer. Aftershave also works. Your skin will look like porcelain."

"Thanks," I said, more like a question.

"Seriously, I have everything in my cottage. I'm in number nine. I'll be there as soon as I figure out how to get these to DeeDee." Summer's earnestness was clear as she touched me on the arm one last time before gliding away to find an officer who might pass along the treasures she'd filched from Aunt DeeDee's room.

At that moment my phone rang with an unknown number, which meant it could have been another debt collector—but it could also have something to do with my aunt. Just in case, I pressed the green button.

"Hello?"

"Ms. Dakota Green?" a man's baritone voice said.

"This is she," I answered.

"This is Officer Micah Spradlin. Your mother took care of my wife when she…"

I vaguely remembered him and his wife, who'd survived breast cancer a few years ago.

"Anyway," he breathed. "I have your aunt here at the station and you're her one call. Would you like to speak with her?"

"Yes," I almost shouted.

"Here she is."

There was some shuffling and then my aunt came on the line. "Dakota?" Her voice quivered.

"I'm here," I said, wishing I could reach through the phone and pull her close.

"Listen, hon. I wanted to tell you... well, I can't really explain..." I could almost see her eyeing the officer listening over her shoulder. "I need you to work with the sheriff."

This was not what I'd expected. "But—"

"I don't get much time, sweetheart, but you need to know that he's just doing his job. I was praying on my way to the station and—"

"All due respect, but this isn't the time for a prayer meeting," I interrupted her. *Oh Lord, not praying.* Aunt DeeDee often referenced God as if he'd sat across from her with a cup of coffee that morning, but unless he was about to show up and spring her out of jail, I wasn't having it today.

"Dakota Deanna Green," she said, using my full name in the way she had when I'd snuck a pack of cookies into my room and attracted the longest-ever trail of ants, which had been my goal. "Listen carefully to me."

"Yes, ma'am," I said, cowering in the hallway.

She took a deep breath. "As I was saying, I was praying and I had one of my feelings." I knew what she meant without her having to explain. She'd often credited it to discernment or "the Holy Ghost," but she was right more often than not, so both Momma and I had learned to listen to her feelings. "The sheriff is just doing his job, and as soon as he has all the missing pieces of whatever is happening here, he'll come to his senses and release me. I can tell: He's a good man."

Even though she might be right about the sheriff's overall character, I'd already found him to be difficult.

"He needs help though," Aunt DeeDee continued. "He's new at this and you know that Aubergine doesn't take kindly to outsiders unless they're in a gown and heels or looking to spend a bunch of touristy money." She paused to let that reality sink in. "You've been adjacent to the pageant world your entire life, and you can help him find what he needs to get me out of here."

"I don't think he wants my help."

"That doesn't matter. I have faith that you can provide him with the evidence he might miss. Do you understand?"

"Yes, ma'am."

"Good, then that's settled," Aunt DeeDee said, taking a calming breath as if she'd checked the final item off her to-do list. "I'll just wait."

THIRTEEN

On the day of Momma's funeral the July sun shone bright, but a surprisingly cool breeze afforded us a beautiful graveside service. I glowered at the blaze above, and I grumbled as the preacher from First Baptist read Psalm 23 to fellow cancer victims, townspeople, and our small family of two. I fought the urge to pop the bunches of Mylar balloons Momma had requested we release at her grave—*To remind you I'm watching from above*.

I'd never thought of myself as a particularly angry person, but that was probably only because I'd had no reason to be mad before that day. I'd been raised in a good family—even if unconventional, with no known father and Momma and Aunt DeeDee acting as my co-parents. My life had been a steady downhill stream of academics and animals, flowing to a future as a successful small-town veterinarian. A bit dull, maybe, but even as a kid that's how I liked it: Set a goal. Work hard. Reach it. Repeat.

With every setback in Momma's treatment though, the angrier I'd grown, so by the time I stood at her graveside, my black dress itching at the zipper, I was spitting mad. I hated the preacher and my aunt and the hospital and this town that would bring pies and "easy to heat up" casseroles. I hated Momma for dying. I hated myself for my powerlessness. I hated life. For one whole week. Then, I ran out of steam. The anger evaporated, and a heaviness settled in my bones, making me sleepy and languid, like I was walking through water all the time.

One of my professors had worked in the wilds of Africa, studying behavioral patterns in elephants. I remember her talking about their grief process, how a young elephant would walk around the matriarch's dead body in circles, how the herd would bury their dead, how they would cry and show signs of depression. I knew that's what I had, but knowing something doesn't fix it.

Sleep really is a lovely escape, as I'd found a month or so after Momma's death, when friends were announcing on social media their return to what would've been my final year of vet school. I'd fall asleep with my phone in hand and stay that way anywhere from twelve to fourteen hours a day, that is until Aunt DeeDee woke me one morning by banging pots and pans around the kitchen. She'd come by at least once a day, often bringing food, but she hadn't made me a full breakfast since weeks before Momma died.

"No more of this," she said when I stumbled into the kitchen and poured myself a cup of day-old coffee. "Today, we're going to the doctor to see about some medication. I also got you a job at the stables until you can find something more permanent, or go back to school."

I was surprised that she'd gone to such lengths, not that I should've been. She'd organized my after-school activities and driven me to doctors' appointments for more than half of my life. Still, this kind of directness, this demanding—this was new.

I tried to brush aside her talk of a job. I planned to live on... well, for the first time in my life, I didn't have a plan. Failing so spectacularly to save my mother's life had knocked all of that right out of me.

As soon as Aunt DeeDee had seen that I'd finished my breakfast, she'd shoved me into the bathroom, handing me a worn pair of jeans and a wrinkled T-shirt she'd probably found on my floor. Later, she shook her head as she located my boots —one in the hallway and the other under the couch—and tisked about how Momma would be ashamed at the state of her house.

That got my attention—a little.

Later that morning, we saw Doctor Palmer, who gave me a prescription for an antidepressant, and that afternoon, I swallowed my first dose before trying to make a list of things I'd need to do to properly clean the house.

At the end of the day, I'd felt better—only two percent better, but still... it was something.

The next day, Aunt DeeDee arrived and we did the entire process all over again, but this time instead of taking me to the doctor, she dropped me at Straight from the Horse's Mouth Stables for an informal orientation and introduction to Bella and the other horses. Ever since that day, I'd had a routine, a place to go, a purpose. Thanks to Aunt DeeDee.

Lacy moved back home a couple of months later—a job in New York hadn't panned out—and started her event planning business for Aubergine and surrounding towns. I never confirmed it, but I wondered if she'd also been encouraged by my aunt to return to open her new business there because of the state of me.

Lacy and my aunt saved me from starving to death or being buried beneath my clutter—and the weight of my own grief— but I hadn't fully rejoined the world again as a whole and functioning person. I hadn't needed to. Yet.

With renewed purpose I told my aunt I loved her and hung up, and I made my way back to the Finch residence. I knocked on the door labeled *The Tickled Pink Apartment*, and Katie called for me to let myself inside.

The name of the apartment did not disappoint. The entryway sported a rosy-pink glow, and blond wood stairs rose half a floor into an open living area. By the door was a hat stand, so I hung up my garment bag. I took in the high domed ceiling and the curved windows before my eyes landed on Mrs. Finch, lying with her legs elevated on a hot-pink velvet settee.

"Thank goodness you're here," Mrs. Finch said. At first I thought she was speaking to me, but then she extended an arm to Katie Gilman. "Doris went back to her own room to take a nap, and Savilla's in the kitchen, making me toast—as if I could eat a bite. I'm here all alone with my thoughts."

Katie gave a pitying smile to Mrs. Finch before motioning for me to take off my boots. My feet sank into a pale pink carpet. Behind us, the walls popped with vertical magenta stripes against a light silver plane. Barbie's Dream House had nothing on this palatial abode. As Momma would've said, *It was something else.*

I had trouble imagining the man I'd chatted with earlier, and who was now missing, in this very pink environment. Not that Mr. Finch had seemed overbearingly masculine, but he also didn't seem like someone who would appreciate pink, Pink, PINK!

"Do you need anything? Can I get you water? Or a drink?" Katie asked Mrs. Finch, falling easily back into her role as former employee.

"My slippers—if you'd be a dear—and then if you could pour me the slightest smidge of Mr. Finch's whiskey."

Katie opened a tall, cherry-wood cabinet that stood regally behind Mrs. Finch's settee and then motioned for me to pour the woman a drink before she strode into the recesses of the apartment to locate the requested slippers.

"Carolina, isn't it?" Mrs. Finch asked me, though with her

arm thrown dramatically across her eyes, I wasn't sure how she could see me clearly enough to know.

"Dakota," I answered, trying not to sound offended that this woman couldn't seem to remember my name.

"That's right. Savilla's friend."

Uh. That might be a stretch, but I'd go with it.

"Just this much," she requested, lifting her other hand and separating her fingers about an inch apart. "It's on the top shelf, behind the books. We haven't been here since December, but still my husband feels the need to hide his whiskey. Says he doesn't like to share his vintage stash... always paranoid people are after his things."

This assessment of her husband was an interesting one, particularly since he'd donated enough money to the town of Aubergine for a premier park and a renovated school, as well as invested in a slew of businesses on Main Street. Not exactly the behavior of a paranoid or stingy man. I wondered how well Mrs. Finch knew her own husband.

I took the books from Mr. Finch's cabinet shelves and stacked them one by one on an end table. Most were expected —*A History of the Pageant World* and *A Pageant Coach's Guide to Being Crowned*—but there were a couple of surprises, namely *Backyard Apiaries* and *How to Rebuild a Broken Home*. Fleetingly, I wondered if this last title was literal or figurative.

As I pulled the whiskey decanter from its resting place, a thin ledger book that could fit in the palm of my hand fell forward. Since Mrs. Finch's forearm was still draped languidly across her eyes, I picked it up and silently turned the pages, which were filled with row after row of numbers.

I slipped it in my back pocket, promising myself that I'd return the item after a closer look.

Opening the bottle, the scent of caramel and vanilla wafted out. A tray of mixers lined the very back of the shelf: ginger, lemon, honey, sweet vermouth, and grapefruit juice. There were two small glasses next to the tray.

"Would you like me to add anything?"

"Is there honey?" she asked.

I opened the lid of the small glass jar which was much like the one I'd been gifted when checking in earlier that day. This one sported a homemade label featuring a tiny purple bee and a small white flower with scarlet dots. As I peered inside, the fragrance of grapevines met my nose. It reminded me of hikes with Momma when she'd taught me to spot nightshade, hellebore, and mandrake. We weren't witches—unfortunately—but Momma had wanted to make sure I would know what not to eat if I ever got lost up there.

"There's a bit left," I told her, just as Katie reappeared.

"Now, Mrs. Finch, you always say that eating sugar makes you anxious," Katie advised, slipping Mrs. Finch's feet into the fuzzy pink slippers. The gesture was surprisingly intimate.

"Never mind, then." Mrs. Finch sighed, seeming frustrated by my slowness as much as by the advice that Katie had offered. "I'll take it neat."

I poured *a smidge* as fast as I could. As I handed it to her, I decided to go with a direct approach. "Mrs. Finch... if your husband left of his own accord, where do you think he might go? Does he ever walk the grounds?"

"Not during pageant week. He's either here with me or downstairs with the contestants." Mrs. Finch took a sip. "The library and the solarium are his favorite places—besides our apartment—but security would've found him if it was that obvious."

"What about the gardens? I'm only asking because I may join the search party," I semi-lied. "I spotted a hedge maze in the center. Perhaps he... got lost?"

"I ordered the team to search high and low, to check every inch of the gardens. I also contacted the front gate, and I called all of our friends in New York as well as the firm that handles our money. No one has heard from him, and he left his phone, wallet, and keys here. It's like he vanished into thin air." She took a swig of her drink and then stared at me over the lip of the glass before continuing: "My husband is aging. He just turned seventy-five, and even though he doesn't look it, he has a list of ailments a mile long. Gout, diabetes, high blood pressure..." She realized to whom she was speaking and trailed off. "Regardless, he doesn't just"—Glenda raised a hand in the air—"wander off without letting me know his whereabouts. You may not realize this, but a twenty-five-year age difference at this point in our marriage means I play nurse far more often than I play wife."

"Of course, Mrs. Finch," Katie said, trying to mollify the woman's mood as she pushed a wingback chair closer to the settee and sat on the edge with her ankles tucked out of the way. "I'm sure Mr. Finch will reappear any minute. Dakota doesn't mean to pry."

But that's exactly what I meant to do. It was the only way to find evidence to get my aunt out of jail and ensure that the show continued so I could have a chance at winning the prize money. I needed those things to happen as soon as humanly possible.

Mrs. Finch ran a finger around the outside of the glass before handing it back to me. "Another, if you don't mind."

I did as bid and gave it back to her.

"That man has loved every minute of his life. Every event, every trip, every woman." Here, she took another long gulp. "If he's gone, there's a reason."

"But there was no sign of a fight. Or of a break-in," Katie said, patting Mrs. Finch's hand in a calming manner. "You really should try to think positively."

"I know my husband. He wouldn't fight. He would use his charm—or his money—to get himself out of a scrape. He may be negotiating with his captor at this very moment."

A sudden possibility hit me. "You said that when you left

him this afternoon, Mr. Finch was finishing a glass of whiskey and about to take a nap, right?" I held out the bottle. "He's a relatively small man. What if—what if the whiskey is drugged, and someone carried him out?"

Mrs. Finch held her glass to the light, looking through it as if she might see particles of husband-disappearing molecules inside. "If the whiskey is drugged, I guess we'll soon find out." Then, she took the final sip.

I was concerned as she held out the glass for another. Did this woman have a death wish? Or was I so off the mark that she was mocking my conjectures? Either way, I was obviously doing great in my first few minutes as an amateur detective.

I refilled her glass and handed it back. Glancing around the room, I tried to keep my itching fingers away from the ledger in my pocket.

A moment later Savilla entered. She'd taken off her hat and outfit from earlier, and she'd changed into a plush pink robe and wound Velcro curlers through her hair. Her face was caked in some kind of mint-green mask, so only her eyes, now makeup-less, were visible. She carried a plate of toast as well as an assortment of tea cakes and scones that I was almost certain no one would eat.

As she served her stepmother, I felt entirely unnoticed, which allowed my eyes to roam to the art hanging around the room.

There were four paintings, each an abstract of a faceless woman wearing a sash and crown. I moved closer to the piece nearest me while Savilla and Katie continued to fuss over Mrs. Finch. In the corner of the first canvas, I caught the name of the subject and the painter.

Miss 1990 by Frederick Finch.

Miss 1990. That was the year that my aunt had won. I inched nearer to the picture to find any defining features of Aunt DeeDee. Beyond the blond hair, which each of the women in the paintings seemed to have, I couldn't find anything... except for... my eyes scanned the subject until they landed on my aunt's collarbone.

There it was. The faintest purple smattering of paint on the right side of her clavicle. My aunt's oval birthmark. *A hemangioma*, my mother had said, telling me the technical term the first time I could remember asking about it as a child when I pointed to a similar mark, this one heart-shaped, on my forearm. It was another physical trait that Aunt DeeDee and I shared. But I knew for a fact that she always disguised hers with makeup; she would've never let her birthmark shine brightly during the pageant, as Mr. Finch had suggested in his painting. I squinted at it again before moving on to the next one.

Miss 2001 by Frederick Finch.

The year of the missing winner and now the stolen crown. There was no way I could determine the person in that painting. No special marks and, like all the others, the subject was blond with a blurred face.

Thankfully, I didn't have to wonder because Mrs. Finch caught me studying the painting and volunteered the information.

"That's me. In my younger years. What do you think?"

Before I could stop myself, I asked, "How do you know it's not the original Miss 2001?"

The three other women in the room halted in mid-motion.

At least twenty seconds passed before Mrs. Finch let out a tinkling laugh. "Of course it's me." She waved a hand as if wafting at a vapor. "Miss 2001 excused herself from the festivities, and I was immediately crowned queen. I've held the honor for years. She had it for... I don't know... a matter of hours." She said the final words as if the initial loss of first place didn't cut deep, which helped me understand how much the wound had actually stung.

"Who was she?" I asked, perhaps too bluntly. "The first Miss 2001?"

Savilla coughed, and Katie held her breath. Apparently, neither of them wanted me talking with Mrs. Finch about her past.

"Sometimes..." Mrs. Finch gestured vaguely in my direction. "Sometimes even the best showrunners don't do their jobs well." She gave me a pointed look, as if I should know to whom she referred.

"Wait... who was in charge? Aunt DeeDee?"

Mrs. Finch shrugged. "For all involved, I think it's best to leave the past in the past. Don't you think, Cheyenne?"

"Dakota," I corrected again. "And, no, I think it's best to—"

"Yes, of course, of course," Mrs. Finch said, cutting me off. "You know, it's an unfortunate reality that sometimes... well, people lie and there are consequences. You are so good to remind us." She gave me a polished smile before continuing. "When that year's queen abdicated her throne, the crown and title fell to me. It could have caused quite a scandal if I hadn't graciously stepped up to the task. As it was, everyone was thrilled with how I handled my duties, especially Mr. Finch."

Savilla seemed to breathe a sigh of relief at her stepmother's summary of events while Katie averted her gaze. Both responses only made me want to know more.

"A lucky break, that's what it was. My parents couldn't even afford to miss work to drive down for the pageant," Mrs. Finch said, nestling into the settee. I sensed her addressing me even as she closed her eyes in remembrance. "I borrowed a couple of dresses from another friend who had more money than we did, and I took the car into Richmond one day to shop with the only credit card Daddy had to his name. I left the tags on everything and planned to return them after the contest."

"But you won—at least, eventually?" I could almost see Mrs. Finch standing onstage as runner-up, salivating for that winning crown before taking it the next day. Why wasn't she the primary suspect here? She clearly didn't care for her husband, and that crown had landed in her greedy hands. I strolled past the third and fourth paintings, these less remarkable and more recent. *Miss 2012. Miss 2019.* Both by Frederick Finch.

Mrs. Finch opened her eyes and studied me as if she'd suddenly become alerted to my nosiness. I wondered for a moment if she might kick me out of her apartment, but she was far too polite—or at least wanted to appear that way. Besides, if she had nothing to hide, I couldn't be a threat. Perhaps she sensed me thinking as much because she continued, "Yes, after a bit of... drama, I won the crown and so much more."

I looked at the three women sitting in a half-moon in this Victorian-era apartment covered in pink. Mrs. Finch lay on what would've been called a fainting couch a hundred years earlier when the pageant had begun. The other two ladies—a fashion-conscious, middle-aged Katie and a chic, young Savilla—looked like Mrs. Finch's ladies in waiting, her loyal companions, her partners in crime.

I tried to squash my wandering thoughts. I couldn't allow the décor and this strange environment to cloud my thinking. For all I knew, the original Miss 2001 had run far away and gone on to live a full and happy life.

But, no, that idea didn't *set well in my gut,* as Momma would've said. The police had found that year's crown in my aunt's room on the very night that Mr. Finch had supposedly written to the "real jewels" of his life, telling them to "go on without" him.

There was more to Miss 2001.

Mrs. Finch finished her little diatribe. "Frederick was smitten." She laughed dryly. "He told me later that he hadn't wanted me to win the crown because he'd already decided to marry me, and it might make people think the pageant was rigged."

"Is it?" I asked.

"Of course not," answered a startled Savilla, her ice-blue eyes boring into me for the first time. Perhaps she wanted her stepmother to rest... or maybe she didn't like my curiosity about her family. She stood abruptly, excusing herself to get ready for the party before hurrying away.

I could almost see Mrs. Finch all those years ago, playing coy, refusing to sleep with Mr. Finch so she could have the real prize—all of this. When Miss 2001 fell off the face of the earth, Mrs. Finch won the man, the estate, and the crown.

Lucky girl.

FOURTEEN

What those people who aren't from rural communities fail to realize is that most people who call themselves *cowboys* or *cowgirls* work day jobs that have nothing to do with tilling the soil or herding the cattle. They are the teacher who lives at the family ranch in the summers, the orthopedic surgeon who drives an hour from the farm she and her husband bought as part of their retirement plan, the kid who wears tennis shoes to school and dons boots at the junior rodeo. Being a cowgirl is a state of mind whose only requirement is a penchant for animals and dusty jeans.

Until her arrest, I'd somehow forgotten that Aunt DeeDee was the one who'd first started telling me stories about a real-life cowgirl and heroine named Kate Warne while Momma worked the late shift at the hospital. For a handful of years Aunt DeeDee took charge of dinner and bedtime, so when the house was quiet, I would snuggle under my blanket speckled with cartoon horses, and she would curl her body around mine and tell me about this first female detective who she claimed was a part-time cowgirl. The stories always featured a different alias—Kitty, Kat, Katie, Kay—and were filled with details about how this woman and her horse thwarted plots against President Lincoln, tracked down a bank robber who'd stolen thousands of dollars, gathered intelligence during the Civil War, and generally set the nineteenth century to right. Surprisingly, Ms. Kate Warne's childhood had been much like mine—brought up by her mother and maiden aunt, a girl who had one close friend and could sense what an animal needed with a glance.

Except some parts were made up. When I reached middle school and decided to do a research report on this famed historical figure, I discovered that Kate Warne died in her mid-thirties and researchers know very little about her—except for the Lincoln story, which is true—and that her horse was entirely a figment of Aunt DeeDee's imagination.

When I'd asked Aunt DeeDee about the fictional additions to the woman's life, she'd shrugged and said she'd *expanded the truth* because she wanted me to know that I was just fine. As a tomboy in a town known for a beauty pageant, she knew I didn't quite fit in with the popular kids, like Savilla Finch and her crew. She wanted me to see that someone like me—a girl who preferred to read *Black Beauty* and draw horses, a girl who cried over deceased goldfish and feared honeybees for the longest time, a sensitive and independent child who didn't fit an exact mold—was a good thing to be.

I was staring at Aunt DeeDee's abstract portrait and remembering these things when my phone vibrated. I excused myself from the Finch living room to check for messages. Three missed calls labeled "Spam" meant the creditors were at it again, and their relentlessness made my stomach churn with the uncertainty of the future. I could see myself standing outside Momma's house next to a foreclosure sign, a few heirlooms and a box of photos in the back of my car.

Aunt DeeDee always said catastrophizing was a waste of time, but I'd literally watched a catastrophe happen with

Momma less than a year ago. In order to avoid another, I had to push forward and I had to win.

I cleared the notifications, unable to deal with that right then, but I was glad for an excuse to get out of that stifling apartment. With an uptight, entitled Mrs. Finch ordering us about and with a nameless Miss 2001 hanging on the wall, I needed to catch my breath.

I grabbed my garment bag at the door, and looked up and down the hallway, wondering how to get back downstairs. I tried one direction but hit a dead end. I retraced my steps, this time feeling along the wall in case there was a hidden door. As I followed the wainscoting, I noticed a break in the wall and pushed it to find the staircase we'd ascended earlier. I shook my head in wonder as I hurried down to the first floor.

The Jewels and Gems party would start soon, but there were no more bustling hallways or women click-clacking across the marble floors. Since I still didn't know how to find my cottage, I decided to sneak into the bathroom nearest the lobby. Even the restroom was opulent, with gleaming brass faucets and gray-speckled marble.

As I sat in one of the stalls, I took the ledger I'd "borrowed" from Mr. Finch's whiskey cabinet, perusing the contents.

The original entry on the first page of the wire-bound book was dated 1982. The letters *R.P.P.*—Rose Palace Pageant—had been written next to a series of numbers, most of them deposits, but a few debits that increased with the years. The next page was dated 1983, the following 1984, and on and on the pages went, a detailed account of that year's pageant and the income brought in and expenses going out. The bottom of each page ended with a profit until the year 2001, when the numbers on the page grew smaller and smaller. Hmmm... so maybe Mrs. Finch had been wrong. Perhaps her saving the throne that year hadn't been as effective as she'd assumed.

I couldn't make out most of the abbreviations in the left-hand column, but a repeated entry labeled "Peabody" started in 1996. At first, the amount next to the name was meager by Finch standards—$16,000. But every few years after, the amount increased.

1996 Peabody: $16,000

2000 Peabody: $35,000

2003 Peabody: $47,000

2007 Peabody: $62,000

Whoever this Peabody was, they'd gotten a lot of money over the years.

I flipped past empty pages and a folded white piece of paper fell to the floor. It was a series of numbers for a policy—a life insurance policy—taken out on Mr. Frederick Finch in the amount of eight million dollars on May 3 of this year. A month and a few days ago.

My eyes scanned the document to the signatures at the very bottom of the page. There were two.

First, Savilla Finch was the guarantor, paying the monthly premium, but why would Savilla need an insurance policy on her father? Wasn't she already set to inherit? Or would everything go to her stepmother?

My eyes landed on the second signature, the witness. It read *Deanna Green.*

Oh Lord, this didn't look good. Again.

Even with signs pointing to the contrary—the crown in her room, the pinky ring in her drawer, her name at the bottom of a recent life insurance policy—I knew Aunt DeeDee wouldn't do anything sinister or underhand. I wished I could talk to her, hear her explanations. I imagined the things I would say to the sheriff to set him straight after all of this was resolved.

My mind skimmed possibilities, many of which I did not want to seriously consider and which would hamper my first goal of getting Aunt DeeDee out of jail. I could march upstairs to the apartment and demand an answer from Savilla, but what good would that do? If she had something to hide, I would've shown my hand. No, better to keep quiet.

I briefly considered tearing up the life insurance policy and the pages of the ledger into tiny pieces and flushing them down the toilet. Instead, I decided to wait and do what was next on my schedule: attend the All That Glitters... Jewels and Gems party.

I checked the time. Twenty minutes, certainly not enough time to find my accommodation out on the grounds, change into whatever was inside the garment bag, and make my way back here on time. And I needed to be on time in order to rack up as many points as possible.

I hesitated only a few seconds before pulling off my jeans and my button-down shirt and wadding them into a ball with the ledger inside. I would hide them in the stall while I made an appearance and collect them before I headed to my room.

I unzipped the garment bag and found a formal romper that blended from a dark graphite color on the bottom into a shimmering explosion of tiny crystals on top. One side was off the shoulder and the other featured delicate straps. It was spectacular, and I knew immediately the narrative that Aunt DeeDee was going for: The graphite-colored bottom was the carbon from which diamonds sprang. Ingenious.

I slid into the romper and grabbed the loose items from the bottom of the bag—rhinestone-studded heels and a small Melbourne Cup-style charcoal hat.

I added the finishing touches and stepped out of the stall to study my sparkling reflection. Aunt DeeDee had outdone herself. I didn't even need more makeup. The woman gazing back at me in the mirror had already changed since Monday, when I'd learned I'd been registered to compete. I looked more mature, more accomplished but, more importantly, I was beginning to rediscover the spark that had always defined me.

I pulled my hair into a stiff ponytail and then decided to wind it into a bun, securing the flyaways with bobby pins from a basket on the counter filled with last-minute necessities. Reminding myself that I had everything I needed to win, or at least place, I made my way into the Primrose Ballroom for the Jewels and Gems party.

FIFTEEN

Two giant geodes with crystal centers, split open to reveal layers of sparkling turquoise, flanked the doors at the entryway of the ballroom, and a pianist played lyrical versions of thematic songs: "Diamonds Are a Girl's Best Friend," "Lucy in the Sky With Diamonds," and "Diamonds on the Water." It was likely Mr. Pratler, my high school choir teacher who accompanied every church Christmas special, community theater production, and children's play in Aubergine.

A woman scanned badges, looking for the tiny rose logo of the pageant, as if there were people just dying to forge credentials and sneak into this place. Not for the first time I wondered how long it would take for news of Mr. Finch to hit media outlets. The man was from a long line of multimillionaires who owned the second-largest estate in the United States, and if he wasn't soon found alive and well in some hidden nook, his disappearance wouldn't go unreported.

As I walked into the ballroom, my eyes took a moment to adjust to the space lit only by twinkling lights above, and all around me a sea of women in gold, finishing off the titular name of the event—*All That Glitters... Is Not Gold*—assaulted my eyes. The few not wearing gold were dressed in jewel tones. No one was wearing anything like what Aunt DeeDee had selected for me, and I knew by the admiring—and jealous—glances that this was a very good thing.

"You look lovely, dear," Miss 1962 said, strolling past with a drink and holding up what must have been her score card. Less than a minute later, Dr. Bellingham caught my eye and gave me a faint nod before scribbling something down. I only needed Katie Gilman's vote of confidence, but she hadn't yet arrived.

We'd been encouraged to invite a date for the evening, so men in tuxes walked the room with golden and glimmering ladies on their arms. Apparently, Mr. Finch's AWOL status wasn't slowing down these women or their show and, if I'd had to guess, I would have said that was the way the sheriff wanted it. People were more likely to let things slip in a loud room with alcohol rather than in a lockdown situation. If anything, recent events were making the staff and contestants more curious and thus more eager to gather in large numbers to confirm they were safe and sound.

I spotted the bar and got in line, grateful for something to get me through the rest of the evening. Pushing back my shoulders, I stood straighter, reminded myself to make sure the judges saw me being confident, comported, and those other two Cs I wouldn't normally care about.

As I waited for the signature drink, something called a Gem and Tonic, I spotted Summer, dressed in a satiny ruby-red dress with lantern sleeves and a plunge neckline, ahead of me in line. She was talking with someone who was almost a foot taller and was wearing a pleated gold dress.

"It's weird, right?" the person said, her voice thin and high-pitched. I soon realized that this statuesque woman with the perfect figure was Jemma. Lovely.

"It has to be a coincidence." Summer's voice lowered. "That

was twenty-something years ago. If the same thing was going to happen, it would've happened before now."

"Or Dr. Bellingham may have been biding his time," Jemma insisted. "I've been in this pageant long enough to know that I should keep an eye on him."

I tilted toward them, trying to overhear their conversation.

Jemma shot me a look over her shoulder. "Oh, hi. Savilla's friend, right?" Somehow she made even this simple question sound condescending.

"Uh... yeah," I said, not wanting to explain my definition of friendship and how Savilla and I didn't quite meet the requirements.

"Oh my goodness, you are gorgeous," Summer said, wrapping me into a hug. She smelled sweet with a hint of peppermint, either from her milk of magnesia or tea bags, I assumed. "I wondered where you were." She lowered her voice. "I found an officer who agreed to get your aunt's supplies to her."

"Supplies?" Jemma asked, narrowing her gaze at the two of us.

Summer drew a finger over her lips as if this was our little secret.

Jemma ignored the gesture and fixed her eyes on my outfit, examining me from head to toe and asking with a sharp edge, "Who picked that out for you?"

"My aunt," I answered honestly, not needing to hide the fact that I couldn't do any of this on my own. I didn't care. I was more interested in the *coincidence* she and Summer had been discussing, but just then their drinks were ready and someone tapped me on the shoulder. It was Lacy, wearing a flowing sunset-colored dress that swished at her ankles. She hadn't dressed according to theme and I loved her for it.

"You look great," I told her, realizing again how well suited my best friend was to run in a pageant. If only she could do this for me.

Lacy struck a pose before she grabbed champagne from a passing waiter and took a long swig.

I motioned to her glass. "Whoa. You okay there? You're drinking on the job."

"Sometimes a girl needs liquid sustenance to make it through an awful day at work." She surveyed the room. "Besides, I've earned it. I'm already getting calls from reporters asking about Mr. Finch's whereabouts. Someone in this organization already leaked it to the press."

I sensed Jemma leaning into our conversation now. Even Summer's ears perked up.

"Also, two of the tents didn't show up for the Decades extravaganza, and I can't find the boxes of legwarmers that we're supposed to give away in the eighties."

Not exactly the titillating details any of us had been awaiting.

I reached the front of the line and grabbed a couple of drinks from the bar. The Gem and Tonic was some sort of concoction layered in jewel tones. I took a small sip and stuck out my tongue against the combination of sweet, bitter, and sour. Jemma made a face as if she was disgusted with me, and Summer handed me a napkin so I could pat away the moisture on my lips.

Lacy, having finished her champagne, gulped her own. She hadn't been a lightweight since her college years.

"Here, have mine," I offered.

"Better not. But I want to. Believe me."

The four of us took a few moments to absorb the forced festivities of the evening. No one had made it onto the dance floor, and though songs echoed from the piano, a sense of hesitation blanketed the room.

I realized that with these three women—Lacy, the event planner; Summer, the eager helper; Jemma, the long-time contestant—I had a trove of pageant knowledge standing right next to me.

"So, what exactly do y'all know about Dr. Bellingham?" I asked as my eyes wandered to where he stood in the curve of the piano. He was surrounded by young women in dresses of varying lengths and plunges. He had a hand on one woman's back, an arm draped over another contestant's shoulder, and if he'd had a third, I bet he'd be using it.

"He seems nice enough, but I've heard through the whisper network that he may be a little..." Summer stalled, unable to say something derogatory even about this man.

"Stay away unless it's strategic," Jemma said curtly. "That's what I tell every newbie." Despite her gruff demeanor, her advice sounded almost sisterly.

"When I started working here, DeeDee told me that he's handsy. Hasn't actually done anything, as far as I know, but he's..." Lacy shivered. "I don't know. Something's off about him."

"You said in his introduction today that he was a judge here in 2001?" I added, thinking about the conversation I'd interrupted between Summer and Jemma.

Lacy nodded and took another sip. "Yeah. He served from 1999 to 2001." She seemed to catch the real question in my voice. "Is this about the crown they found in your aunt's room? It belonged to Miss 2001, right?"

I nodded, adding, "I thought it was weird when I arrived today and Miss 2001's cutout was the only one missing from the entryway."

This surprised Jemma and Summer, who must not have noticed.

"Then, Aunt DeeDee is accused of stealing the crown just as Mr. Finch leaves a note mentioning Miss 2001," I continued. "I can't quite put my finger on it, but if the last time Dr.

Bellingham served as judge someone else went missing... I don't know. Seems suspicious."

"A missing pageant owner and a missing pageant queen are very different kinds of people," Jemma pointed out. She might have been a bit rude, but she was savvy. "One holds all the power, and one holds none."

This, I knew. Though Momma had given me the sex talk all the way back in second grade, right before my first high-school dance Aunt DeeDee had sat me down and explained to me in vague language the things that a man could force upon a woman if he so chose. All I remembered from the talk was that I'd wanted her to stop, but she'd insisted I needed to know the reality. *I've seen too much*, she'd said at least three times. I hadn't thought of that moment in years, but now it rushed back at me.

What had my aunt seen in all of her years in this pageant? What had she personally experienced in her week-long stints here? It hadn't been enough to drive her away, but it had certainly been enough for her to want to protect me.

I thought of her warning, of Mr. Finch and his odd little family, of my aunt in a jail cell, and of Miss 2001 disappearing more than two decades earlier. All of these details had to be pointing at something I just couldn't yet see.

"Have you ever seen my aunt's office?" I asked all of them.

Jemma shook her head, but Summer nodded eagerly, saying, "She let me hang out there last year after I messed up my song during the talent show dress rehearsals. I was blubbing like a baby, and she was so nice." She drew out the word *soooo* in a way that so fit her personality.

Lacy studied me. "What do you have in mind?"

I was embarrassed to admit that I had very little in mind. "I'm not sure."

"I'd be surprised if it's locked, but if so, my key might get us in. You want to check things out?" Lacy waved a hand in the general direction of the crowd. "I think we've made an appearance."

I swallowed back one last sip of the Gem and Tonic and immediately regretted it.

"Let's go then," Lacy said, setting down both her glasses and leading us out of the party filled with living jewels.

Without being invited, Jemma, likely out of nosiness, and Summer, likely out of concern, readily followed in our wake.

SIXTEEN

The four of us were sneaking out of the party just as Savilla Finch was walking inside.

"Leaving so soon?" she asked, confronting us with a curious glance. Her face no longer sported the mask I'd last seen her wearing, and the rollers had made her hair spring to life. She held a scepter and was dressed as a beauty queen—crown and all—which would have seemed haughty except for the fact that she was merely an honorary contestant.

"Oh... um..." I struggled to find an excuse and realized I could ask a question instead. "Any news of your father?"

"No, nothing yet." Savilla's eyebrows turned down, and she watched me carefully. "Where are you going?"

"I need help with... waxing," Summer said, creating another bulletproof excuse. "It's so hard to find time during the school year and—"

Lacy pretended to stifle a yawn, a move that I found unnecessarily dramatic. "Just a few more things to check before turning in for the night."

Savilla studied us as if she couldn't quite understand where we could possibly be running off to. "Whatever. Dakota, come with me so I can introduce you to Dr. Bellingham. I know you already met Doris"—by which she meant Miss 1962—"and Nanny Kate"— by which she meant Katie Gilman—"but you haven't had a chance for an intergeneration with Daddy's old friend."

Intergeneration? I wasn't even touching that one. And Daddy's old friend, huh? I peered around the door at Dr. Bellingham, who was pinching a woman's cheeks and raising them ever so slightly while the girl attempted to smile at him.

"Maybe tomorrow."

"Oh, please, please, please, please," Savilla urged, placing her hands together in the form of a prayer.

Jemma stepped forward. "I'll talk to him," she offered, surprising me with this act of self-sacrifice, before I realized that this was more likely an opportunity for her to get face time with one of the judges while other people were around. Jemma was a sly fox.

Savilla accepted Jemma as a conciliatory sacrifice for Dr. Bellingham and then bent forward to give me an air-kiss— because heaven forbid she smudge her makeup or my nonexistent concealer.

As I pulled back from her quick embrace, Savilla grabbed my arm and stopped me. "Thank you."

I had no idea why she was thanking me.

"Upstairs with StepMommy. I'm sure Daddy will show up soon enough. He's done this kind of thing before—flown off to Paris for the night or taken the car into town at the worst moment—though I suppose that was years ago. Still, she can be a bit melodramatic. Has a bit of history of onyx, you know, but she means well."

History of onyx? I glanced at Lacy, but she hadn't heard Savilla's misuse of the English language. Then it hit me. *Histri-onics.* Her stepmother was prone to histrionics. No one could say Savilla wasn't trying to use those big words, although perhaps with tonight's glittering theme she'd actually meant what she'd said. I was beginning to suspect her odd phrases might be intentional. Maybe she was a Shakespeare in the making.

"I'm sure your stepmother is..." How to describe what Mrs. Finch must be feeling? "I'm sure she's processing."

Savilla patted my arm before someone caught her eye from across the room and waved her over. She yanked Jemma along behind her, and the gold-clad Barbie look-alike went willingly.

Before anyone else could interfere, Lacy, Summer, and I darted through the foyer, down a wide corridor, and toward the library where my aunt's office was apparently housed.

The library doors were thick and wooden and, through those, shaded sconces cast a soft yellow glow across the floor-to-ceiling rows of books of all colors and sizes. A full wall of outward-facing paperbacks on display appeared to have been written by former pageant queens. I picked up two of them: *Heavy Lies the Crown* had been written by Miss 1983 and *How to Give Yourself a Self-Perm* by Miss 1978. Very different topics. At least twenty other varied titles were lined up beside these.

"The pageant had its own publishing press for about twenty years, starting in the seventies," Lacy said. "Winners were required to write a memoir of their experience or a 'tip guide' for future contestants."

"I've read all of them," Summer enthused. "You can get them on Kindle too."

I shouldn't have been surprised since First Baptist hosted a literary festival celebrating one of our town's many obscure claims to fame: revivalist John Cartwright, a nineteenth-century preacher who wrote mostly about fire and brimstone and who set up a printing press at our town hall in 1834 to distribute pamphlets across Virginia. We were nothing if not literary.

"So where exactly is her office?" I asked.

"On the other side of the fireplace," Lacy answered, nodding at a high white mantel above black grating. "The door is remote-controlled." She reached under the mantel, pulled out a slim device, and pressed in a code. The fireplace wall began to move, turning ninety degrees to let us walk inside.

In front of us were slatted steps leading to a second floor with another door.

"Her office is up there," Lacy said, pulling a key from around her neck as she led me and Summer up the steep stairs, which creaked in a sort of singsong melody. "They built the palace with hidden rooms and tunnels in anticipation of the next war. DeeDee told me that most of the spaces are now used as offices, storage, or as a way to get quick access to other parts of the property."

I thought of the secret world around, above, and under me as I breathed in the musty scent of books. That was the kind of thing I'd dreamed about when we'd been invited to Savilla's tenth birthday sleepover here as kids, but all Savilla had wanted to do was gossip, eat brownies, and play with a Ouija board that told all of us that we were going to marry someone whose name started with the letter C. I thought of the sheriff—Charlie—and swallowed hard.

Maybe Savilla had been a lonely child, surrounded by toys and diamonds and a household staff and little else. Maybe she'd felt neglected in this huge house with only a doting nanny for company. Maybe she'd simply been trying to connect. I was beginning to realize that people's realities—Aunt DeeDee's included—might be all kinds of different than I'd imagined.

Lacy used her key to open the door. Once inside, she felt along the wall until she found a light switch. The overhead fixture was a sunburst pattern in copper tones with a globe emanating from the center. It looked original to the 1910s, when it would've been installed.

The décor inside Aunt DeeDee's office was tasteful, as I

would've expected. A reprint of Monet's *Woman with a Parasol* hung next to Renoir's *Luncheon of the Boating Party*. I knew them because every summer Aunt DeeDee dragged me and Momma to her favorite art museum in Richmond, and one year I'd spent hours staring at the originals that were on loan from some faraway place. In between the paintings hung her framed pageant-winner's sash.

"What should we look for this time?" Summer asked.

"This time?" Lacy asked, her brow quizzical.

"Summer and I explored Aunt DeeDee's guest room earlier," I explained.

Lacy seemed to accept this and peered over my shoulder as I opened the tall filing cabinet behind my aunt's orderly desk, which was lined with a jar of pens, a stack of pageant programs, and photos of our family.

Inside the cabinet I was glad to see everything neatly labeled by year with colored tags indicating marketing material, contestants, and winners.

"Looks like files on each of the contestants," I said as I flipped to 1990 and saw photos of Aunt DeeDee, as well as an application scrawled in her handwriting. Next to the question, *Why do you want to be the next Rose Palace Queen?* she'd written, *To be a good role model to young women by letting them know they can be themselves.*

I smiled faintly at the answer. That was actually pretty good, and not something I'd thought a place like this would aspire to do. Makeup tips, sure. How to lose ten pounds in ten days, that too. But maybe Aunt DeeDee's goals here had been more grounded and altruistic than I'd considered.

I handed Lacy the stack, and Summer opened the bottom drawer to pull out Miss 1938. She laughed and held the folder out to me. "Look at this swimsuit."

Miss 1938's get-up was essentially a sundress, complete

with a matching swim cap that covered every inch of her scalp and ears.

"I'm sure Dakota would much rather wear that than whatever Aunt DeeDee ordered for her," Lacy told Summer, as I combed through the files until I found the date I was actually searching for.

Miss 2001, a suspiciously light folder. I opened it, and only two items fell out, facedown on the floor. I stooped to pick them up and flipped them over.

A wedding announcement from *Aubergine Weekly*, dated December 15, 2001, read, "Mr. Frederick Finch married his blushing bride in an intimate candlelit ceremony at The Rose, the same place where she was declared the official winner of this year's pageant only a few months earlier. Those in attendance included Mr. Finch's daughter and the staff at the estate. Frederick and Glenda Finch will honeymoon in Venice."

Oddly, the second item was a class photo, my class photo. Well, mine and Lacy's and Savilla's. There were the three of us, arranged by height with our kindergarten peers. Miss Gladiola's class. I remembered loving the teacher from the first moment Momma told me her name. My eyes scanned other classmates, most of whom I recognized. Then, my eyes fell on two figures that were, of course, familiar, but didn't fit in this context. Aunt DeeDee stood at one edge of the photo and Savilla's nanny at the other.

I handed it to Lacy. "What do you make of this?"

"Aw, picture day is my favorite. All those fresh faces and little suits and dresses. They look like tiny grown-ups," Summer crooned. "You two were so cute."

"We really were." Lacy studied the image for a few seconds. "And there's Aunt DeeDee. She was one of our room mothers that year, remember? You were terrified of starting school, so DeeDee volunteered to help."

I gave my oldest friend a curious look. "I don't remember that."

"I do. You cried every day for a month when your mom dropped you off, and then one day Aunt DeeDee appeared at snack time to read us a story, and you were fine after that."

I only remembered Momma leaving after a warm hug, me longing for her to stay, and Aunt DeeDee picking me up, commenting on how much dirt I'd smeared all over my clothes and how messy my hands looked with Play-Doh crammed in my nail beds. Even then, I hadn't understood her obsession with cleanliness.

But had Aunt DeeDee volunteered at school? Had she been watching over me? Could it be that I didn't remember a piece of my childhood with my aunt? If the answer to any of these was yes, as I was coming to believe, then what else did I not know about my aunt?

THURSDAY
THE ROSE PALACE PAGEANT SCHEDULE: DAY 2

JEMMA'S BROADWAY BUTT-BUSTING WORKOUT: 7 to 8 a.m. Join contestant Jemma Jenkins as she sings and dances her booty to beauty in the main garden. All body types and personages—even those not competing—are welcome.

MORNING TEA: 9 to 11 a.m. Contestants will be scheduled to meet in the solarium with each judge for a formal tea that will act as a preliminary interview. Conversation and comportment are key as you interact with your fellow contestants and the judges. Please follow precise etiquette and be prepared to answer hard-hitting questions. This event traditionally elevates certain young women to a special tier of the competition.

TEAM PREP TIME: Noon to 3 p.m. Contestants should arrive promptly at their assigned tent to prepare for Saturday's showcase, "Through the Decades Centennial Show." This much-anticipated centennial treat will walk attendees through the past hundred years and demonstrate how the pageant has grown and changed. A light lunch will be provided.

HAPPY HOUR AND DINNER: 6 to 8 p.m. Contestants are invited to pick up dinner from the Main Ballroom and eat on the grounds.

SUNDOWN YOGA: 9 to 10 p.m. Contestants are invited to a peaceful and toning yoga session on the front lawn before heading to bed.

Dakota's To-Do List (in order of priority):

1. Uncover the person framing Aunt DeeDee.
2. Find Mr. Finch—dead or alive?
3. Who is Miss 2001?
4. Win pageant.

Possible Suspects:

1. Dr. Bellingham
2. Mrs. Finch
3. Savilla?
4. ~~Aunt DeeDee~~—Never.

SEVENTEEN

Momma had been born with one blue eye and one brown eye, but after being diagnosed with ocular melanoma at seventeen, they'd taken her blue eye and replaced it with a glass one. She chose to match the color to her remaining eye in order to draw less attention to her new disability but she told me that, even in her sixties, she'd never gotten used to looking in the mirror and seeing the same-color eyes on her face. *I liked what made me different*, she would say. *So should you.*

Without the two distinct colors, Aunt DeeDee always forgot which eye was which. *They did such a good job that I can hardly tell the fake*, she'd say from time to time.

Momma's cancer lay dormant for decades before roaring back to life with a vengeance. After trying all of the mainstream options, she and Aunt DeeDee and I traveled to Oklahoma City for her last chance at a cure. In those days, I often regretted not having a sibling, someone who would travel with us, be another pair of ears to hear the news with us. Aunt DeeDee was great, but sometimes, despite her efforts, I felt like a third wheel as she and her sister—my mother—chatted in a kind of shorthand from their own childhood together.

During the week at the experimental treatment facility, the incessant drip of the IV and the beeping of the monitors became our soundtrack.

On our third day there, Aunt DeeDee walked in with an armful of magazines and game books—sudoku, crosswords, and word finds kept her mind young, she claimed. Momma was fast asleep because the drugs they pumped into her were strong, and her body was exhausted. I figured Aunt DeeDee would settle herself next to Momma and keep quiet until she awakened. Instead, my aunt's cheeks burned pink, and a bead of sweat broke out along her hairline as she started fiddling with the machines, pressing buttons and glancing at the emergency call. I could practically see her heartbeat elevate as I thumbed through a *Better Homes & Gardens* someone had left in the lobby.

"I don't think you're supposed to press those," I whispered as my eyes darted back and forth from her to Momma, who seemed perfectly fine from my vantage point and not worth Aunt DeeDee's angst.

When Aunt DeeDee moved closer to my mother's face, shining the light from her phone into Momma's eye to better examine her, I knew what was wrong. The eyelid covering Momma's glass eye had popped open, and with the unmoving pupil, Aunt DeeDee had thought for a few terrifying seconds that she'd died.

"Allow me," I said, leaning over my mother and shutting the eyelid with two fingers. "It's a bit like a lever. Remember?"

Aunt DeeDee grabbed her heart in relief and rushed out of the room to find a bathroom and splash water on her face.

When Momma woke up, it tickled her to no end. Aunt DeeDee was appalled at our hilarity.

It's not funny. I just... I got turned around and forgot which eye... I haven't slept through the night in weeks... I thought you were dead and gone, she ranted, loudly enough that a nurse came to quiet the three of us down. *I swear. You two will be the death of me*, Aunt DeeDee said, pointing at us.

Momma and I guffawed. That was the kind of person Momma was—able to stare death in the face and keep in good spirits.

I didn't inherit that trait from her.

That's why I'd lain awake ruminating in my tiny cottage on the first night of the pageant, trying to put pieces together, trying to figure out how Mr. Finch's disappearance could possibly relate to a stolen crown and my aunt. But more than that, I feared that someone else—namely me or Lacy or even one of the Finches—might be next to disappear. We were, after all, closest to the case.

Last night I'd grabbed my clothes from the bathroom and stolen back to the Finch apartments to place the ledger back in the liquor cabinet right before returning to my cottage. Thankfully, I was still awake when Katie Gilman had swung by to check on me. She'd given me a long hug from my aunt and encouraged me to get a good night's sleep, so I'd be fresh in the morning.

I needed that sort of motherly advice and, after tossing my fancy romper onto the floor, I finally fell asleep for four or five hours before waking up to the screeching caw of peacocks.

If you think of peacocks as silent creatures of majestic wonder, the only way I can think to explain their early morning sound is like this: With one hand, scratch your nails against a chalkboard—hard, really dig in—and with the other, ring two discordant bells against your ear. That's how my eyes opened to my second day at the Rose Palace.

A puddle of drool had escaped the side of my mouth sometime during the night, and I creaked one eye open as I stretched out a hand, patting the empty side of the queen bed.

As I fondled the pillow, my fingers landed on something

cool and plasticky. I sat up and rubbed sleep out of my eyes before picking up the thin, square object. It was a photo, a Polaroid, a blurry one that had a finger covering half of the frame. I blinked as my eyes attempted to adjust to the muted sunlight streaming through a thin window that ran along the top of the loft wall.

I flipped on the lamp, but before I had the chance to look closely, a peacock shrieked again and a knock sounded at my door.

I threw the photo back onto the pillow and yelled, "Coming!" before stumbling down the stairs, my head still sloshy from last night.

"Delivery," Lacy called from the other side.

When I swung open the door, she stood with a giant tote on her shoulder and her hand propped on a long metal rack filled with garment bags of all shapes and sizes. Aunt DeeDee's pageant order had come through even though she was locked up.

"I brought coffee too." Lacy handed me a hot to-go cup. "From the dining room bar. It's pretty good."

"I hope you've got a cyanide pill to go with it," I said as I took a sip of the hot brew, and winced as it scalded my tongue.

"You and me both, friend."

"Any news on Mr. Finch?" I asked.

"Not yet. Over breakfast, some of the contestants were whispering that he probably ran off with a previous winner, and others thought he must be dead in the woods at the edge of the estate."

I tried to swallow another gulp of coffee but choked on it this time.

"DeeDee was on my mind the entire night, particularly since I was up until three making sure the missing tents arrived and all ten were properly erected." Lacy pointed a finger at me.

"Did you just wake up? You haven't showered yet? Or attended Jemma's Broadway Butt-Busting workout?" She pretended to be shocked.

"I literally just got out of bed." I went to the sink, set down my coffee, and splashed water on my face. "Did you work out?"

"I did, actually," she answered, looking pleased with herself as she plopped on the couch. "We listened to 'Memory' and crawled around like cats. It was surprisingly difficult to stay on all fours until the last note, but Jemma did a great job—showed us all the moves and yelled encouragement at us for the entire hour."

The yelling part made sense, but the encouragement part, not so much.

"Well, best get to it." Lacy nudged me toward the bathroom. "I've got stuff to do, but I know DeeDee would want me to oversee your hair and makeup." She placed her tote on the two-person stained-wood kitchen table. "Do you have everything you need?"

"It's all upstairs," I answered, not wanting to think about possible beauty torture devices my aunt had packed for me.

The hot shower did wake me up, and the specialty lavender shampoo and mint body wash left me smelling like something Bella wouldn't have recognized. I thought about the stables on the Rose Palace property and wondered if I could sneak out and bribe someone into letting me go for a ride. The blessed escape of riding through the foothills called to me, but instead I had two jobs to do: win a pageant and solve a mystery.

As I imagined exploring every inch of the grounds, searching for a man who may have left of his own accord, I used the brand-new loofa and scrubbed all the parts that one is supposed to leave bare and shiny at a pageant.

I peeked my head outside the door. "Do you have my outfit ready?"

"You'll need to wait to dress until after we do hair and

makeup. Just come out in your underwear and towel," Lacy answered, as the stairs creaked above me.

I figured she was spying to see which shoes I'd brought. She would be disappointed.

I'd almost closed the bathroom door again when I heard Lacy scream.

I tightened the towel around myself as I rushed up the stairs, but when I got to the top, she hadn't fallen or found a gigantic spider. Instead, she was standing next to the bed, holding the photo I'd found and promptly forgotten.

"That was here when I woke up," I said, waving away her dramatic response. "The last person here must've left it."

Lacy shook her head and pointed at the bedspread. "I saw it lying on the pillow and pulled back the duvet to get a closer look. Then I saw..." Her voice faded.

I went to stand next to her and lifted the covers gently, expecting to find a dead rat or a newspaper headline saying that all the coffee in the entire world had been depleted.

Instead, it was a handful of Polaroids with one word written in capital letters at the bottom of each of them. I read them in the order that they lay.

BOTH KILLED THEM OF SHE

"What does that mean?" Lacy asked. "I just saw the word 'killed' and freaked out."

I studied the image in the photos: a close-up of a worn sash reading *Miss 1990*.

At the bottom of each of the photos on the white frame surrounding the image, as well as the one word, there was a number indicating the proper order in which to read them.

"Wait," I said, shuffling the photos until all five were in order. The note now read:

SHE KILLED BOTH OF THEM

Someone had taken time to make this message. To accuse Miss 1990—Aunt DeeDee—of killing two people. Perhaps Miss 2001? And then, more recently, Mr. Finch?

The accuser had snuck into my room, either before I'd arrived or after I'd fallen asleep, to leave the message. I growled and threw the Polaroids on the floor, mentally cursing.

"I should've checked my bed last night, but I just fell asleep. Who would leave something like this?"

"Someone who wants your aunt behind bars."

"But why?"

I knew the literal answer. Someone wanted her behind bars either because they were out to get her… or she'd actually committed murder, and they were too scared to come forward. But I knew it had to be the first: someone was continuing to frame my aunt. I tried to see Aunt DeeDee holding any kind of weapon aimed at Mr. Finch, but the image wouldn't compute.

My heart began to beat more rapidly, the staccato picking up pace as my palms grew sweaty and my vision began to swim.

The last time I'd had a panic attack was the day we'd found out that the experimental treatment—Momma's last chance— hadn't worked. Just like that day, my chest muscles constricted, my heart pummeled my ribcage, and my hands grew clammier by the second. Black spots floated into my vision. Except unlike that time, Momma wasn't there to calm me down.

Lacy spotted the signs and made me sit, then shoved my head between my legs. "You're okay. Breathe, Dakota. Breathe. In, out. In, out. Good girl."

"I feel like I'm going to…"

"I know, I know. You're okay."

Can I just take a second to say what a badass Lacy proves to be again and again? She graduated from our class as valedictorian, earned an MBA from Georgetown, and convinced the Finches to give her the largest contract yet for her fledgling event planning company. All that and still, here she stood, rubbing circles into my back as she helped bring me back to myself.

Minutes passed and my body, worn out, began to calm, finding its baseline, which—while overthinking and slightly anxious—was not typically on the verge of hysteria.

Lacy traded my coffee for a glass of water and sat on the bed next to me, scattering the Polaroids.

"I'm sorry," I said, moving my wet hair. "I soaked your shirt."

"It'll dry soon." She pulled the AllSaints top away from her skin. "Look, I know you and the sheriff didn't exactly hit things off," Lacy said, breathing out something she'd been holding back. "But hand these photos over to him. He can help."

I thought of Aunt DeeDee telling me to trust the man who'd put her behind bars. I still hated that suggestion just as much.

"Give him these photos, and then proceed as usual?" I asked. That seemed to be a common theme at the Rose Palace.

"Pretty much. Do your job. Win the crown. And in the meantime, keep listening and watching and gathering clues to figure out where Mr. Finch could be. You and I both know Aunt DeeDee is innocent, so we operate from that starting point."

"This is way bigger than what Momma expected when she wrote that letter and paid my entry fees," I told her.

Lacy considered that statement as she lay back on the bed and turned on her side. "Yeah, but she would've gotten a kick out of all of this. I mean, not your aunt in jail, but, you know, the puzzle of it all."

"She did love puzzles of all kinds." I put my hand over Lacy's and gripped it as I fell beside her. "If someone is trying to scare me away... it's kind of working. I mean... a missing crown is one thing, but... murder?"

Lacy leaned on her elbow, looking me in the eye. "But you're gonna stay, right?"

I hesitated. A couple of years ago, Lacy wouldn't have needed to ask a question like that.

"You'll make yourself stay, won't you?" Lacy asked again.

"I have to be here for Aunt DeeDee," I answered. "And we still need the money... I just need to place... if that's even a possibility now."

"Sure it is." Lacy pushed a strand of hair out of my eyes. "Let's get you dressed." She gathered the Polaroids into a stack and handed them to me before leading me back downstairs. When she reached the bottom, she spun and asked me a question, confusion on her face. "Why don't you want the sheriff's help?"

I thought of the pinky ring in my aunt's room. "Because if I hand these to him, he'll give me nothing, and I could be feeding him material to use against Aunt DeeDee."

"I don't think he's working against you," Lacy mused without sounding condescending. "Do you know what his platform was?"

"No."

"It was, 'Help me help you.'"

I snorted. "That's dumb."

"But it worked," Lacy said. "And more importantly, I think he means it."

"I don't know," I said, imagining him leading my aunt away in handcuffs.

"He's requiring additional training for all officers and he's implementing de-escalation tactics and body cameras," Lacy added.

"How do you know all that?"

"I'm a concerned citizen," Lacy answered.

I gave her a look that asked for the real reason.

"I had to hire some of his officers for security detail this weekend. They like him, or if they don't, they at least respect him." She put a hand on my shoulder as if to reassure me. "Despite what you saw yesterday, I think he's a good guy."

EIGHTEEN

In my imagination, the Blue Ridge Mountains have always had a mood, an air, if you will. On the day I won first place for my chicken coop in sixth grade, they were proud and majestic. On the day I started working at the stables in high school, they were tentative but enthusiastic, and on the day I left home for college, they were pensive. On the day Momma died, they were somber, mourning with me.

Today the mountains were confused as I gripped my fingers around a clutch Lacy had given me and held it over my head on the way to the morning tea. A sprinkle of rain—almost a mist—had descended over the Rose Palace and I could barely see the peaks in the distance. I could only imagine the frustrated contestants, railing against the humid air teasing their coifs.

My clutch contained lip gloss—Lacy's idea—and the five Polaroids with the accusation—also her idea.

SHE KILLED BOTH OF THEM. These five words ran through my mind, repeating over and over like a mantra. I tried to consider all the ways I could figure out who had placed them in my bed without telling the sheriff—who was suddenly at my side.

Sheriff Strong wore the same uniform, but he'd added a cowboy hat that made him look like a sheriff from the Wild West. His brow was knitted and his eyes were on his feet, ignoring me completely.

"Good morning to you too," I said, causing him to stop.

He stared at me as if puzzled about who I was.

"Dakota Green," I reminded him. "You gave my aunt some fancy new bracelets before hauling her to jail."

"I know who you are, Ms. Green," he said, as if I was the one being rude.

"Okay. At ease," I told him, confused by his rigid stance. I thought that perhaps there'd been a spark of something yesterday—but that had been before he'd arrested my aunt.

"I apologize. I'm on my way to..." He pointed toward the mansion. "Did you need something?" Impatience practically oozed from him. There was no way this man deserved my evidence.

"No, nothing from you," I said, my tone icy.

"As solitary as a fisher," he mused, almost to himself.

"Excuse me?" I scoffed. "I hate fishing."

"No... a fisher, as in the mammal that lives in Canada. My grandparents are from Alberta and used to say that."

"I prefer the term 'lone wolf.' Much scrappier."

He almost smiled and I realized that I liked how his shoulders relaxed when he was on the verge of slipping into a more personable manner. Then, his walkie-talkie beeped and he was back to business mode.

He listened to the static. "The transmission here is terrible."

I nodded to show I wasn't the one keeping him and he turned and walked away.

I shook off the interaction as I neared the morning tea, trying to convince myself that despite the fact that someone had snuck into my room, I didn't need the sheriff's help... yet.

The windows of the solarium let in morning light, but the

framework around them looked like giant black spider legs branching above the women. Along the walls were plants of every variety and size: Carolina jasmine, wisteria vines, Boston ferns, even a few succulents.

Colorfully dressed women streamed into the room for our first official event of the day, and I couldn't help but look at them with renewed suspicion. Had one of them left the message in my bed? I'd considered the possibility that Dr. Bellingham may have planted the photos, but I wasn't convinced. He would've had to enter a female contestant's cottage without being spotted or reported. That would be a lot easier to do if the culprit was a woman, especially another contestant.

Perhaps he was working with someone?

I checked in at a table beneath the center of the glass dome just in time for tea with the judges. The sunlight created a gauzy glow and a kind of halo around the other ladies, particularly the blond ones, of which there were statistically far too many.

Lacy had done my makeup, used the tiniest glisten of Vaseline across my upper teeth, and dressed me in a light blue Sachin & Babi toile maxi sundress—I only know this because she'd coached me how to answer "who" I was wearing. She'd brought over her own shoes—a pair of strappy Valentino sandals—and pulled my hair into a half-braid that reached mid-back. While she'd worked her magic, she'd given me a few practice questions so I would be ready to impress the judges.

"What are your goals for this weekend?" Lacy had asked while brushing on a nude eyeshadow—of which I'd asked, "Nude? Then what's the point?" The answer was that we used nude to look natural, which sounded like some kind of doublespeak to me.

I'd answered honestly—to win money, find Mr. Finch, and spring Aunt DeeDee out of jail, legally or otherwise—which, based on the look Lacy had given me, wasn't the right answer for any question this weekend. "Fine. My goal this weekend is to meet other women and become my best self."

"Better," Lacy had said. "But next time say it like you mean it."

My dress swished against my ankles as I tried to prance rather than gallop through the room. This was a far cry from my usual attire, but even I had to admit that I looked like someone who belonged here.

"Good morning, Dakota," a woman said as she handed me a 4x6 card with my table number and the time slots in which I would meet the judges. I recognized her as she put a hand to her chest and said softly, "I'm Aubrey's mom."

"Oh... yes... good to see you."

Aubrey was one of the students at the stables, an elementary-aged kid on the spectrum who took riding lessons as therapy. I didn't conduct the sessions, but I did help her care for Bella before and after her lessons. Aubrey didn't speak much, but she and Bella would cuddle and stare into one another's eyes for hours if we let them. I liked the little girl. Neither of us made demands on the other, and we shared an interest in all things equine.

"You know that she talks about you and Bella all the time... well, I mean, she's not a chatterbox, but every other time she speaks, it's to mention Bella or 'Coda,' that nice lady who lets her use the brush and hoof pick."

After every difficult moment from the past sixteen hours or so, those words made me feel something other than unqualified or inept.

"Thanks for saying that," I told her.

"Thank you for being patient. Not everyone is."

The last sentence was weighted with things I couldn't begin to unpack in that moment, so I smiled and asked her to point me in the right direction.

"Yes, of course." Aubrey's mom returned to the matter at

hand with a knowing grin. "The judges have been here for the past hour, eating breakfast and deliberating about all of you. I'm pretty sure I overheard your name a time or two."

I looked at where she was pointing to see the three judges' heads close together in conversation. I could only hope they were saying nice things as I turned to find my assigned seat. Four chairs had been set up at each round table, so judges could rotate through the contestants in batches, notecards and pen in hand to record anything profound or unseemly that we said during our brief interlude. An assortment of pastries no one would eat, as well as a teapot and a pitcher of water had been stationed at each table, and three roses—one red, one pink, one yellow—had been bunched together and placed in a thin white vase in the center.

When I arrived at my assigned spot, Jemma was already seated. She wore a lavender dress that billowed around her feet, and she sat with perfect posture and a bored expression on her face.

"Oh, goody," Jemma said, her voice not betraying any actual sign of enjoyment at seeing me.

"Good morning," I said. "How was Dr. Bellingham?"

"He likes me," she said simply, studying her cuticles. "That's what matters."

I didn't have time to ask more because just then Summer hurried to my other side.

"Yay! Together again!" Summer's enthusiasm was almost contagious.

"Except we're missing someone from our little bonding exercise," Jemma noted.

"Right." Summer's face fell. She was as expressive as Jemma was not. "Poor Savilla. I wonder how she's doing. I would be absolutely bereft if my father disappeared."

I found this statement interesting for a variety of reasons, primarily because I'd never had a father. I mean, I had a father in the biological sense, but whenever I'd asked Momma about him, she would pull me onto her lap and tell me a story about how she'd found me in a basket floating down the river or how the fireflies had led her to me in the deep, dark forest on one moonless night. Eventually, I didn't think it important enough to keep asking. Besides, it wasn't like I was missing something. Momma was the best friend a girl could have, and Aunt DeeDee made the best fried chicken and banana pudding a girl could want. What else did I need?

"I'm sure Savilla will recover," Jemma said flatly.

"I know it's ungenerous, but..." Summer paused and tilted her head as if considering her words carefully. "I really hope they don't cancel the pageant."

"I think most of us feel that way," I said, motioning toward the other women readying themselves to interact with the judges.

"I'm getting married," Summer said, almost as if it was a secret.

"Oh, congrats," I said, imagining that she was planning to use her winnings on a fancy wedding.

"My fiancé is in med school and wants us to go abroad when he graduates."

I tried not to make a face at her obvious wealth.

"He wants to repair cleft palates for children whose families can't afford it," Summer continued. "I'll be a teacher wherever he sets up his practice."

My face fell as I realized that I'd misjudged her, and I reminded myself once again that not all contestants were alike.

Jemma didn't seem interested in Summer's plans, but she *was* interested in winning. She leaned forward, lowering her voice. "Okay, I'm going to be straight with you. I don't really see either of you as real competition."

Both Summer and I startled at the words.

"I'm not trying to be cruel," Jemma continued. "But it

usually takes a few years before a contestant stands a chance at being a top contender, and neither of you has competed in this particular pageant as long as I have."

"What about beginner's luck?" I asked.

Jemma didn't deign to answer that question, and Summer shrank into herself as she seemed to notice the competitive gleam in Jemma's eyes.

"How many times have you competed at The Rose?" I asked.

Jemma seemed to debate whether or not she wanted to answer. "I started at twenty-two, and I just turned twenty-nine."

This was her last chance at the crown. Summer's mouth morphed into an "Oh" and her eyes widened.

Jemma stared at me for a second too long. "That's why I need you both to take this seriously."

"I am," I told her, thinking about the debt collectors calling incessantly and the number of messages I would need to return next week, hopefully with good news that I could pay the debts. "I need the money probably more than anyone else, and my aunt is in jail. Why are you here?"

"None of your concern," Jemma answered.

"Except it is our business if you want us to have a nice chat with the judges this morning," I informed her as I leaned back and crossed my arms, before continuing in a singsong voice: "Remember that conversation and comportment are the order of the day."

"It's okay if you don't want to share," Summer said, trying to put a hand on Jemma's forearm—she jerked it away. "Sometimes it's hard to talk about our emotions."

I wanted to tell Summer good job at using her teacher voice, but Jemma broke in again.

"It's not hard," she insisted. "I just..." Jemma inhaled. "I'd like to produce my own show. Off-Broadway, but even that's expensive. I wrote it years ago about my brother's battle with recovery, but no producer has shown the slightest interest, so..."

I was surprised. Jemma actually had a goal and a family—and maybe even a semblance of a heart?

"That's a good reason to be here," I admitted.

"This is my third year at The Rose, but I've done thirteen pageants," Summer said almost like a confession. "The only show I won was the very first when I was five and no talent was required. What does that say about me?"

Oh Lord. This was turning into a beauty queen support group.

"Since we all have reasons for winning, let's work together," Jemma said, a gleam in her eyes as she formulated a plan. "In all my years at The Rose, I've noticed one thing is consistent: The judges love it when we seem like we're best friends." Jemma mouth rose into what looked like a smile.

Huh. I hadn't known she had that expression in her.

"They have these little score cards that they jot notes and numbers on whenever they leave an event, and this one is particularly important because it's your best chance at scoring the conversation points. When they make their way to our table, turn on the charm. Talk each other up."

Summer nodded eagerly, and I shrugged. Whatever would make this go smoothly.

A chime sounded, and all of us turned toward the woman who had handed us our schedules.

"All right, ladies. Today is a chance for the judges to get to know you beyond what you listed on your application. We'll be treating this as a speed-dating situation in which the judges rotate from table to table, and they will be keeping score of the best conversationalists. You'll have seven minutes to chat it up, but because there are so many of you this year, you won't have a judge at your table each round, so be patient. I'll ring a bell to start and stop the sessions, and we must stick to a strict schedule in order to accommodate everyone. Are we ready?"

Heads nodded across the solarium, and the energy in the room amped up.

"Let's begin."

The first judge at our table was Miss 1962, aka Doris Davis, dressed from head to toe in various shades of pink except for a bright orange silk scarf wound around her neck.

"Hello, young'uns," Doris said as she inched her way into her chair. I could almost hear her hips creaking. "How are we today?"

"Great," Jemma answered.

"Fabulous," Summer said.

"I've been better," I answered, too honestly for my table-mates.

Jemma nudged me under the table, and Summer's mouth turned down into a rare frown.

"But I'm so glad to have made new friends," I added, attempting a lighter tone.

"Hogwash," Miss 1962 blurted. "Your aunt's in the clinker for the suspected murder of Mr. Finch. That's not nothing."

My eyes widened at her no-nonsense assessment. Once again, I liked this lady, despite her brashness.

Summer leaned forward. "Do you think Mr. Finch is actually... dead?" she asked, her eyes beginning to water with unshed tears.

"Frederick Finch dead?" Doris mused on the question. "Perhaps. He was beloved here, but a philandering son of a bitch outside these halls, so I wouldn't be surprised if some woman finally got fed up with his cheating ways."

"Some woman like Mrs. Finch?" I asked.

Doris narrowed one eye. "Perhaps."

"I'm sure all that will be determined soon enough," Jemma said, attempting to steer us back on course. "I am such a history buff, have always loved those documentaries about then and now, about how close we are in history to big events like the World Wars..." She chattered on for at least thirty seconds before realizing she was losing her audience. "I'd love to hear about the amazing changes you've seen in the pageant over the years."

Miss 1962 paused, thinking for a moment about significant changes she'd seen. "The bras used to be much pointier, and you had to go commando before those thong-thingies that you bunch now wear."

I loved that answer. "What about the kind of girl who competes?" I asked. "In the past couple of decades, how have the contestants changed?"

Doris had an immediate answer. "You all feel like you've got to have some kind of platform. Don't eat meat! Vote progressive! MeToo! In my time, we were happy if society let us talk about anything other than becoming a wife or mother. My own mother was lucky to get the right to vote, and she certainly didn't go around announcing her political party. Different times."

I studied this woman who had been part of the pageant in some capacity for almost seventy-five years. She'd seen and heard everything by now.

I decided to shift gears. "What about being a judge? Were you here in 2001, the year that Mrs. Finch was crowned?"

Miss 1962's mind seemingly shifted to the past like a Rolodex flipping backward. "Yes, siree. Was a judge that year too, in fact, but Mrs. Finch wasn't crowned."

Now we were getting somewhere.

"Oh?" I tried to act surprised.

"That's right. It was... what was it she called herself? Cathy... Cathy P-something. Cathy Pierce?" She tapped a pointer against her chin. "No, that's not it." She searched the table as if the name was waiting there for her. "Peabody," she finally said, snapping a finger. "That's right. Cathy Peabody won that year, but then she disappeared the next morning."

Peabody. That was the name in the ledger, a line item going back years in the Rose Palace accounts.

"Anyhoo, judging is fairly easy. We watch and listen in the days leading up to the show and then tally scores on the big day." Miss 1962 licked her lips before clearing her throat. "Though this year, two of us know what the hell we're doing, and one of us is only here to drum up business. As per usual." She gestured pointedly to the right, where Dr. Bellingham sat sketching a new face on a napkin for a contestant. The girl was beaming as if she couldn't wait for him to get his scalpel in her.

"It must be such a difficult decision with so many great contestants." Jemma kept her focus on Miss 1962, pushed back her shoulders, and put on a smile as she tried to change the subject. She was a pro, I'd give her that much. "I'm just so glad that I can be here for Dakota while her aunt's in jail."

Miss 1962 tilted her head. "I suppose DeeDee did it to herself, getting on the bad side of you-know-who."

I was surprised by the statement. "Wait... who do you mean? Dr. Bellingham?"

"I'm not saying a word," Doris said as the bell rang, forcing Miss 1962 back to her shaky feet and to her next table. I caught a glimpse of her scorecard and was shocked to see that I had received all five of the conversation points, while Jemma had four and Summer had only one.

"That was good," Jemma said, offering the two of us a rare genuine smile. Maybe working together on a common goal was releasing some of her angst. "Just two more to go."

We sat through three rounds without a judge, and Jemma turned to me and fixed a misplaced strand of my hair. At first I thought she was going to pull it out of my head, but she laughed softly. "I'm not that bad," she smirked.

Both of us watched Summer re-adjust the neckline of her

dress a number of times, and beat a tune on the table with her fingertips.

At last our second judge, Ms. Katie Gilman, strode to our table. "Oh my word, I keep thinking about you," she said to me as she tucked her ample frame into the chair. Katie's hands fluttered in front of her as she seemingly remembered the events of the previous evening. "Poor Mr. Finch gone missing, and our very own Deanna Green led away in handcuffs. You know you can count on me as a character witness. Your aunt and I—we go way back. Even before I started selling her pieces at my store, we were friends."

"I appreciate that," I told her.

"Your aunt is a great pageant MC," Jemma admitted. Then she began talking about how many years she'd competed, about how proud her family was, about how close she felt to each of us. The minutes passed quickly as she rambled on, and Katie listened politely until the two-minute warning bell rang, and I jumped in.

"I'm sorry for interrupting, but..." I struggled to determine the most pressing question. I needed to know things about the Finches: what had happened to Miss 2001 and what Miss 1962 had meant when she'd said that my aunt was on someone's bad side. I inched closer to Katie Gilman. "I was wondering..."

"Yes?"

"I was wondering how well you know Dr. Bellingham." It wasn't exactly the question I wanted answered, but I hoped she would volunteer even a speck of information like Miss 1962 had done. The universe was pointing me toward him, and I wanted to ensure I heard correctly.

"Jim, oh... I've known him... gosh, forever." Katie looked around the solarium. "Mostly harmless, but just... watch yourself around him. If he's not trying to sell you on a 'beauty-enhancing procedure' he may be trying to woo you—or worse."

The bell rang a final time as she said the last two words. I wanted to stop her, to call her back, but Dr. Bellingham was approaching our table.

He gave Jemma a quick rub on the shoulder, and she flinched ever so slightly. I was grateful again for her intervention with him last night, even if she had been selfishly motivated, at least in part.

"I know you," he said to Jemma with an affectionate grin. "Did you have time to think about the Botox we discussed? Actresses need to keep their youthful vigor for as long as possible."

Jemma nudged away his hand and put on a smile. "I can't wait to visit your office in New York to get started."

I hoped she was lying.

Dr. Bellingham sat and rested his hands on the table. I noticed something strange on his pinky finger. A faint white line.

"Do you wear a ring?" I asked as Jemma and Summer both listened, their faces briefly showing their puzzlement at my train of thought.

"Not married, as you can see," he said, wiggling his fingers in front of me. His Adam's apple bobbed as he answered. "But, yes, I left my judge's ring back in my room in my hurry to get out here with all of you beautiful girls."

Gross. But... a judge's ring?

I thought about last night, about what Katie and I had discovered in Aunt DeeDee's drawer. I'd assumed that the ring we'd found belonged to Mr. Finch, but what if it was Dr. Bellingham's? The two men were buddies, and he was a long-time friend of the pageant.

"Fred gave it to me as a memento for my years of service here." He studied me and then reached out to touch the bridge of my nose before I could pull away. "I could fix that bump with a very simple procedure..."

I dodged him with my wit. "And here I thought my cheekbones would compensate for my bumpy nose."

Dr. Bellingham studied me. "You do have a remarkable bone structure."

The three of us women sat quietly, not knowing how to proceed. Even Jemma seemed at a loss.

"Right-o!" Dr. Bellingham took a deep breath and changed the subject. "So, I'd love to hear anything and everything you girls want to share. Your deepest, darkest secrets..." He looked at us with a playful gleam in his eye. "Or your naughtiest fantasies."

Jemma was the only one of the three of us able to act like he was winning her over. She launched into her childhood pageant days and teen years before going into detail about this year's show schedule, about how we would all have to undress from our opening costumes in a matter of minutes, how she would need to crawl into her red bikini. She gave him a lot to imagine as Summer and I squirmed uncomfortably.

"I might vacate my judge's seat and join you all backstage." He was titillated. "Don't tempt me."

Bile rose as I marveled that this man could get away with such comments in this day and age. Summer and I had nothing to contribute to this conversation, and when the bell rang, the two of us scooted as far away from the man as humanly possible.

He reached out a palm to shake my hand, and when I reluctantly took it, he covered it with his other. He leaned forward and whispered in my ear, his breath damp. "I wanted to say... I'm so very sorry your aunt has gotten herself caught up in this mess. It really is unfortunate."

My jaw clenched as I backed away to study his face, to see if his word choice matched his expression. *Has gotten herself caught up?* What did that mean? Was he blaming Aunt DeeDee for putting herself in jail?

He was at the next table so quickly that I didn't get to ask him. Instead, I turned to Jemma. "What was that?"

"What?"

"Describing us changing backstage. It was gross."

"I was doing the job. He gave all three of us the full five points."

That did not justify the conversation in my mind.

"Don't you need the money?" Jemma asked, and both Summer and I slumped into our seats because, deep down, we knew she'd done what she thought was necessary. This pageant world was so strange, but also like a mirror to the world in which women found themselves every day.

I studied Jemma more closely and noted the fatigue behind the makeup. She'd been at this for years, and had her own reasons to win.

I couldn't dwell too long on justifying Jemma's behavior because just then Savilla Finch ran into the solarium, her eyes wide with concern. She was breathtaking, far more beautiful than any woman in this sunlit room, in a silky ivory halter dress and champagne pumps with an open toe, the soles of which were muddy, marring an otherwise perfect picture of femininity.

Savilla, clenching and unclenching her fingers, searched the room before hurrying to my side. Everyone turned to watch, likely wondering what she could possibly want with someone like me.

In that moment I realized that I was probably the closest friend Savilla had at the pageant.

"I'm sorry to interrupt, but I... I need you to come with me." Savilla's words were tremulous and uncertain. "It's Step-Mommy. She's..." Savilla paused and sniffled. "She won't wake up."

NINETEEN

Jemma and Summer didn't hesitate, nor did they ask whether or not they should follow me and Savilla on the same path I'd taken the day before to the Finch apartment, the walls around us turning from tasteful modernity to ornate gaudiness in a matter of steps.

As the four of us entered the long hallway to the Tickled Pink Apartment we stopped in our tracks. Two medics, one on each side of a gurney, wheeled an unconscious Mrs. Finch toward us, an oxygen mask over her mouth.

"Oh my God," Savilla said. "She was breathing... she just wouldn't..."

"She seems stable," the medic reassured her. I recognized him as a fellow student who'd graduated a few years ahead of us, and I wondered if he'd worked at the hospital with Momma. There was no time to ask. "The oxygen is a precaution. We'll take care of her, Miss Finch."

"Can... can I come with her?" Savilla asked, her voice shaky.

"You can follow us there in your own car."

Summer raised a hand. "I have a rental. I'll drive you."

Savilla looked to me. "Will you be okay? I think the sheriff will be at the apartment any minute."

That must've been why Sheriff Strong had been hurried earlier this morning. A pang of guilt rushed through me.

I could see Savilla trying to keep her emotions under control. First her father. Now her stepmother... I also sensed not only the concern for her parents but a deeper fear: a fear that she might be next.

"You go," Jemma told Savilla and Summer. "I'll stay with Dakota."

I was grateful not to be left on my own, even if my new companion was Jemma. My thoughts turned to Dr. Bellingham then—how he'd smiled and flirted coquettishly with Jemma only moments ago. He was quickly becoming my top suspect in whatever was happening here, but how would he have had access to Mrs. Finch this morning? How could he have been down there preparing to meet with us and at the same time doing whatever had been done to the pageant owner's wife?

The medics rushed the gurney down the hall. Summer led Savilla away while Jemma followed me into the Finch apartments, and for a fleeting moment I imagined Jemma attacking me from behind. But I was being dramatic, silly with the lack of sleep and ongoing intrigue.

We crossed the threshold into the silver and magenta sitting room at the front of the residence.

"I've never been in here," Jemma marveled.

White powder from fingerprinting marred the furniture, and shattered glass had been splintered across the floor. "What do you think happened?"

"It looks like she was enjoying a morning aperitif that didn't settle well," Jemma speculated.

"That's an understatement."

Just then a figure came from one of the back rooms. Charlie Strong.

"Good morning again, ladies," he said by way of greeting. His eyes still had bags underneath, but he seemed to be making an effort at some sort of nicety. "Sleep well?"

"With my aunt in jail at your directive? Nope."

"Your aunt is in jail because she's a suspect to theft and possible kidnapping—or murder," he reminded me. "Unless you'd like to confess something?"

I couldn't tell if he was joking, but either way, I didn't appreciate the question. "Hilarious, Sheriff."

"I'm nothing if not a tease," he said dryly before his tone shifted and his expression grew more concentrated.

I decided to focus on the real issue. "So, what happened here this morning?"

"Savilla woke up, got dressed, and then found her step-mother unconscious. She called the ambulance, who informed me."

"And after you arrived, she came to look for me at the morning tea," I finished for him.

"Right. She thought you might have some insights to share with me." He considered the general layout of the apartment and any clues it might offer, and I couldn't tell how he felt about me—or Jemma—actually being here.

I cleared my throat. "I'm... I'm sorry I was a little curt earlier. I had no idea you were dealing with... this."

His eyes darted to me. He was either confused by the apology or unwilling to accept it, because he didn't say anything.

"Well, it looks as if whatever was in Mrs. Finch's glass was the problem," Jemma said, before extending her hand to the sheriff, never missing an opportunity to make a good impression. "I'm Jemma Jenkins, long-time contestant and"—she paused as if the word was hard to get out—"friend of Dakota."

The sheriff nodded in acknowledgement, but he didn't shake her hand.

I would've laughed if the situation hadn't seemed so ridiculous. My beauty pageant nemesis was now on the case, trying to outwit the handsome but grumpy sheriff with me. What a riot.

The sheriff addressed me. "Savilla mentioned that you were up here last night, serving Mrs. Finch drinks."

"Am I a suspect now?" I choked out the words.

"Whether we like it or not, everyone is." He inhaled deeply, tired or frustrated or both. "But I was asking because I'd like your perspective... as an insider, as a person who was with the victim only hours ago."

I didn't have to give him this information, but maybe if I shared what I knew, he'd give me something in return. I squatted down and put a finger to the pale pink carpet, which had been drenched in spatters of brown liquid. I lifted my fingers and sniffed. "It's whiskey, the same thing she was drinking last night."

"Here's the bottle," Jemma said, reaching toward the end table, almost grabbing the container and putting her prints all over it.

The sheriff held out a hand to stop her. "Right, but Savilla said her stepmother didn't usually drink except for a glass of wine with dinner."

I thought of the three glasses Mrs. Finch had downed yesterday and wondered how much of an anomaly that had actually been. I moved closer, to scan the contents of the decanter without touching anything.

The books in front of the bottle had been removed and stacked neatly on the end table just as I'd done, and I could see the row of mixers—ginger, lemon, sweet vermouth, grapefruit juice—except... My eyes roamed back over them.

Something was missing.

I closed my eyes and imagined the conversation with Mrs. Finch, the scent of vanilla and caramel and something else.

"It's not a secret that she and Mr. Finch enjoy their liquor," Jemma said.

"My predecessor was called out here a couple of years ago when things got too rowdy one night after the pageant," the sheriff acknowledged. "But the police report didn't mention Mrs. Finch."

"Who did it mention?" I asked.

"I'm afraid that's classified."

"But this crime scene, or whatever it is, isn't classified?"

"I can use my discretion about who I allow to help me with a case."

"And you've selected me, a family member of a primary suspect?"

"You know what they say: Keep your friends close and your enemies closer." He seemed to immediately regret the words. "Not that you're the enemy."

Jemma was watching us like this was a tennis match, her head bobbing back and forth between us, a small smile on her lips.

"Look, I haven't slept in almost thirty hours and..." He let out a long breath. "I'm not exactly beloved in Aubergine after beating one of their hometown boys for the job. This is my first real incident"—I wasn't sure that was the word I would use for whatever this pageant had become, but sure—"and I would appreciate any insights you can give."

It wasn't exactly a truce, but it was a show of vulnerability.

My eyes fell on something I'd noticed last night when pouring Mrs. Finch glass after glass. Open on the side table was the honeypot with the purple bee and white flower.

I took a tissue from a box nearby and picked up the honey jar, sniffing it. Grapes. That was the missing scent. "Last night Mrs. Finch took her whiskey neat, but it looks like she used honey this morning." I handed the jar to the sheriff. "Better have this tested."

"And maybe a few shards of glass," Jemma added. "Just in case something was in the cup before she poured the drink."

"My officers are already on it." The sheriff scratched at his jaw. "Can you tell me who else was in her apartment yesterday evening?"

"Savilla, Katie Gilman, Doris Davis—but she left after a few minutes."

"Was Dr. Bellingham here?" the sheriff asked, startling me. Did his list of suspects match mine? When I didn't answer, he clarified his thinking. "The other two judges were present, so I assumed..."

"No, but later, I was with Dr. Bellingham in the ballroom," Jemma interjected. "He was on the dance floor with contestants all evening."

"At the Jewels and Gems party," I added. "I was there too but left early." I skipped mentioning the ledger I'd taken from the Finches' cabinet or the insurance policy I'd found. But I recalled the Polaroids in my purse.

Lacy was right. He needed to know about those.

"Hopefully whatever the lab finds will match whatever is in Mrs. Finch's system."

I opened my clutch. "What were her symptoms?"

"The medics said she was unconscious. Elevated blood pressure, irregular heartbeat. She'd broken out in a cold sweat. Signs of poisoning."

Before I could talk myself out of it, I pulled out the Polaroids and read the message—the words implying that my Aunt DeeDee had killed not one but two people—one more time, before handing them over to him. I considered briefly whether or not I wanted Jemma to see the coded message, but I was fairly certain that she'd had nothing to do with them. Yes, she wanted to win, but I felt in my gut that she wouldn't risk being caught cheating—or murdering—to do so.

"These were in my bed when I woke up this morning, but

they could've been placed there before I got to my cottage last night." I laid them on the settee.

The sheriff studied the images. "This thing in the center of the photos... it's a sash?"

"A pageant winner's sash. My aunt's, specifically. It's hanging in her office."

"Has anyone else seen these?"

Jemma peered over, her brows drawn. Now I was convinced she'd never laid eyes on these images.

"Just Lacy," I answered. "But she won't say anything."

"Let's keep it that way for now." He gave us both a pointed look as he picked up the images.

"Look, Sheriff, I know my aunt is innocent. I'm certain that whoever put these in my room also planted that crown in hers. I also spotted a ring missing from Dr. Bellingham's pinky—he has a noticeable tan line. I think he may be behind all of this. The last stint he had as a judge ended the same year that Miss 2001 went missing."

"Dr. Bellingham," he repeated as he stared at the ground, trying out the accusation. He pulled out his notebook and flipped through the contents—information he didn't offer to share with me.

"What have you got there? A top ten list?" Jemma asked, and I wondered if she'd meant to sound sarcastic. Perhaps she'd spoken that way for so long that she couldn't really help herself.

The sheriff ignored the question.

"Dr. Bellingham is also... He's a man that my aunt warned me to stay away from," I said. "He's got to have something to do with all of this."

"Why would she want you to stay away from him?" His tone sounded inquisitive but also... protective? I wondered if that was because he was specifically concerned for me, but no, he was concerned for everyone. That was his job. The sheriff made eye contact with me, and I hated that I noticed the color.

Hazel rather than brown or green. Figured. Even his own eyes couldn't make a decision about how to be. "This is an insider, someone who has access to a key," he finally said. "Someone who knows their way around."

"An insider could be someone like a judge," Jemma suggested.

"Or security, or housekeeping, or... someone like Dr. Bellingham... or like DeeDee Green," the sheriff added, making me hate him again.

"Why would my aunt put photos of her own sash in my bed and then accuse herself of murdering two people?"

He seemed to read my mind before he took a halting step toward me. "I understand that you're determined to believe in your aunt's innocence." He studied me, and my face heated under his gaze. "But you have to hear me: My job is to consider all angles, to think like a criminal *and* a law enforcement officer at the same time. If your aunt is innocent, you have my word, she will be released. If she's not, then..."

The words jarred me. "Wait... are you saying that you would consider those photos—the message about killing people —as some kind of evidence against my aunt?"

"Not necessarily, but—"

"I cannot believe this," Jemma said, her voice rising in both pitch and volume.

Slack-jawed, I listened to Jemma come to my defense.

"Dakota came to you, gave you these photos, told you about Dr. Bellingham, and you stand there and say that this could be used against her aunt if—"

"Let me stop you right there, Miss Jenkins. I'm not saying any such thing. I'm not in the business of helping the family of the accused—or of working against them. All I meant was that we need all the facts before we draw any conclusions."

His tone sounded reasonable, and it made me feel like I might explode.

Facts? This man wanted facts?

"Fine. I'll give you facts," I said through clenched teeth. "The woman that you put in jail is the only family I have left. After my mother died, she..." I was almost crying now, but I didn't want him to see, so I wiped at my eyes and caught my breath. "Deanna Green was the person who came over every day and cooked and cleaned and got me out of bed. She made sure that I had somewhere to go, that I acted like a functional human being..."

As I said the words, memories of her swarmed my brain—of that first week without Momma in the house, of making me sit up and eat, of her running a hot bath for me, of her embroidering in my room while I napped. She'd never been the one I'd confided in or sought out when I'd fallen down or had a broken heart. That had always been Momma, my emotional support system in so many ways. But, for my entire life, Aunt DeeDee had been showing me that she loved me, just not in the ways that I'd thought to notice.

"She loves this pageant, God help her, and she wouldn't take so much as a pencil from the front desk, much less a crown or a... a person's life. Whoever put that crown in her room and these photos in my bed has something against my aunt. My eye is on Dr. Bellingham, and I suggest you start looking there as well, because if I find out who's behind all of this before you do, I just might do something reckless."

The sheriff seemed surprised by my little speech as he stared at me. "Miss Green," he said calmly, "I know you're frustrated, but please don't do anything rash."

TWENTY

I needed to go for a ride. I needed to pat Bella's nose and let her carry me to the edge of the woods and into the foothills of the Blue Ridge Mountains like I used to do with Momma. The wind would cool my flaming cheeks and my sweaty palms, and the shadows dancing through the oak leaves would calm my anxious spirit. This week was getting to be too much.

I tried to quiet my mind as I hurried outside, Jemma trailing behind me. I hated my lack of control in all of this. My aunt was behind bars, my attempts to help her may have backfired, and I still had to stick to a strict schedule and beauty routine.

"Do you have the schedule?" I asked Jemma, looking toward the mountains that had an air of watchfulness as if they were awaiting news from me.

She handed it to me without a word, her gaze also fixed on the distant peaks.

"We have rehearsals in a half-hour," Jemma said, as if I couldn't read my responsibilities in black font on the page. "If you miss that—"

"I won't miss it," I said through clenched teeth. "I just need a few minutes to collect myself." I scanned the list of activities—I had no time for a ride. I would have to be content stomping out my rage against the sheriff before my next obligation.

"Fine. I'll see you in a few. Wash your face and buck up, cowgirl," Jemma said. Then, she walked ahead, leaving me alone.

I took several deep breaths and a few laps around the gardens before stepping onto the wide back lawn and into the first Through the Decades tent.

It was astounding. The space following an obvious organizational structure from the 1920s through to the 2010s: five massive tents on one side and five on the other of a wide strip of green. I was right on time, and a mix of contestants and staff was milling about. I breathed deeply and then made my way down to the 1950s for rehearsal.

At the entrance to the tent a sign reading *Rose Pageant Soda Shop* stood next to a life-size cutout of a soda jerk in full uniform, holding two malted milkshakes. As I looked around for someone in charge, my eyes took in what must've been every shade of pastel known to man. It was like the 1950s wanted visitors to know just how perfect things had been before it threw up all over you.

Not only was there a malt shop with a giant menu of ice cream flavors, a counter, and rounded stools, but the 1950s tent also featured the interior of a small mid-century home complete with light yellow walls, baby-blue cabinets, and low-slung, blocky furniture. Giant cutouts of a smiling Elvis, Elizabeth Taylor, and James Dean stood between the front of the stage and a dance floor stenciled with giant letters that read *SOCK HOP*.

Women rushed around the stage, a few of them with costumes flung over their arms. I spotted Jemma standing in front of a full-length mirror, bobby-pinning an orange domed hat that looked a bit like a repurposed cereal bowl to her head.

She seemed to have recovered better than me from our chat with the sheriff.

"Hey," Summer called, waving me over in front of a cart loaded with boxes and hanging bags. The cart was rusted in places and had been splattered with paint along the bottom edge. "You need to grab your costume."

I looked around at the stacked containers near the stage. "From there?"

"Those are the giveaways for everyone who comes to the fifties," Summer said, tapping the top of the cardboard.

"What's the prize?" I asked, thinking about that decade's icons and inventions. "Oooo... I know! Birth control pills?"

"Nope. Too suggestive." She laughed. "I believe these are hula hoops."

"How's Savilla?" I asked.

"I dropped her at the hospital, and she went straight inside to be with her stepmother, so I drove back here. I'm hopeful."

I couldn't help but smile at Summer's optimistic outlook.

The sheriff, talking with one of his officers, ambled to the outskirts of our tent, but when he stopped and took in the surroundings, bewilderment settled across his face. I caught the other women watching him, a couple of them starting his way, most likely trying to either flirt or find out what happened to Mrs. Finch.

I hated the amusement creeping onto Sheriff Strong's face as he took in the colorful 1950s décor, the multiplicity of staged settings, the barrage of lights and music. This was the Aubergine I'd always known and loved, the town that would be incomplete without its Spooky Tricks & Treats Fall Festival, the Living History Presidential Parade, the Pink and White Valentine Sock Hop, or the Hide a Bunny Easter Festival. I'd participated in all of them during my childhood, and here, through a new-in-town man's eyes, I suddenly felt protective of where my family had lived for generations. He had a lot to learn if he was planning to be sheriff in this county for long. To start, he needed to realize that, in Aubergine, we go all in.

I tried to dismiss the sheriff from my thoughts as Summer ran over and handed me a dress originally labeled *Savilla Finch*. Her name had been crossed out, and mine had been added. This dress, a size too small for me, was red with white polka dots, a lacy short collar, and had a white apron. In it, I would appear to be a moving target that screamed, "Kill Me Next."

I thanked Summer, who scurried away, and I wandered toward Jemma, who was once again a girl-boss—although in a flared yellow skirt, she looked like a 1950s housewife version, if ever there was such a thing.

Gone was the concerned and almost vulnerable girl from the Finch apartments. Instead, Jemma gave me the rundown in her usual authoritative tone: Along with two girls named Gina and Nina—which wasn't at all confusing—we were set to perform a living history skit a few hours after the tents opened to guests on Saturday. The decades tents and the show, which seemed a pretty generous term for ten minutes of subpar acting, was a "treat" for the centennial, according to the pageant program.

Jemma handed me pages as I walked into a kitchen with a fake stove and pink laminate countertops. The set—complete with the kitchen, a living area, an entryway, and a front door—was all a façade. Nothing functioned. "Learn your lines. We rehearse in a few minutes."

"Any acting notes?" I joked.

Jemma stared at me for several seconds, taking my question seriously. "It's the 1950s. Embody the decade. Everything in this tent is legit from that era, and everything we do should bring people back to that point in time."

"Suppressed proto-feminist. Got it," I said, skimming the first page.

<u>1950s Living History: A Rose Palace Pageant Girl's Typical Cares & Concerns</u>

Narrator (Nina): The 1950s pageant contestant encountered the same cares and concerns that twenty-first century gals experience today. Take Mildred, for example. (*Motions to Host*)

She just finished college with a degree in Art History, and she's returned home to live with her parents until she finds *The One*. What's a girl to do between learning to care for a home and waiting for a proposal? Perhaps compete in a pageant that will help with both of these endeavors? Let's take a look.

Host (~~Savilla~~ Dakota): (*In the kitchen, frustrated but composed. Makeup and hair should be perfect*) Gosh darn it! I can't believe my soufflé fell again. What will the judges think at the baking portion of the show when I can't serve them anything edible? And what will Robert think when he comes over tonight? He'll never ask me to marry him if I can't learn how to cook. He might even tan my hide!

Uh. No. No, no, no, no.

I paused, looking at my fellow actresses, who were taking their positions and adjusting their props—glasses of iced tea and records—in their hands. A singer onstage began lilting Doris Day's "A Guy Is a Guy." I flipped through the next two pages of the script and, as I expected, it didn't get any better with Robert teetering on the brink of abuse charges.

"Can we make some changes to the script?" I asked, walking up to Jemma. "Perhaps take out Robert wanting his girlfriend to be a size four? We could focus more on Mildred's desire to learn the art of baking."

Jemma narrowed her eyes as if she'd expected as much from

me. "Mr. Finch approved this himself. Think of the skit as a tribute to him."

"It's about a nonexistent perfect pageant girl and some jackass named Robert being upset because his 'girl' burned his dessert and actually ate calories." I flipped to the third page. "And she's terrified of being an old maid if she doesn't win this year?"

"This is about stepping back into another era and experiencing life as these ladies did," Jemma said, a hand on her hip.

My Rural Women's Studies course at Cornell had never painted women in this light. "Okay, then where's the 1950s fight against segregation and the petition to President Eisenhower for cabinet positions for women?"

A pause.

"Listen, Gloria Steinem, I can't deal with this today," Jemma spouted. "I'm sure this isn't what all women talked about, but it's what we're working with. Got it?"

Nope. I didn't have it, but I also wasn't going to stand a chance at the prize by being difficult.

Jemma called for us to take our places, and I made it through the entire script. Then, I ran it again, trying my best to take Jemma's unsolicited advice about my tone and mannerisms.

"Let's do it one more time," Jemma said, almost as soon as we'd finished.

"Fine," I said, my heart rate accelerating. The combination of my money worries, my aunt behind bars, and the general safety concerns of this pageant were mounting. This ridiculous production might be the thing to break me. "Let's run it again." I stomped into the kitchen and hurled my first line, long and loud and flat, every word plodding and monotone.

"Gosh darn it. I can't believe my soufflé fell again."

I began opening and slamming cupboards with nothing inside, not even shelves. "Robert will tan my hide if I can't learn how to cook. And fast." I yanked on the drawers, but they were all just fronts, so I moved to the bottom cabinets. "How did you catch your husband?"

The final word stuck in my mouth. Because there, in the bottom cabinet, on display for lovers of all things 1950s, was a body, dressed in a suit with a crumbling dead rose in the lapel.

I backed away from the cabinet and barreled into the kitchen counter behind me. Pain spread across my hip as the body fell head first out of the cabinet, landing with a thud.

I stared in horror at the dead man, his muscles rigid and his arms folded on his chest. His right eye was no longer in the socket, and a stream of blood had dried down his face, along his right pants leg, all the way to the toe of his brown loafer.

I'd found Mr. Finch, and he was still wearing his pinky ring.

TWENTY-ONE

I couldn't walk or turn or call for help. When Jemma, flustered and frustrated, entered the kitchen, ready to scold me again, she instead let out a blood-curdling scream. After that, the word got out. Gina and Nina and Summer came running, and soon contestants poured in from other decades while staff members rushed to and fro in golf carts.

Summer pulled me away as the sheriff appeared, calling for his officers to cordon off the area. "Come with me," she whispered, taking my arm and leading me outside the canopy and to a park bench set up between the 1970s and 1980s.

My hands were shaking, and I could only stare into nothing. Birds in the trees continued to sing, and the summer sun still beat down, but this day had irrevocably changed for me. Even the mountains now hid behind gray-tinged clouds.

"Mr. Finch was..." I swallowed, trying to speak. "His eye... his blood was..."

"I know. It's okay," Summer said, her small hand on my back, anchoring me as the sheriff approached us.

He crouched down to my level and spoke with the kindest tone that I'd yet heard from him. "Miss Green, I know that

173

you're in shock." His voice was steady, the resonance oddly comforting, but his next words unmoored me again. "Do you think you can tell me in your own words what you found?"

"I found..." I couldn't finish, and I didn't meet his eyes.

Summer put her arm protectively over my shoulder. "It's all right, Dakota. You found Mr. Finch's body, right?"

I think I nodded.

"And where was it located?" the sheriff asked.

We were standing yards away from where the man's lifeless body had fallen from the kitchen cabinet. Couldn't the sheriff walk over and see it for himself? I tried to recall Aunt DeeDee's claims that I should trust him, but this new wrinkle didn't help matters, particularly if I had to give a vivid description of what he could discern on his own. I did not want to relive another death.

He followed my eyes. "I just need a quick statement. For the paperwork."

I pointed vaguely. "You can ask Jemma. She came in right after... right after Mr. Finch's body... fell."

The sheriff scribbled down the information and then touched my shoulder lightly as he looked to Summer. "Can you stay with her?"

"Sure."

I sat on my hands to stop the shaking and watched the crowd part around the sheriff. I knew next to nothing about dead bodies, but Mr. Finch couldn't have been gone long. From what I knew about animals—at thirteen years old, I'd had a brief stint of thinking I wanted to be a taxidermist—I was pretty confident that rigor mortis was all but gone after twelve hours. His arms hadn't budged even as he'd inelegantly plopped onto the ground, which meant that a very-alive Mr. Finch had been somewhere, most likely nearby, since he'd gone missing nineteen or so hours earlier.

The sheriff peeled away while Summer escorted me to my

guest cottage. I was in such a daze that I had no idea how much time had passed when Lacy arrived with lunch.

The two women conversed in whispers for a few minutes before Summer gave me a hug and a brief goodbye, and Lacy remained with me in the cottage, urging me to eat something. I picked up and put down a sandwich, nibbling at the edges to satisfy her. In between tiny bites, I detailed the evidence—the Polaroids, the honey, the ledger—watching her expressions shift as she listened to my conundrum.

"I think Mr. Finch died less than twelve hours ago, sometime after two a.m."

"Which is good, right?" Lacy asked.

"It means that Aunt DeeDee was led away in handcuffs before he died, so she can't be guilty of killing him. I just need the autopsy to confirm the time of death." I took a sip of water. "But the other things—Miss 2001's crown in her room and the fact that the original winner, Cathy Peabody, disappeared while Aunt DeeDee was in charge of the pageant... I don't even know where to start with that."

"It was so long ago," Lacy said, taking another bite of her sandwich.

"Do you remember hearing about the original Finch house? Out on the back side of the property?" I vaguely recalled Mr. Finch mentioning the old estate, saying they were considering converting it into a pageant museum.

Lacy took a sip of Diet Coke. "I've never been out there, but sure. I've heard of it. Your aunt said it can't be torn down because it's historical."

"I wonder if any of the archives would be out there, especially if the Finches are planning to convert it into a place for tourists to visit."

"Maybe," Lacy said, turning toward the window. "But I have a million things to do today, and you don't seem in any state to... to search the woods."

She was right. I was mentally and physically exhausted and probably still in shock at seeing Mr. Finch's corpse. I also had no desire to possibly put my own life in danger by wandering around the unused and untrimmed outskirts of the property alone. I could almost hear Aunt DeeDee and Momma agreeing in their admonishments: *You better stay put, young lady, until you see the sunrise.* This time I was more than happy to comply.

"Let's do this: I have to go check on a couple more tent issues," Lacy said. "Promise you won't go anywhere without me."

"I won't, but..." I knew Lacy, being fiercely independent, might balk at what I was about to ask. "Are you sure it's safe?"

"I'm sure." To my surprise, Lacy just gave me a soft smile. "I have pepper spray, and I'm not afraid to use it."

I didn't like the idea of her out there alone—or of me inside alone. "But can you come back here to spend the night when you're finished? I want to head to the back side of the property."

I didn't mention that I was also afraid to be on my own, but she seemed to sense as much. Lacy hugged me one last time before she locked me inside with no other company than my churning thoughts.

I closed my eyes to try to clear my mind, but one memory in particular kept rising to the surface. Six weeks after Momma died, on a Saturday evening in early September, I emerged from my fog long enough to have an actual conversation with Aunt DeeDee.

"I've already started sorting through your mother's belongings," she said to me from the door of my childhood bedroom. She'd tried to pry me out of bed for dinner but had eventually given up and started rummaging through my mother's things. "Feel free to take anything you want with you when you leave."

When you leave... Those last three words made me shoot up in bed. "Where do you think I'm going?"

Aunt DeeDee pursed her lips, confused by my question.

"Back to school. You have a year left of your program, so I thought..."

I forced back the tears threatening to escape. My aunt—the very woman who had just lost her sister—was expecting me to re-enlist in the real world, to head back to school as if I hadn't spent the last year as a caregiver, to restart my life as if my mother hadn't died. I remembered hearing once that people grieve differently, but it had only been a few weeks. How could this be the conversation my aunt was already having with me?

I didn't want to cry in front of her when she was bustling around the house, sorting through Momma's belongings like they were part and parcel for Goodwill, but holding back my tears contorted my features into a kind of frozen spasm.

To her credit, as soon as she saw my bereft confusion, Aunt DeeDee hurried into my room, dropping my mother's favorite purple scarf in the doorway. She threw hers arm around me and pulled me into her breast, swaying back and forth as she must've done when I was a baby. After that day, Aunt DeeDee and I performed our individual dances with grief, and I began to realize that our approaches to loss are worlds apart. Aunt DeeDee gets in there, gets her hands dirty, gets down to brass tacks. I tend to sink into the sadness, to wallow for as long as possible.

Take Mr. Finch's death as a micro-example of our natural reactions. When I saw his body on the ground at my feet, my instinct was to run to my cottage, to crawl beneath the comforter, to hibernate until spring. On the other side of town, even in her dire situation, Aunt DeeDee would be pacing the cell, thinking about all the steps she would take to find out who'd done such a thing. All the while, we both knew she was relying on me to work with the sheriff to find the truth.

But maybe knowing how she would react helped push me forward. I had to process the facts. First, my aunt was in jail for theft, and second, someone had accused her of killing two people: Mr. Finch, whose body now lay in some sort of repose and Miss 2001, aka Cathy Peabody.

Those two realities raced back and forth in my thoughts before I finally and mercifully fell asleep on the couch. I didn't wake up until long after the peacocks squawked the next morning.

FRIDAY

THE ROSE PALACE PAGEANT SCHEDULE:
DAY 3

JEMMA'S BROADWAY BUTT-BUSTING WORKOUT: 7 to 8 a.m. Join Jemma once again as she sings and dances her booty to beauty.

BREAKFAST: 9 to 10 a.m. A breakfast spread will be served in the Primrose Ballroom.

INTERVIEW PRACTICE: 11 a.m. to 2 p.m. Contestants are invited to mingle in the gardens of the Rose Palace and are encouraged to run through practice interview questions. The judges will be available for specific concerns as needed. A light lunch will be provided.

PRACTICE AND PREPARATIONS: 2 to 4 p.m. The ballroom stage will be open to allow contestants the opportunity to do sound checks and confirm the timing of their performance.

Remember that all numbers must be kept to under three minutes.

GILDED AGE DINNER: 6 to 9 p.m. Enjoy a specially curated meal with authentic Gilded Age menu, décor, and attire. The guests will include contestants, staff, and the judges.

On Saturday, gates open for the public to peruse the "Through the Decades Centennial Show" tents and attend the grand finale.

Dakota's To-Do List (in order of priority—maybe):

1. ~~Find Mr. Finch, dead or alive?~~ Found him.
   Definitely dead.
2. Get Aunt DeeDee out of jail. Who would
   frame her?
3. What happened to Mrs. Finch? Drink? Poison?
   Other?
4. Win pageant.

Possible Suspects:

1. Dr. Bellingham
2. Savilla
3. Mrs. Finch (also victim)

TWENTY-TWO

Dust motes floated through the beams of sunlight, hitting my face. At first I thought I was back home, that Aunt DeeDee would stop by later that day with a trayful of food she would try to force-feed me. But no.

I lay on the couch across from Lacy, who'd fallen asleep curled in an uncomfortable position on the wing chair.

I checked the time—it was already 7:42 a.m. I sprang from the cushion I'd wedged under my head as a pillow. We needed to finally connect the dots between the crown in my aunt's room, the Polaroids in my bed, and Mr. Finch's dead body.

I nudged Lacy awake, and within minutes we were both on our feet. After we sprayed on fresh deodorant and took a quick look at ourselves in the mirror, ignoring what we didn't have time to fix, we were out the door and headed to the stables.

On the way we spotted the group of butt-busters shaking and jiving to "Master of the House" from *Les Mis*. Jemma was grinning and in her element, moving between the sweaty contestants and showing them the perfect squat. Whatever made her happy, I supposed.

The stable master recognized Lacy, so he agreed—after

asking me several questions about my experience with horses—
that we could take out a couple of the gentler mares.

Polly had a rusty-red coat and a dark brown mane. I intro-
duced myself and told her about Bella as I stroked her nose and
gave her a good rubdown, letting her sniff me before placing the
saddle pad across her back.

When I asked the stable master where I could find a saddle,
he pointed to a door in the barn. Inside I counted seven rows
with five or six saddles each. Mr. Finch had said they had quite
a collection, but I couldn't have imagined anything like the
leather craftsmanship covering the entire wall. I ran a hand over
the nearest one—soft and supple. Only the finest for the
Finches.

There were messages inscribed on the cantle of most of the
saddles: everything from simple dedications to ones so personal
I wouldn't let my eyes linger.

To My Diamond

To My Rose

Love You Forever

Love, Your Mom

Love You Always

To Another 20 Years

What a Wild Ride

I was reminded that in all the bustle yesterday, I'd never
finalized what my talent would be in the show tomorrow.

A myriad showstoppers had scored big points over the years,

according to Aunt DeeDee: a performance of "La Macarena" in the style of ballet, "Für Elise" played with wind chimes, Macbeth's soliloquy given while dressed as Harry Potter. The show certainly seemed to award creativity.

I spotted a bucket and several cleaning supplies in the corner and considered requesting them backstage. If worse came to worse, I'd be able to give a detailed tutorial on the proper way to clean a saddle. Aunt DeeDee would be proud or horrified—I wasn't sure which.

Lacy grabbed the first saddle she saw. She didn't particularly like horses, but her parents had forced her to take dressage classes for a year, thinking she could specialize in a less-known sport for college scholarships. The first time she'd accidentally stepped in horse poop, she'd gagged for five minutes and known it would never be a lifelong passion.

I turned toward her. "Do you think I can borrow one of these for my talent?"

Her brow wrinkled. "I guess, but why would you?"

"I want to wow the judges."

She put up a hand. "Whatever you think's best."

After we ensured a secure fit for the saddles, Lacy threw her leg over the back of a quarter horse named Ginger as I climbed astride Polly.

The path to the back of the property wasn't a straight shot, and branches poked at our arms as if reaching to hold us back. Neither of us talked much as we navigated fallen branches and trees that had been struck by lightning. There wasn't much of a breeze and I wished for a bandana to wipe the sweat beginning to drench my face. Thankfully, the dense foliage soon thinned and the scent of honeysuckle perfumed the air.

A stone wall at least ten feet high towered in front of us, topped by spindly wrought-iron spikes ready to impale intruders. The only break in the wall was a gate with more narrow spires an inch or two apart.

Lacy led Ginger toward it. "Do you think it opens?"

"One way to find out." I hopped down and walked Polly to the metal slats, pushing against them, but the gate wouldn't give because of the vines growing beneath the entrance. I dropped the reins and put my shoulder into the effort, but it barely budged. After yanking up the weeds while trying to avoid the prickly ones, I tried again. This time, the gate opened enough for me and Lacy to squeeze through. "I guess we can tie the horses here while we check things out."

"It's strange what the Finches want to do with this part of the property," Lacy said, once we were inside the gated perimeters.

"Yeah, it's weird, right? Putting a pageant museum out here when no one has been through this gate in a long time."

"Unless there's another way back here," Lacy added. "Maybe that's part of the appeal—a secret passageway. Mr. Finch seemed just eccentric enough to appreciate something like that."

A few steps more and we realized we'd arrived at the edge of an expansive garden, wild and untamed, stretching for acres in every direction. Directly ahead of us was a glass greenhouse with a dome rising from the center. Panes had been shattered and some were missing, creating a kind of gap-toothed grin. A picturesque hillock rose and fell, and behind it stood an abandoned two-story stone structure with steps ascending to a front door.

"This is the original house where the Finch family stayed while the Rose Palace was being built," Lacy noted as we ambled toward it. The looming mountains made this space feel nestled and held, and I realized that the acres featuring a beautiful home, a greenhouse, an overgrown grassy expanse, and a spacious garden had been "roughing it" for the Gilded Age Finch family.

We stepped up the stairs and opened the door to the house,

our eyes adjusting quickly to the low light. The style of construction reminded me of the historical homes in Williamsburg. Every Christmas Aunt DeeDee asked me and Momma to tag along with her while she walked through house after house, decorated with evergreens, candles, and holly berries. Momma and I would make it through two mansions before leaving to find hot chocolate until Aunt DeeDee finished.

In this house there were rooms branching off a long breezeway that stretched all the way from the front to the back door, a design that had allowed air to circulate before the era of air conditioning. A musty scent of closed rooms and abandoned belongings permeated the house. I ran my hand along the peeling sage-green paint on the wall and tried to envision the late-nineteenth-century family who'd walked these halls. Each room's entryway featured crown molding, and only one had a modern door. From behind it, I could hear a motor running.

"I bet that one room is temp-controlled to preserve whatever is inside," Lacy said as she approached. "In college when I shelved books at the on-campus library, the archivist had a repository like that."

I could see the Finches bringing out a crew to install AC in just one room in order to preserve history. But then, why not keep the items in the main house at the front of the property? Unless there was something they didn't want visitors stumbling across?

I jiggled the handle, but it didn't budge.

"Allow me," Lacy said, stepping forward. She took an ID badge from her pocket and slid it between the doorframe and the lock mechanism. It took her a full minute of wiggling the card, but the click eventually let us know that her method had worked.

We walked inside a room that must have been the dining area at one point. The rectangular layout would have seemed spacious if not crammed with boxes and random pageant para-phernalia. I shivered in the much cooler air.

"Jackpot," Lacy said, coming up behind me, studying the stacked metal boxes around the room. "This must be where they keep the goods."

The space was filled with memories of the pageant world. I lifted a drop cloth in the corner to find a guitar that had been signed, "To the Rose Palace Pageant, Love Dolly Parton." Next to it was a large, framed photo of a young Dolly singing her heart out on the pageant stage. There were a few dresses on wire mannequins, and cutouts of all kinds of people who'd visited the show over the years: movie stars, politicians, singers.

"I could've used these for the tent decorations," Lacy mused, running a hand along Elizabeth Taylor's cardboard hair.

I tapped my fingers against the lid of one of the black metal storage boxes before I took the one on top, lifted it, and peered inside... to find a handful of items scattered along the bottom: a Rose Palace cookbook from 1964, charcoal sketches of women in gowns, a sweatshirt with the words *We're All Queens* written across the bust.

"That's a bit..." Lacy started.

"Unimpressive? Unhelpful?" I finished.

We moved to other boxes.

The next one contained stacks of rough-edged file folders from 1982 to 1988 filled with faded receipts and crumbling bank statements. The box after that had a litany of pageant advertisements, some decent and some downright sexist. *You can be pretty or smart at the Rose Palace*, one read from 1993. *Which one will you choose?*

I shook my head as I pushed aside the material and kept searching.

It took me seven boxes until I found what I was looking for, and I almost skipped it because the label read, *Misc.* I figured the contents would be more of the same, but when I lifted the lid, I almost froze when I realized what I was holding.

"Lacy," I said, gasping as I thumbed through material harkening back to the 2001 pageant. Here was the welcome packet, the contestant itinerary, and the program. The papers had yellowed and the edges were crinkled, but every word was legible. "Why would they keep an entire box for this one show? And label it as miscellaneous?"

"Maybe they're planning a whole exhibit around it? To explain what happened to Miss 2001?" Lacy suggested. "It could make for an interesting story."

"Or maybe they wanted to ensure all of the evidence is in one tidy box that they can get rid of if needed," I suggested less generously.

I flipped through the program and the alphabetical order of contestants, going straight to the Ps for Peabody, but someone had taken a pair of fine-point scissors to where her name and biographical information should've been. This person had excised Cathy Peabody from the pageant.

Lacy came to my side and squatted next to me, taking the program from my hand. "Why would anyone go to such painstaking effort to remove all traces of this woman?"

"A better question might be *who* would go to such lengths?" In my mind, the likeliest culprit was the runner-up that year: Mrs. Glenda Finch.

"Wait... here's something." Lacy handed me Cathy Peabody's application. "Her address is listed as a PO box in Richmond."

Richmond was an hour and a half from Aubergine, but the closest large city.

"Which tells us she could've been local. Relatively, anyway."

I set aside the application for now and pulled out sleeve after sleeve of preserved photos of contestants in their gowns and sashes, all of them featuring one person: Dr. James Belling-ham, his arm around a woman's waist or shoulder. Mr. Finch made an appearance in a few of the photos, including a candid shot in which he wore a blank look, as if someone had caught him unaware.

Another photo had been ripped, effectively decapitating the woman whose sash read *Miss 2001*, and instead of an arm around her, Dr. Bellingham held her hand like a paramour, their fingers interlaced and woven together.

"Cathy Peabody, I presume." I held up the image. "Without a head."

I dropped it next to the stack of pages and reached into the bottom of the box, finding a police report labeled with four words: *POI FOUND. CASE DISMISSED.*

"What's a POI?" I asked.

"Person of interest," Lacy said, without missing a beat. When I looked at her, she shrugged. "I've seen *SVU*."

"Miss 2001 has been missing for more than two decades, so why would it say she'd been found?" I mumbled, scanning the page. "Okay, here we go: Cathy Peabody was reported missing at seven a.m. on Sunday, July 8, which was the morning after that year's pageant. Found at eleven a.m. on the same day." I squinted. "Why would someone report her missing so quickly and why would they—?" I stopped as my eyes fell on the most important piece of information.

"What is it?" Lacy asked when I didn't finish the sentence.

"She was reported missing because she took something with her."

"The crown?" Lacy asked, echoing my initial thoughts.

"Yes, but..." I bit my lip. "On July 8, 2001, she also took... four-year-old Savilla Finch."

TWENTY-THREE

The shock of the discovery didn't wear off as we continued through the remainder of the boxes, but none of them provided further material on Cathy Peabody, aka the original Miss 2001, or her short-lived kidnapping of Savilla Finch.

As we put everything back how we'd found it and shut the door behind us, my mind kept spinning.

Someone named Cathy Peabody had won the 2001 crown. The morning after her big win, she'd kidnapped Savilla Finch but, a few hours later, the four-year-old had been found at a McDonald's just outside of town. Mr. Finch hadn't pressed charges and, according to his ledger that I'd found near the whiskey bottle, he'd paid the kidnapper and original pageant queen for decades. And most—if not all—of this had gone under the public's radar. It had possibly even been hidden from my aunt, someone who'd dedicated her life to this world.

The Finches were a strange bunch, sure, but this was beyond strange, and the one living person closest to it all—Savilla Finch—would likely have been almost too young to remember.

We made our way into the warm air outside, and the goose-bumps on my arm settled as I stood in the sunshine, grateful now for the heat. I took out my phone and searched a variety of terms that included "Cathy Peabody."

There wasn't much to find. One catch-all pageant website that looked defunct listed Cathy Peabody as the first and only "de-throned" pageant winner, but provided no relevant personal information. No social media accounts appeared, which wasn't surprising since Myspace hadn't even been invented until 2003. I typed in a few new iterations of search terms.

Cathy Peabody, police report
Cathy Peabody, missing
Cathy Peabody, Virginia

Results came up—birth records and obits, but none of them matched the age range she would have been in 2001. When I typed in "2001 Winner of Rose Palace Pageant," it appeared as if the Internet had been scrubbed of anything—besides the defunct website—that alluded to anyone other than Mrs. Glenda Finch receiving the crown. Mrs. Glenda Finch... but that wouldn't have been her name in 2001 because she hadn't yet married, much less dated, Frederick Finch. I searched for her maiden name, but the Internet also seemed to have lost that info.

"What are you thinking?" Lacy asked, looking up from her phone, where she'd been researching the same.

"I'm thinking that Cathy Peabody isn't this woman's real name, and that under her fake name, she received some kind of payout from the Finches. Maybe she was blackmailing them."

Lacy pursed her lips. "Or maybe she had a bone to pick."

"A lot of people could have something against someone that rich," I mused.

Lacy and I decided to look around to see if we could find

any other info. We poked our heads into the kitchen house, which was dark and dank but empty; then, we started toward the half-hidden structures, only to find trees and overgrowth. We made our way farther into the loblolly pines and red maples, finding wooden boxes that looked as if they were sprouting right out of the ground, like waist-high quadrilateral plants.

Lacy held a hand over her eyes to block the glare from above us. "What do you think those are?"

The slatted edifices were too small to be playhouses. A slight hum emanated from the one nearest me and, as I moved closer to inspect it, being sure to dodge three-pronged poison ivy, a bee escaped and landed on my forearm.

My heart began to pound as it had when I'd been young and watched Pooh Bear sing about being a storm cloud as he floated toward the bees. I closed my eyes and recalled my trip with Momma to the Sweet Hive, the apiary where she'd taken me when I was ten in an attempt to face my fears.

It's okay to go slow, but it's not okay to not go at all, Momma had said as I'd hesitated to even get out of the car, much less put on the white beekeeping suit while bees swarmed around me. That day had required extraordinary patience and stalwart fortitude from my mother as we both donned the gear—me, glacially, since I had to stop periodically to shoot her frantic looks and beg to go back to the car.

You are stronger, smarter, and braver than this hive, she'd said over and over, the words baptizing me as we'd finally followed the beekeeper out to his modern apiary, all white lines and curated glass, and watched him blow puffs of smoke at the entrance to the hive.

While Momma and I had waited for the bees to calm enough not to sting us, I'd closed my eyes, felt the fabric against my skin, listened to the sounds. At ten years old, I couldn't express the vulnerability I'd felt even though the white costume mostly protected me from the bees' stingers. I couldn't begin to understand that Momma hadn't been teaching me to be unafraid of bees nearly as much as she'd been teaching me to be unafraid of life. In the end, Momma had been right: Living through and in spite of the fear was the best way forward.

Back in the here and now, I breathed in the scent of honey-suckles, opened my eyes, and watched the bee flit away without stinging me. I knew what I was looking at.

This was an apiary, though a simple one, possibly dating back to the original house. These structures housed the bees, quite a small hive based on the low hum nearby. There were eight houses, but the sounds were only coming from the box closest to me.

"I knew that Mr. Finch liked to make his own honey, but I had no idea..." I remembered the book I'd seen in Mr. Finch's whiskey cabinet, *Backyard Apiaries*. "Must be his hobby... or must've been. But I can't imagine Glenda Finch letting him out of her sight long enough to come back here." She'd been panicked after not seeing him for a couple of hours.

"So you think this is where he was? Before he died?" Lacy asked.

"I don't know," I answered. "But in our welcome packet, there were specialty bottles of honey. I saw one of them in the Finches' apartment too. Maybe he was trying to contribute something personal, something he'd made with his own two hands, to the contestants."

The idea made sense. Frederick Finch had been a beloved member of the pageant community, and this place, this show, was his baby in many ways.

"What do you think is back there?" Lacy asked, pointing to a shed just past the apiary, where ivy hung over a one-room structure that looked as if it might have been a smokehouse at one time. Now, it appeared more like a ramshackle shed with its slanted roof and a few missing exterior slats.

"Let's find out," I said, starting in that direction.

The hinges screeched as the door to the shed swung open, sending a thin stream of light into the windowless space. The hair stood on the back of my neck. Instinctively, we both pulled out our phones and switched on the flashlights, lighting up the space in small bursts.

Lacy pulled at a string above us and a yellow bulb glowed half-heartedly. As my eyes adjusted to the dim light, I studied the paltry contents of the room. I knew what I'd been hoping to find: clear-cut evidence that Mr. Finch had been here and that someone other than my aunt had been involved. But there was no blood-soaked chair with a rope hanging over the side. There were no weapons or torture devices thrown about. There wasn't even a good place to sit.

I closed my eyes and reminded myself to use all of my senses as I attempted to picture Mr. Finch in this space. I sniffed. A hint of smoke lingered in the air, which meant the apiary had been recently harvested for honey.

I opened my eyes, and they landed on a white suit with a plastic mask folded in the corner. Beside it was a tarnished silver bucket with a funneled lid, and behind these objects ran three shelves filled with jars of honey labeled with a purple cartoon bee. The first two shelves held jars just like the one I'd received on arrival, but the jars on the third shelf featured a white-petaled flower with scarlet marks: an exact match to the one in Mr. Finch's cabinet.

I picked up a jar from the bottom shelf and held it in my hand. I ran through the flowers Momma had taught me grew around this area. Swamp roses, of course. Black-eyed Susans. Queen Anne's lace. That white flower with the pinprick dots wasn't any of those. I thought through the list several times, adding to it as I went: azaleas, rhododendron, dogwood, sourwood, black gum.

Then it came to me: This was a sketch of a mountain laurel, a cup-like white flower with a rim of scarlet drops. Dots of darkness. I remembered the lesson Momma had taught me about mountain laurels on one of our hikes, how she'd told me to think of the dark spots as blood, a warning to steer clear. If I'd even touched the flower, I had to wash my hands before eating or drinking.

I side-eyed Lacy. "This label, it's different than the others. I think that flower is a mountain laurel." I opened the jar and sniffed at the contents. It had the tell-tale scent of grape-flavored candy, the same thing I'd smelled in the Finch apartment when I'd lifted the honey jar to my nose.

"What's wrong with mountain laurel?"

"Poisonous," I said, screwing the lid back on and setting it on the shelf. My eyes traveled down to a boxed kit on the ground. I shone my light on the words that read, *Toxicity Test*. Thin strips of litmus paper had fallen to the floor like petals from a flower. "There's our proof," I said, taking a photo of the kit, the test strips, and the honey jars to show the sheriff later. "One time a beekeeper told me he had to test the honey around these parts, to make sure it wasn't toxic. Too many mountain laurels had invaded the area, and the pollen carried poison. The honey was usually fine but, occasionally, he'd get a bad batch." I pointed to the bottom shelf. "Like those."

Someone had been tending the hive, and that same person had been testing the bees' wares, seeing if any of the collected honey had too much mountain laurel pollen, the element that would make a batch poisonous.

The four jars on the bottom shelf—the ones with the white flower—must've contained the right amount to tip the oozy liquid into the danger zone for human consumption, and one of those jars had been placed in Mr. Finch's liquor cabinet. But by Mr. Finch himself? Or someone else?

That's when I saw a small metal case lying on the ground, one of those that holds a few pills at a time. It was empty, but an inscription had been etched into the corner.

To my favorite Dr. B!

Love,
Savilla

TWENTY-FOUR

All signs were pointing to Dr. Bellingham—and now, quite possibly, his patient, Savilla Finch. I needed to let the sheriff know what we'd found, but I wanted to do it carefully so as not to unintentionally point any fingers in the direction of Aunt DeeDee.

After arriving back at the main part of the property, I tried to think like the sheriff, if that was even possible, as I cooled down the horses and settled them in their stalls, while Lacy stepped away to call the hospital. I didn't have long to consider because a few minutes later, as I was filling the water trough, Sheriff Strong walked into the stables.

My first reaction to his presence was to wonder if he'd been tracking me, if somehow he knew where I'd been.

"How are you?" His expression was open, genuinely concerned.

I wasn't sure how to answer that. "Did Lacy tell you what we found?"

"The honey? Yes, she briefly mentioned it when I saw her just now." He hesitated as if weighing his next words carefully. "But I wanted to check on you too."

"You need another official statement?"

"No," he breathed, frustration evident. "I have to do my job, but I also... I care."

I narrowed my eyes, trying to read what he actually meant. "Aubergine will come around. They just need some time to adjust to an outsider."

"All that's fine, but I meant... I care about you."

"Me?" I looked at Polly to see if she had any insights into Sheriff Grinch's heart growing two sizes.

"Yesterday, you seemed"—he tried to find the words—"overcome."

In that moment I knew I had a choice: risk vulnerability, or keep on the same trajectory I'd taken for the past year or so.

I almost told him I was good and he should mind his own beeswax, like I was in middle school, but something about his wide eyes and something about being in an event that I'd assumed was all about selfishness and superficiality—but was actually more about camaraderie and community—made me reconsider.

"My mom died last year. Cancer," I said bluntly, too tired to couch my words. I took a deep breath and leaned against Polly. "She wanted me to compete, so I'm here. But seeing Mr. Finch, lifeless..."

"It took you back," the sheriff said softly.

"I have no idea why. He and Momma were nothing alike."

"Grief doesn't follow a neat trajectory, doesn't always make sense." He gazed into my eyes and those deep wells called to me.

"Have you lost someone?" I asked before I could change my mind.

His lip twitched as if he wasn't used to such direct questions. Giving them, yes, but not receiving them. Still, he answered.

"My dad. He was in the force where I grew up in New Jersey. We moved to Virginia after he retired."

"Very different kind of police work down here, I'm guessing."

"Yeah." He gave a hint of a smile. "He was older when I was born, about to quit working, so I grew up with him at every basketball game, every campout. He would tell stories of his time in uniform and I ate them up; he was the superhero I wanted to be. I lost him five years ago. It's gotten better—the missing—but I'd give anything to hear his stories one more time."

Momma would tell the best stories about her patients, about the funny things they'd said even in the dark moments. She'd made the families come alive in vivid detail, so I knew what he meant.

"I'm sorry for your loss," he said. "That's what I wanted to say yesterday but somehow couldn't."

"But you didn't know about my mom yesterday."

"I could see you'd lost someone."

So, he was perceptive, compassionate, and sexy. Good Lord, I had no chance at hating this man.

He took a step back and resumed his more official stance. "Lacy was hurrying away. Anything I should know about? Like, exactly where you two have been all morning?"

"I didn't know Big Brother was watching," I teased him, turning away to brush down Polly.

"Not watching." He leaned his forearms against the wooden half-door and bent forward to stroke Polly's nose. She nuzzled against him, which signaled that he might be a good person after all. Horses can often read people better than lie detectors. "I'm just curious."

"You know what they say," I started. "Curiosity killed the—"

"—the sheriff?" Sheriff Strong finished. "That's rather

insensitive, Miss Green." His tone was lighter than I expected, almost as if we were old friends.

"Probably too soon to joke about killing anyone," I said, giving him a pointed look.

"Fair," he conceded. "I mentioned this to Lacy, but the hospital called a few minutes ago. Mrs. Finch is conscious. She told the doctor that she passed out after drinking a smidge of whiskey. She'd mixed it with honey."

I paused mid-brush. Then my suspicions were correct. Someone had known the honey was toxic and intentionally put it in the Finches' cabinets, waiting for one—or both—of them to consume it.

"Lacy and I found some of that honey at the back of the property. It was poisonous—and, remember, I've seen her definition of a 'smidge.' It's enough to off a horse."

"The doctor says she'll be okay, that there wasn't enough of whatever was in her system to do permanent damage—just to make her lose consciousness and feel terrible. She might even be back in time for the show tomorrow night."

"The show is still happening?" I asked. Despite the fact that my priority had to be clearing my aunt's name, I knew I also desperately needed to place in this pageant.

"The show must go on." The sheriff scratched at the back of his neck. "As soon as she regained consciousness, Mrs. Finch insisted that everything would continue, and since it won't interfere with the investigation, I'll allow it, though we will have more security this weekend. She insisted that the pageant has never shut down before—not during World War II, financial collapses, or COVID. She said it's what her husband would've wanted."

I thought about that response. It sounded like those words could carry two disparate meanings: either she didn't care much that her husband had died, or she really wanted to honor her husband's love for the pageant. I wasn't sure which I believed, but I was leaning toward the former.

"You said this is your first show?"

I nodded, dragging a brush gently along Polly's back.

"You seem like a natural," he said without condescension or sarcasm. "You're poised, and the judges—as well as some of the other contestants—seem impressed."

I peeked over Polly to check his expression, and he caught me looking at him.

"I'm complimenting you, Miss Green."

"You sure you don't want to make some snide remark about how all pageant contestants are blond bimbos?" I asked, realizing that this was close to what I'd been thinking until this week.

"You're neither blond nor a bimbo," the sheriff said evenly. "In fact, I'm hoping that you'll continue to share with me anything important that you find about Mr. Finch or his murder."

"And why would I do that?" I asked, my head tilted.

He cleared his throat and considered how to best answer the question. "I think that our interests are more aligned than you realize. I want to find evidence pertaining to Mr. Finch's murderer, and you want the same."

"Though for different reasons."

"Maybe," he conceded, kicking the toe of his boot into the ground. "But as an act of goodwill, I thought I'd tell you that I received the coroner's report this morning."

That caught my attention.

"It appears as if Mr. Finch died sometime after midnight last night."

After midnight... that was what I'd expected—and well after Aunt DeeDee had been taken into custody. A thrill went through me. "Does that mean my aunt's in the clear?"

He put out a hand. "For the direct cause of death, yes, but she still stole a crown."

"Allegedly," I said. "Anyone could've put that in her room."

"True. Allegedly." His brow furrowed. "The coroner also determined Mr. Finch's cause of death. A blow to the head through the right eye socket."

It's what I would've guessed, what with the missing eyeball and the stream of blood down one side of his body.

"Any idea what the weapon might've been?" I asked, as I put a blanket over Polly's back and then moved to Ginger's stall.

"It was a pointed object. Not sharp like a knife. Something blunt." The sheriff skirted out of my way and cocked his head. "The strange thing is that they found traces of mud and grass at the site of the wound."

I hit the toe of my own boot against the ground a few times before an idea came to me. "How long do they think the object may have been?"

"Four to six inches."

"Could it have been a shoe? Like a high heel or a stiletto? Something pointy, four to six inches in length, that would be in contact with mud and grass on the regular out here."

He considered the possibility. "That's a decent guess."

"Which means the murderer would likely be a woman, right?" Savilla's face came to mind again. So too did the gold heels she'd shown off on our first meeting, and the champagne heels she'd been wearing yesterday. Open-toed heels caked with mud.

As if to remind me of the fact that he wouldn't draw aimless conclusions, the sheriff stated, "Just because the murderer used a shoe as the weapon doesn't mean it was a woman. Around here anyone can get their hands on a high heel."

"Except the mud and grass indicate that this shoe was worn recently." I thought about how Lacy treated her footwear like they were precious gems. She wore them, cleaned them, and displayed them like works of art in her closet. "If the heel belonged to a contestant, it wouldn't have had mud or grass on it —unless the woman had recently been out on the grounds and had no choice but to tromp through the dirt."

"Perhaps," the sheriff conceded.

"So, what do we do?" I asked. "Check everyone's shoes for mud and dirt—and blood?"

"Scouring closets probably isn't the way to go. I can have forensics dig deeper, see if they can more closely identify a specific plant or type of soil, but that will take days if not weeks."

"Well, you know it wasn't me because I don't even own a pair of heels."

"Like I said, anyone around here can get their hands on a high heel," he said, his eyes crinkling at the corners as a curl fell across his forehead. I had to keep my hand from instinctively brushing it away, but in an instant, his brow furrowed as he refocused on the complexities of this case. "Now I'd like to figure out who did."

TWENTY-FIVE

With her stepmother's recovery expected and her father's body discovered, Savilla Finch arrived back on-site and officially declared that the pageant would proceed as planned.

A gaggle of girls dressed in workout gear did not look like they were doing the scheduled interview prep as they lifted light weights and strolled the gardens. Summer was among them.

"At least the money is still up for grabs," one woman, who I was fairly certain was named Piper, said as I trailed behind the three contestants.

"Winning is not about the money. It's about being a role model," Summer reminded the other two as she lifted a five-pound dumbbell over her head.

Maybe-Piper laughed as she halted and lunged forward, swinging her arms. "Spoken like someone who already has plenty of money."

"We all have money," said a third girl who marched in place. "But my actual concern is... do you think it's safe to stay here?" I couldn't see the woman's face, but I could hear the fear underpinning her words. "I've been wondering *that* since Mr. Finch disappeared... and now..."

Maybe-Piper jumped in again. "Someone is after the Finches, not us."

The ladies went quiet, seeming to weigh the wisdom of the sentiment.

"But what if the killer is here? Among us?" the third girl asked, this time with a tremor in her voice.

"What if the killer *is* one of us?" Maybe-Piper laughed and turned to each of her compadres before noticing me listening in. "What if it's her?" She pointed at me. "You know what they say: Families that steal together, kill together."

Summer swatted at her hand. "Not funny, Piper."

Definitely-Piper was joking, of course she was, but she now stared at me with a condescending smile. If I hadn't overheard the conversation, I would've assumed her distaste for me sprang from the flyaways sticking out of my ponytail and the mud splatters covering my jeans, but it felt more personal than that. Like she knew that with my aunt in jail I was an easy target for laughs—or for compassion from the judges, which could be even worse. So maybe some of the contestants didn't have a heart, but I reminded myself this had to be the exception to the rule.

Summer took her dumbbells and peeled away from the girls, who strutted to the other side of the garden where they set down their weights and began to bend into yoga poses. "She didn't mean it. We're all just nervous and trying to find a way to make all of this less scary."

I attempted to shake off the comment. Did the other contestants actually think my aunt was guilty? And that I might know more than I was letting on? Or were they just jealous that I was performing surprisingly well despite no previous pageant experience? Was the pageant world that cut-throat? I couldn't bring myself to ask the questions out loud.

"How are you feeling after... everything?" Summer asked.

"Ready to see Aunt DeeDee," I answered. "You?"

"Ready to win," Summer said. "Or support the winner. Either is fine."

I believed that last part when Summer said it.

"Oh..." Summer's eyes lit up and she dropped the weights at her feet. "I found something that I thought might interest you. It's about Miss 2001." She took a book from a workout bag that had been slung across her back. "From the library. I was in there this morning, looking for something to read, and I came across this."

I took the slim, bound-canvas volume that fit in the palm of my hand. It was titled *The Twenty-First Century Queen*, and when I opened to the cover page, I saw that it had been published by Aubergine Press, the same publisher who ran the weekly newspaper. Instead of one single author, there were multiple contributors.

"It starts talking about the 2001 pageant on page twenty-two," Summer directed.

I opened it and skimmed the first full paragraph.

Unlike the first seventy-five years or so of the pageant's history of blue-blooded contestants, today's girls come from all backgrounds and all walks of life...

"I'm not sure if it's anything you don't already know," Summer added. "But I recognized the year and thought it could be useful."

"Yeah, thanks," I said, relishing every detail I could find about Miss 2001.

I continued reading.

At the Miss 2001 competition, I spoke with a young woman named Cathy Peabody, who grew up in the nearby mountains on a farm with her family. Instead of blue-blood, she's from a blue-

collar family, but she hopes to one day work on the Parisian runways.

After that, the writing switched focus to other young women before coming back to quote Peabody.

"My child will grow up in a different kind of world than even I did," Ms. Peabody said. "I'm here at this pageant to create a better world for her."

"Her child?" I asked. "But contestants can't have kids. It's in the rules."

Summer looked over my shoulder. "She probably meant a future kid."

"But it says 'a better world for her.' Like she already has a daughter."

"Could be a figure of speech, but who knows?" Summer shrugged and began doing high kicks, antsy to finish her workout.

"Right. Maybe," I agreed.

"Can you just get that back to the library when you're done with it?"

"Sure," I said.

She gave me a one-sided air-kiss. "Remember that tonight's all about comportment and costumes, so be ready, okay?" Summer's brown eyes sparkled in the afternoon sun. "I'll swing by to see if you need help with any finishing touches, but it will take me a while to freshen up."

"Sounds good."

I watched her walk away and then scanned the other fifty-odd pages of the short book as I made my way back to my cottage. Cathy Peabody wasn't mentioned again.

When I reached my room, I glanced at the clock. We'd missed breakfast and lunch, and now evening was fast approaching. Lacy had texted to say she'd notified the sheriff and the hospital about our findings and then been called away for another tent emergency.

I started digging through one of my bags to find a melted protein bar when a knock sounded at my door. It was Katie Gilman.

"I don't have much time, but I saw you across the garden with the other contestants. I have no idea what those gals said to you, but I could see that it wasn't great."

"Thank you," I said, wishing my body language wasn't so transparent.

Katie looked behind her as if perhaps she shouldn't step inside, but then she put one foot across the threshold. "Listen, hon. I've known your aunt... well, forever... and since I don't think it's technically against the rules, I wondered if you needed any help getting presentable for this evening. It's an important event, lots of points at stake."

Help? I wasn't sure what Ms. Gilman was offering, but I probably needed all the help I could get.

"With your makeup," Katie said, answering my unasked question. "At the Gilded Age dinner. Certain contestants are seated with the judges, and I may have shuffled things around a bit to get you at the main table." She smiled. "When I saw Lacy running around with boxes of who knows what over by the 1930s tent, I thought I should come check on you."

I wanted to tell her I was fine, but we both knew that wasn't true. My independent streak hadn't served me well this past year. I did need her—and the rest of my community, small though it might be.

"Can you do hair too?" I asked, running a hand through the strands as I slid my scrunchie out of the ponytail.

Katie's face softened as if she was relieved to have me ask. "I think a high-set updo would be just the thing." She rushed inside, sat me in front of her, and got to work quickly, using a hodge-podge of supplies that Aunt DeeDee had given me and that Lacy had left behind, as well as bobby pins and rhinestone clips she'd brought with her.

"What did you think of the Jewels and Gems party on the first night?" Katie asked as she combed a coconut-scented oil through my hair.

"I didn't stay for long."

"I understand. The soiree was rather anticlimactic with everything else that day," she said, pinning pieces of my hair to my head before she plugged in a straightener. "I came down with Mrs. Finch for a few minutes at the very end but, honestly, I was exhausted. That night, I slept like the dead." She put a hand over her mouth. "I guess I shouldn't use phrases like that in our current situation." The product in my hair steamed as she worked. "Can I ask you something? About Savilla?"

"Sure," I told her.

"Did you see her with anyone in particular that night?"

"No, but she mentioned wanting me to meet Dr. Bellingham." I didn't add that I went to my aunt's office to find out information instead. The way Katie's hand fluttered nervously made me realize she was concerned for her former charge. "Why do you ask?"

"It's just... before Savilla left for the party, I thought I heard her tell her stepmother that she was planning to spend time with Dr. Bellingham afterward. I wanted to step in, to tell her to stay away from him, but when Mrs. Finch didn't say anything, I didn't feel it was my place."

I could sense her question of whether or not she'd made the right call by staying silent.

"Why do you think Savilla wanted to meet with him?" I asked.

Katie unpinned a strand of hair, straightened it, and then picked up the curling iron. "I'm not sure, but that's what concerns me." She bit her lip, thinking as she wound my hair around the hot iron. "Savilla's father met Jim—Dr. Bellingham —in New York at an art gallery back in the nineties. Despite the age difference, the two of them hit it off, bonded over shared interests in investments, that kind of thing. Mr. Finch took him under his wing, taught him about shrewd business skills, helped him set up a successful practice, invited him into the pageant world to meet potential clients with plenty of money to spend. I can't help but assume Savilla heard or saw something that led her to believe Dr. Bellingham might know the whereabouts of her father, but I'd much prefer for her to let the police do their job and for her to stay out of the whole thing."

The two of us sat with that information for a few minutes until I noticed that Katie had done wonders with my hair. Her own cheeks were flushed and her lips set in a line, a similar expression to that of my aunt when she'd told me to *stay away from that man*.

I turned in my chair to face her, thinking about the idea of Savilla and Dr. Bellingham spending time together on the very night that Mr. Finch died.

"Anyway, probably just a middle-aged woman's fears. I was young and beautiful once, so I know how it can be." Katie tried to relax her shoulders and push aside her concerns as she finished her work.

I caught her hand as she tamed a final strand of hair. "Savilla's lucky to have you." I wasn't able to express in words how much she reminded me of Aunt DeeDee in that moment. I also couldn't bring myself to tell her that Savilla, along with Dr. Bellingham, had ascended to the top of my list of suspects.

She didn't say anything more as she began applying foundation and powders and all the things I needed to enhance my features that evening.

When I looked at myself in the mirror a few minutes later, I was astonished.

"You look like you came from the set of *Downton Abbey*," Katie breathed, obviously impressed with her work.

I was reminded of how Momma always said that I had nice eyes. I could see, especially with Ms. Gilman's magic, that the green in them did pop. I knew nothing about contouring or lightening, but Katie did, and my skin appeared almost porcelain. My hair had been its own beast, fluffy and windblown from the ride, but she'd wrangled it into a sort of high bun with tendrils falling around my face. Within a half-hour, she'd turned me into a new woman.

"Oh dear, I best be getting into my outfit for the evening," Katie said as a text came through and she lifted her phone so I could see it. "That's Savilla. She wants me to stop by her room for a quick chat."

"Maybe you can tell her that you're worried about her?"

"Maybe." Katie took a deep breath. "Do you think you can manage the gown on your own?"

My outfits were labeled by event, so all I had to do was take the silver dress from the hanger and wiggle into it. Delicate lace ran across the bodice, and seed pearls dripped along the waist and down the skirt. Of course, it wasn't what I would have chosen to wear—that would've been my jeans and a red plaid button down—but if it simultaneously made me blend in and catch the other two judges' attention, that was key.

"I've got this," I told her.

Katie gave me one last pat on the shoulder and then saw herself out. "Good luck tonight." She leaned forward conspiratorially. "Don't tell anyone, but I'm rooting for you—and your aunt."

My heart warmed at the mention of someone besides me and Lacy being on Aunt DeeDee's side. "Thanks... for everything."

She gave a half-smile and shut the door behind her.

I turned to the dress. "Looks like it's just you and me," I said as I took it from the hanger.

I climbed inside the get-up and tried to pull the back together. Aunt DeeDee had done a great job with my measurements, but after a couple of minutes, I'd still only been able to get the bottom five buttons fastened. I turned around and studied the rest of the open back in the mirror. There were at least ten more buttons climbing up my spine. I'd spoken too soon about being able to dress myself. I could almost see the horror on the other women's faces if I stepped into the Gilded Age that evening with an open-back dress that should be very closed. This wouldn't do.

I texted Lacy to see if she had time to finish pulling me together, but she was now in the 2010s, setting up the K-pop band cutouts. Resisting the urge to beg, I rifled through the other gowns, thinking maybe I could switch them out. I found a slinky dress with colorful flowers fanning across the front, and another one that looked like something bridezilla might wear. The last was in a bag, and when I unzipped it, yellow—a lot of yellow—assaulted my eyes. These clothes were suited for other purposes, and I needed to fit in tonight.

I glanced at my open back in the mirror again, and then desperate, I cracked my front door to see if I could spot a fellow contestant walking past. This was a sisterhood, right? Surely someone—even Piper or Jemma—would take pity on me and my unreachable buttons.

A light rain had begun to fall again. I looked at the black flats and then down at the bottom of the gown. The dress was so long that I bet I could wear boots and no one would know. But it wouldn't matter unless I could finish dressing.

I couldn't quite make out the shadowy figure passing with an umbrella, but I had no choice.

"Hey!" I called. The figure stopped, and I called out again. "Hey, can I get some help?"

I saw the person turn and head toward my voice, but the umbrella still hid their face. When they were only a couple yards from the cottage, a man lifted his head. Sheriff Charlie Strong. Shoot.

"Oh, sorry. Never mind," I said, nearly shutting the door on his foot as he started through the entryway. I did not want him to see me quite this... exposed.

"It's fine. What do you need?"

Nothing from you, I wanted to blurt. But that wasn't quite true.

When I didn't answer, he seemed almost embarrassed for me. "I was just on my way to the dinner. I was invited as a special guest."

The sheriff had changed out of his uniform and wore all black with a high-necked scarf-tie thingy. He'd combed the curly hair atop his head, and it grazed the shaved sides. He looked way better than I wanted to admit.

"I'm off duty tonight—as much as I can be." He lifted his jacket and pointed to the holster he still wore around his back. "A couple of my guys will be patrolling the grounds, so not to worry."

I hadn't had time to worry, though perhaps I should've been more concerned.

I studied the sheriff's face in the lamplight of my cottage, realizing that he'd been working for most of the past forty-eight hours. The circles rimming his eyes showed his fatigue.

"Did you get some sleep?" I asked.

He smiled, appreciating my question. "A couple hours."

"I was... I was trying to button this," I stammered, moving my hand behind me. "And I thought Lacy would be here to help, but I guess she's busy and—"

He turned me around, his hand drifting over my shoulder. "These are kind of tricky." His fingers brushed against the small of my back as he struggled with the buttons. "I'm impressed that you got this far on your own."

His breath was warm on my neck, and a rush of heat ran down my entire body. He fumbled with one or two, but for the most part, his hands were quick and efficient as his fingers roamed up my spine, pausing for a few seconds at each button-hole. Moments later he spun me around, and his eyes grazed my breasts before darting to the ground. A flutter low in my belly wasn't helping matters.

"You're good to go," he said, seeming to force himself to take the smallest step away from me. "You look... you look lovely."

"Thanks, Sheriff."

"You can call me Charlie... if you want." He halted. "I'm glad I ran into you."

"You didn't exactly run into me."

"Well, then, I'm glad you desperately needed to be buttoned." He gave a quick smile.

"How's my aunt?" I asked, trying not to frown at him since he'd offered me much-needed help.

"She's fine. I spoke to her about an hour ago."

"You mean you questioned her?"

He almost blushed. "Well, yes. It's just, she's also insisting that Dr. Bellingham is somehow involved in all of this. I was wondering if—as a contestant—you've had any run-ins with him?"

"Nothing beyond the tea yesterday morning. There, he struck me as... sleazy."

"Sleazy," the sheriff repeated.

"Not exactly criminal," I mumbled.

"No, not exactly, but it's something."

Seeming not to know what else to say, the sheriff offered a stiff bow that was both ridiculous and somehow endearing. He paused for a moment, then locked eyes with mine as he moved toward me. "Miss Green, you really are beau—"

My breath caught.

His mouth was only inches from my lips and I wanted to close the gap.

Before either of us could move, Summer, wearing a pale gray gown, burst through my unlocked door. "Do you have an umbrella?" She halted mid-sentence when she saw the sheriff standing close to me.

"I have one, but we'll need to share," I said too brightly, practically jumping away from Sheriff Strong. I grabbed my boots, slipping them on before I could even consider those flimsy flats again.

Summer seemed surprised by my selection.

"Don't say a word. It's muddy out there." I caught my phrasing, remembering that the weapon of choice for the killer had likely tromped through the same dark earth I'd be traversing. I looked from my shoes to the sheriff, wondering if I could trust him with the new intel I'd discovered that day. I decided to try. "I wanted to put a name on your radar. Cathy Peabody?"

As he turned I waited for his reaction, which I hoped would tell me what I needed to know: whether this woman's name had been entirely wiped off the system.

"It already is," he said, raising an eyebrow.

TWENTY-SIX

After we reached the open door of the Rose Palace, Summer and I turned right and walked down a long veranda with a high glass ceiling that let in the remnants of sunlight. The distant mountains gave edges to the clouds, and lights in the topiaries lined the windows, twinkling and shimmering like stars peeking through a waxy green sky. We lost the sheriff at some point as he peeled off to speak to one of his officers.

The man standing guard at the door took our names and we were each handed a box with a label: *Open Me, Property of Finch Jewelers.* Mine contained a long strand of pearls with a diamond-crested rose in the center, and Summer slid on an emerald bracelet.

"Are these the party favors?" Summer joked.

The man standing guard answered with a rote statement he'd likely repeated all evening. "The Finches generously arranged for accessories to be provided. Please return at the end of the dinner." He spoke without inflection and while somehow barely moving his mouth.

I looped the strand over my head a couple of times. "Fancy," I said as I wondered how much money this strand was worth.

Probably enough to pay several months of my mortgage, but for better or worse, I was no thief.

"I could get used to this," Summer giggled.

After bejeweling ourselves, we entered a spacious banquet hall and saw the Gilded Age come to life: a vaulted entryway, ornately carved crown molding, gold-painted accents, a crystal chandelier. It was the epitome of gaudy wonder.

Jemma approached as if she'd been watching for us. She wore a pair of amethyst earrings and motioned to our right. "We're seated through that door. All three of us are at the main table." She took a sip of champagne. "The winner for every show has always been seated there on the night of the dinner, though it's not always a Gilded Age theme."

"I can't believe I made it to the main table," Summer said, eyes wide with wonder.

"I can't either," Jemma said in a tone that was so matter-of-fact it somehow didn't seem offensive. Jemma studied me. "You, too. You're doing surprisingly well. Your authenticity at the morning tea—I could tell that Miss 1962 ate it up, and of course, Katie Gilman is a fan. I heard she helped you get ready this evening?"

"How do you know—?"

Jemma lifted a shoulder with a single seed-pearl studded strap. "Everyone's watching everyone at this point. This is when it gets fun."

A bell rang, and we were asked to take our seats. As we entered the room, the women around us glided to their uphol-stered chairs, most of them passing the center table with a look of longing. One of the girls from earlier—Piper—rolled her eyes as Jemma, Summer, and I pulled out our seats and sat at the same table as the judges.

I looked at my name, heavy with calligraphy: *Miss Dakota Green of Aubergine, Contestant.* Only a moment later I noticed that Charlie was pulling out the chair on my left. Even seated, he was nearly half a foot taller than me, and this close, I noticed how long his eyelashes were. He rested his hand only inches from mine and I could feel the heat radiating from him, though perhaps I was the only one who sensed it.

Control yourself, Dakota. Focus on the prize.

"Miss Green, so good to see you this evening," Dr. Bellingham said from across the table, lifting a glass in my direction. "You look as fresh as the evening breeze."

The sheriff's hand curled into a fist, but he didn't say anything.

"Thank you. It's an honor to be here at this table with all of the judges this evening," I said, doing my best impersonation of pageant royalty.

"And, my dear, how was your day?" Dr. Bellingham asked, his eyes still fixed on me as he leaned his elbows on the table, likely hoping for something clever from me.

"Oh, you know. The usual. I spent the morning reading my *Beauty Queen's Guide to Murder and Mayhem.*"

The other contestants at the table—including Jemma and Summer, who looked like they might do a spit-take—stilled at my quip, one I hadn't even considered before letting it pop out of my mouth. But Dr. Bellingham laughed, full-throated and hearty. "*Beauty Queen's Guide...* that is very clever. Very clever." He continued laughing as he moved on to Jemma to inquire about her afternoon, and that's when I noticed the pinky ring on his finger, which meant that it hadn't been the one in my aunt's room.

I was relieved to have the spotlight off me, and I turned to Charlie, who wore a look of surprise, which reminded me how out of practice I was at conversation. It was certainly too early to joke about Mr. Finch's murder, especially not with the man who I thought might be involved in his death.

"Sorry. I'm not great at this," I said quietly to the sheriff.

"No need to apologize to me." He looked around at the

other guests talking among themselves. "This isn't exactly my usual scene either."

"You don't regularly dress like you're from a hundred years ago and try to solve murders?"

"I reserve this outfit for only the most special occasions," Charlie answered, patting the pocket on the front of his suit.

"Then I'm glad you could join us," I said, surprising myself with how much I meant it.

At that moment the hum of conversation paused as Savilla Finch stepped into the dining room wearing a blood-red gown that trailed behind her. She made her way to Dr. Bellingham, who stood to receive her. She gave him her hand, and he folded it within his own. A second later, he moved close to her ear and whispered something before she let out a silvery laugh.

Jemma, Summer, and I exchanged glances from our spots around the table. The dynamics between Savilla and Dr. Bellingham, this shared intimacy, seemed to be a new development.

I tried to *fix my face*, as Momma would say.

As Dr. Bellingham seated Savilla, I took a sip of my wine, wondering what Momma would think if she could see this scene—and me in it. Just as immediately, I pictured Aunt DeeDee sitting in her jail cell, waiting for me to do something. I set aside the wine and drank water. I needed to stay sharp. The sheriff also seemed to be keeping a watchful eye on Savilla and Dr. Bellingham, which gave me some measure of comfort.

Within seconds of being seated, Savilla tapped a spoon against the edge of her crystal stemware, summoning the attention of the women gathered in the massive dining hall as well as a smattering of guests and staff.

All eyes turned to her as she spoke, commanding the room as well as, if not better than, her father or stepmother had ever done.

"I asked Doris Davis, as the longest-running judge of the

pageant"—Savilla nodded in Miss 1962's direction—"if she'd like to do the honors of welcoming you all here this evening, but she insisted that I do them instead."

Miss 1962 was oblivious. She took a long gulp from her wine glass, and I wondered if she'd turned off her hearing aids so she could enjoy her evening in peace.

"I spoke to StepMommy on the phone a few minutes ago, and she wanted you all to know that she plans to be back on the premises for showtime tomorrow night."

The room applauded. Savilla took a few moments to look at each of the faces in the room—the dozen or so at our table as well as those scattered across the dining space.

"This—the centennial year—has brought with it a magnif-tude of sorrow. My father's death is a grave loss, not only to myself and my stepmother, but to the pageant world. Even though I'm grateful we can be together and share this amazing meal, I can't help but picture my father in the midst of you all. He would have loved to see this room filled, the wine flowing. I do want to acknowledge that we are doing all of this with a hint of dilapidation."

Magnifitude? Dilapidation? I considered the malapropisms before recalling that Savilla seemed to have an explanation for every odd word she spoke.

Dr. Bellingham raised a glass in support of Savilla and the beautiful women around him. He was grinning far too much for my liking.

"To that end, I would ask anyone who might know anything about my father's death... or my stepmother's poisoning..." She choked back a small cry. "Please, if you know anything, immedi-ately come forward and tell Sheriff Strong." Here, Savilla looked across the table at Charlie before her eyes fell on me, and she gave the slightest indication that she had noticed the two of us seated together. "Any amount of information—no matter how ridicule..."

Ridicule? Perhaps a combination of minuscule and ridiculous? I could see it.

"... could be helpful to the sheriff in determining if we have a killer among us. I trust him to do a thorough job to bring justice to my family and this pageant."

At the conclusion of her speech, I almost gave a standing ovation. It was as if Savilla had only been waiting to take her rightful role on the stage of her family's pageant.

"To Mr. Finch," Miss 1962 said. So her hearing aids were on after all.

"To justice," Katie Gilman added, raising her wineglass.

"To all of you lovely ladies," Dr. Bellingham said, nearly giddy. This man had either started on the alcohol long before everyone else, or he was a criminal relieved to have gotten away with his dastardly deed.

Across the room, glasses rose.

As I toasted the former owner of the pageant, I thought about these guests, the contestants, the judges, and the staff. Were any of them likely to know the property as well as the Finches? Would any of them have a stronger motive to kill Mr. Finch and poison Mrs. Finch than his very own daughter, the one person eventually set to inherit all of this? And was anyone else paying as much attention to Savilla as her father's dearest friend, Dr. Bellingham?

Still, even with signs pointing to the two of them as the culprits, I couldn't help but wonder why she would need to involve DeeDee in any of this. Why would Savilla plant a crown in Aunt DeeDee's room? Why place Polaroids in my bed? Why accuse my aunt of killing her father and Miss 2001? As far as I could tell, Savilla Finch had no reason to involve my aunt—or me—in any of this.

But someone else might. A grudge that had turned into something stronger, perhaps.

My head turned to Dr. Bellingham. He'd been around a

long time—since 1999, when he'd been a judge for three years. That stint had culminated with the disappearance of Miss 2001, and he had only recently returned, two decades later. Could he be the missing link between a winner vanishing in 2001 and the systematic takedown of the elder Finches in the past two days?

My eyes trailed back to Jemma and Summer, both of whom were focused on Savilla in her blood-red gown.

My cheeks heated as I watched Dr. Bellingham's eyes rove across her body. *Could* they be working together? Or, if he was working alone, might Savilla Finch, for reasons I had yet to discover, be his next victim?

TWENTY-SEVEN

Momma always said that the best way to handle a problem was usually the most direct way. This was when I'd just gotten my license, and the boy I liked—and who happened to be a year older than me—was sending me mixed signals, flirting with me in physics one minute and ignoring me by lunchtime.

"You should ask him out," Momma advised as the two of us sat at the kitchen table while Aunt DeeDee whipped cream to top the blackberry dumplings. Momma's suggestion didn't surprise me because she herself had casually dated a couple of men who worked at the hospital. Nothing serious ever came of it, but she had a nice time.

Aunt DeeDee's mouth set in a thin line.

"What is it, Dee? You disagree?" Momma asked.

"I think it's the young man's duty to ask her out, that's all," Aunt DeeDee answered as she finished whisking her arm frantically around the bowl and pulling up creamy peaks.

"But why do I need to wait around for him?" I asked as she handed me the whisk and let me lick the sweetness from the spoon, as she'd always done.

At this, Aunt DeeDee threw Momma a look to say that she

hadn't wanted to be involved in this conversation in the first place. Then she sighed and tugged at her apron strings. I expected her to say something trite like, *Because it's the proper thing to do.*

Instead, she surprised me by saying, "Because, men really aren't worth all the fuss, so I'd rather let them put forth the most effort."

Momma and I couldn't argue with that line of thinking, and the three of us had enjoyed our pinto beans and cornbread followed by blackberry goodness.

I thought of this advice now as I watched Dr. Bellingham with Savilla. This man was easily in his mid-fifties, so Savilla, at twenty-eight, was about half his age. He'd been good friends with her father, he had a plastic surgery practice in New York— that much I knew. Savilla was his patient, and they were close enough that she'd even inscribed a pill case for him. But, no, with the way he studied her, the way he watched her every movement—this was something else, a kind of intensity and focus as if his eye was on a prize to be won. Before tonight, he'd flitted from flower to flower, albeit wanting to adjust their petals. Now, he seemed eager to hang about Savilla like a lovelorn bee.

Money had to be part of what he was after. He may or may not have known about the insurance policy Savilla had taken out on her father, but it was no secret that if both Mr. and Mrs. Finch died, Savilla would be next to inherit.

I studied the man, seeing him in this new light: the glint of his gold cufflinks, the trim suit, the Rolex on his wrist. He already had money, but it wouldn't surprise me if he wanted more.

As I ate my seasoned chicken and wondered what Mrs. Finch would think of Dr. Bellingham's interest in her step-daughter, I spotted Katie monitoring the two of them. Every time he leaned in to better hear Savilla's laugh, Katie touched his arm or tugged at his sleeve, drawing him back into her orbit and distracting him from her former charge. Good Nanny.

That's why I wasn't as surprised as I might've been when I turned to see Dr. Bellingham walking out with Katie Gilman on his arm. Savilla remained seated, chatting with another contestant.

I caught Summer's and Jemma's eyes, asking a silent question of my two sister-contestants. They gave me a quick nod and I stood to follow Katie and Dr. Bellingham. Within a minute, one by one, Summer and Jemma followed suit.

We made our way out the door as the pair of judges headed into the garden, but a man's voice kept us from trailing them.

"Pardon me. Excuse me. Ma'am, I must insist you stop immediately."

I paused and spun around to see the guard who'd handed me the box of pearls earlier that evening. Jemma yanked the earrings from her lobes, and Summer pulled off the emerald bracelet, handing them over.

"I really need to—" I glanced back in the direction of the judges, who were heading toward the maze.

"Please, ma'am." The guard's tone was tinged with a threat, so I hurried over, unwound the strand of pearls from my neck, and practically threw them at the man.

"One moment, please," he said as he located the original box, took the necklace from me, and inspected it with a loupe.

I tapped my foot impatiently.

"They won't get far," Jemma said as we waited.

After what must have been five minutes, the guard seemed satisfied as he slid the boxes back into a compartment and told us we were free to go. Without a word, Summer and Jemma followed me down the steps and into the moonlit night.

TWENTY-EIGHT

We stood in the garden, our eyes adjusting to the low light. I'd seen Katie and Dr. Bellingham come outside, but even though no other buildings stood nearby, there was no trace of them.

"Where do you suppose they went?"

Jemma pointed to the maze. "The only place they could've gone."

"If that's true, they shouldn't be in there long, right? Or should we...?" I hesitated, noticing clouds floating overhead, making the night darker. Inside the maze, it would be almost pitch-black.

"Why don't we go around and wait on the other side?" Summer suggested.

We picked up our pace, skirting the rose hedge maze. When I stretched my fingers to press the petals of a rose, I discovered it was a sturdy fabric without scent, and the leaves were waxy and unreal.

"It looks so authentic," I mused.

"I don't see why Mr. Finch would even build it if it's just a fake," Jemma said, distastefully.

"My mother had a green thumb," I said. "And I remember

her and Aunt DeeDee talking about the maze. In this climate it would mildew, and the roses wouldn't get enough sun. Still, Aunt DeeDee said that Mr. Finch insisted he had to have one, so years ago, before I was born, he had this built."

"I guess Mr. Finch wants—wanted—everything to look a certain way," Summer added.

I thought of his annual tradition of filling a ballroom full of women desperate for a crown—including me this year—before echoing her. "I guess so."

A cloud moved past the moon, and the garden became more visible again. An owl hooted in the distance. Minutes passed. Still no sign of Dr. Bellingham or Katie Gilman. I wasn't sure what we planned to do when the two of them emerged. Pounce on Dr. Bellingham? Interrogate him? Demand that he confess that he'd planted a crown in my aunt's room? That he was a murderer?

I paced in front of a bench. "They've been in there for a while."

"Do you think Katie is okay?" Summer asked.

"She seemed pretty strong at my morning workout," Jemma answered.

I was impressed. "She attended your Broadway Butt-Buster?"

"It's for all ages," Jemma informed me. "The glutes are one of the most important muscles as one ages."

As I looked from my two companions to the maze, something Lacy had said came to mind. "On Wednesday, when we were poking around my aunt's office, she mentioned that the Finches built tunnels all across the grounds."

I also recalled how Mrs. Finch had told us in her apartments that she'd had every inch of the garden searched, high and low, which was strange if it was just a garden. But if a tunnel lay underground, one would need to search every inch, even beneath where we stood.

Without another word, I started toward the greenery, and Jemma and Summer matched my pace.

As we entered the maze, the high trellises blocked out much of the moonlight. A chill settled around us even though the night air remained warm, and for a flickering moment my mind was awash with the image of a bloody Katie Gilman, Dr. Bellingham standing over her lifeless body in the heart of the maze—or somehow underneath it. I blinked back the thoughts and focused instead on the scattered electric tea lights, interwoven into the foliage and glowing faintly.

We walked for several yards and hit one dead end and then another.

"Do you have any idea where to go?" Summer asked.

Jemma shook her head. "I've never been in here."

"Really?" I was surprised that navigating the maze wasn't some kind of pageant tradition. "In all these years?"

"I'm not a child, Dakota. I don't do mazes."

I could only imagine the look of derision on Jemma's face because I could barely see the farther we went.

"This is more complicated than I expected," Summer said as we felt our way along the faux greenery. Briefly, we split off, going in opposite directions, but within a minute, we were back together. A few steps more, and I was certain we were in the innermost part of the maze. Here, the hedge rose around and above us, blocking out any remaining light. The electric tea lights hadn't even made it this far into the maze, so we were struggling to see our hands in front of us. If I'd been alone, I would've been afraid.

In the darkness, I stumbled into a wall. Summer reached out to catch me, but as her hand found mine, the wall swung open, revealing a tiny room with one single lightbulb—turned on, thankfully—in the heart of the maze.

I paused and stared at Summer before calling to Jemma, who was close behind. I stepped through first, Summer next, and when Jemma hesitated, we grabbed her arm and pulled her behind us.

The door closed, and the three of us stood arms' length apart, insulated and hemmed in. I looked up to see a grated ceiling covered with ivy. At our feet an outdoor carpet had been spread and then thrown aside, half-draped across a wooden door in the ground. It reminded me of the tornado bunker Lacy's family had installed in their yard when we were growing up.

I stood over the sealed door, glad that I'd worn my boots instead of a pair of Lacy's heels as I planted my feet, threw the hem of my gown over my shoulder, and bent to reach for the metal handle.

The door moved easily, creaking as it went. Our eyes opened wide as we froze. A light shone from the cement hole beneath us.

I peered over the edge of the entryway, letting my eyes adjust. That's when I saw it: a thin trail of crimson dried on stone steps that led into the earth.

TWENTY-NINE

I considered running back to the main house and trying to find the sheriff, but who knew how much time that would take? And I was beginning to think that time might be a precious commodity for Katie Gilman. The stairs were steep, and all three of us tried to prevent our gowns from touching the dried blood.

I spoke first. "Since that's not fresh, I'm guessing it belongs to Mr. Finch rather than Katie Gilman."

Jemma didn't respond, and Summer was either turning green or reacting really poorly to the dim lighting. When she leaned forward and threw up, I knew it was the former.

"Oh Lord, Summer. Do you need to go back to your cottage?" Jemma asked, her hand on Summer's back. She somehow sounded both concerned and annoyed.

Summer wiped at the edges of her mouth before responding. "No. I'll be okay. We need to... we need to find Katie."

The walls felt like they were closing around us; no dirt or tree roots peeked from the cement, and Jemma, the tallest of us, had to duck as we moved farther into the enclosed space. She took the lead and Summer the rear, so I was sandwiched between them.

Whoever had designed this tunnel had done a good job sealing the tomb-like cavern and leaving just enough room for a person to walk single file from the heart of the rose hedge maze to... wherever the tunnel let out. There must've been some kind of ventilation, and the lighting was dim but sufficient. Still, no living thing—no gnats or spiders or cockroaches—came in or out, which wasn't exactly comforting.

A narrow strip of halogen ran along the ceiling, so we could now follow the drops of blood along the ground several yards into the tunnel. When we reached the end of the bloody trail, tossed against the curve of the tunnel wall lay a shoe.

I bent down to study it. Rows of sparkles ran across gold fabric. "Do you think that was the—" I started as I crouched near the footwear.

"—the murder weapon?" Jemma finished for me, skirting the heel and bending closer. Sure enough, blood had dried along the edges, and there seemed to be mud caked into the fabric.

"Do you think the murderer was wearing it?" Summer sounded like she might be sick again.

"I sure hope not because I know that shoe," I told them. It was one half of the pair that Savilla had been wearing when I first met her in the entryway of the estate late Wednesday afternoon. I looked around for the other one, but it was missing. "Savilla wouldn't kill her own father, right?"

Summer bit her lip, but Jemma shook her head. "All signs point to Dr. Bellingham. He could've easily procured the shoe, brought Mr. Finch down here, and murdered him."

As I tried to envision the scene, Jemma studied the area, walking a few feet beyond us. "Maybe this is something," she said as she bent down to pick up a piece of paper that had been folded into a tight square and dropped on the ground. She opened it carefully and held it toward the light so she could read the faint scrawl.

"It's a list of names." Jemma began reading aloud. "Dakota, Jemma, Gina, Pam..."

I took the sheet from her. A numbered list of thirty names—all of them pageant contestants—lined the page. And I was first on the list.

"Only one name is crossed off," I noted.

Summer met my eye. "Dakota."

I could tell from her expression that she was trying to think of a way to reassure me, but she wasn't quite convinced herself.

The air in the tunnel was cooler than the night above us, but heat prickled behind my ears, at the base of my neck, under my arms. I thought of who else had been metaphorically crossed off the pageant list so far—Mr. Finch, dead; Mrs. Finch, poisoned; Aunt DeeDee, behind bars. The familiar feeling that I might be next shook me.

"Perhaps it's some kind of pageant ranking?" Jemma suggested.

"Or..." Summer began. "What if it's a list of who Dr. Bellingham is coming after next?"

The three of us let that thought sink in. Until we could prove that this man was Mr. Finch's killer, I wouldn't be able to rest easy.

"This is a list of contestants," I thought aloud. "Whatever it means, I can only imagine that one of the judges wrote this, which suggests that Dr. Bellingham was down here."

I imagined him in this space, the way he could easily navigate the confines with his thin frame and spry physique. After befriending Mr. Finch and acting as a judge for two different stints across more than two decades, he would know this property. Mr. and Mrs. Finch trusted him. He could get into places

—shoe closets, whiskey cabinets, guest rooms, secret tunnels—
that others had no idea even existed, let alone how to access.

"It has to be Bellingham," I said, picking up the shoe with
one finger inside the toe. I held it with one hand and the list in
the other. "Let's see where this ends."

THIRTY

As we walked farther into the tunnel, I could feel my heart rate speeding, and it wasn't only because of the briskness of Jemma's stride. We were headed straight toward a killer, and the walls were definitely narrowing.

"Aren't tunnels supposed to be the same size throughout?" Summer sounded like she was trying to keep the tremor out of her voice.

"We can turn around if you need to," I told her, even though I certainly didn't want to stop now.

Jemma, unexpectedly, began to sing. Her voice, tentative at first, rose, echoing off the walls. We stalled at first but then settled into the tune and kept moving forward, comforted by the sound. The melody was pure and clear, the words about knowing and being known, and some of the tension left my body as the song rang out for several minutes.

"That was beautiful," Summer said when she'd finished.

It had been, and I was struck by the power that Jemma held with her voice.

"Music helps me calm down," Jemma said, neither acknowledging the praise nor dismissing it. "It helps me distract myself, helps me think about something else." She turned in a circle and pushed forward as if she hadn't just astounded us. "Like, I don't know... how long have you lived in Aubergine?"

I was grateful for the distraction but also had to blink a few times to refocus on the task at hand. If Jemma got up onstage and sang like that, I might never stand a chance. "I've lived here my entire life. My ancestors supposedly came over on the *Mayflower*." I pushed past the lump in my throat. "Momma raised me in the house that her great-grandfather built, but last year, she... she died."

The two other women remained quiet.

"What about both of you?" I asked.

Jemma answered, "I grew up in Rhode Island, went to school in New Haven, majored in pre-law, hated it, and now I work at Starbucks near Times Square while I'm trying to find money to produce my show... the one about my brother."

Wait. New Haven? "You went to Yale? And became a barista?"

Jemma's voice was rigid. "That's almost exactly what my parents said."

"I mean... it's... it's fine. It's just that—"

"I didn't use my degree? Reach my potential?" I could hear the self-deprecating tone in Jemma's voice, and I wondered if she realized how much more likeable it made her. "My parents said that too. After my brother's struggles, I was the grand hope of the family. So far, I've just disappointed them."

"I was a pre-med major and switched to education, so no judgment here," Summer chipped in. "I couldn't manage anatomy and physiology. I felt like a dummy."

Jemma chuckled. "I'm laughing because the only way I got through pre-law was by testing out of college algebra. I passed by one point." She considered. "I can't believe we never talked the last two years you've been here."

"You weren't exactly approachable," Summer said, in a burst of raw honesty.

"Fair," Jemma admitted. "After my first year competing, I gave up all chances of being Miss Rosie."

"I guess it takes a murder to bring out your friendlier side," I said, half-jokingly.

We walked several paces without speaking.

"What about you, Dakota?" Jemma asked. "What was your life aspiration?"

I couldn't find the words to tell them that I'd wanted to open a veterinary practice in Aubergine since middle school when one of Momma's friends, who had a practice a half-hour away, had let me shadow her for the weekend. I'd watched the doctor deliver a foal and stitch a puppy's injured paw. I'd held a goat around the neck while she'd administered antibiotics, and I'd helped her diagnose a cat with heartworm before it was too late. Helping these creatures was the closest I'd ever been to experiencing any sort of divine calling, and that purpose had driven me for years—until I couldn't help my own mother.

"I wanted... I went to vet school. I planned to work with animals. Horses, mainly."

"I've heard that vet school is as tough as med school," Summer said. "You could work here at The Rose with the stable full of horses."

"If it's not shut down as the scene of a deadly crime," Jemma added.

I tried to change the subject as I ran a hand along the cement wall. "I have no idea how much farther this tunnel goes, but maybe we could... um... review what we know so far about Mr. Finch's death."

"Good idea," Jemma said, obviously more comfortable discussing the business of murder rather than more personal things, which was fine since the former was currently more important.

"Okay," I started. "So Mrs. Finch last saw her husband in their apartment drinking whiskey around five p.m. on Wednesday afternoon. Then, she came to see the contestants, chat, and make an appearance. She left, but an hour or so later, she came back into the Primrose Ballroom and collapsed."

"When she came to, she said she couldn't find her husband," Jemma said.

"But she'd found the note," Summer added.

"That's right, and then according to the sheriff, sometime after midnight Mr. Finch was stabbed through the eye socket"—I paused, reflecting on the new information we'd discovered minutes ago—"in this tunnel, with a high heel now in our possession."

"Before guests were milling about the grounds the next morning for the judges' tea, he was shoved into the kitchen cabinets in the 1950s tent," Summer concluded.

"Lacy was setting up tents until three a.m., so whoever put him there had to have done it after that."

"Which means he was likely killed in the early morning hours," Summer mused. "He had to be placed in the cabinets sometime between three and…"

"Seven a.m.," Jemma said. "That's when I led my Broadway Butt-Buster."

"So, after midnight, he died, and between three and seven a.m. his body was moved," I finished.

Moved was a gentler word than what had likely happened, especially if this was a one-man operation. Mr. Finch's body would have been pulled up the stairs, yanked out of the rose hedge maze, and shoved into the 1950s kitchen cabinets. I could imagine the manhandling that must've happened to get Mr. Finch's body where I'd found it.

"Around nine the next morning, Savilla found her stepmother collapsed in the Finches' apartment," Summer continued.

I thought about Savilla finding her stepmother. Had she been shocked? Or had she expected to find her dead? Had she planned all of this with Dr. Bellingham?

As I wondered, Jemma called our attention to what stood only a few yards away now: the end of the tunnel, with a stairway leading up to a door, similar to the one through which we'd entered.

"Thank God. I was beginning to wonder—" I stopped when Jemma put a finger to her lips and pointed above us.

Listen, she mouthed.

Faintly, I heard an echo of voices beyond the door. As the three of us stood still and listened, first came the jumbled voice of a woman. Then a man's.

It was Dr. Bellingham.

THIRTY-ONE

"You're hurting me," Katie Gilman screamed from the shaft above us.

"You deserve whatever they throw at you," Dr. Bellingham spat back at her.

As Jemma and I leaned forward against the door, trying to open it, Summer crouched low and gave a hard shove.

The three of us sprang out of the earth, and I lunged in front, whether to protect the others or to jump into the fray first, I wasn't sure. I could hear sounds of a struggle, grunting and kicks and huffs. I could easily imagine which of the two judges was winning, and thinking of Dr. Bellingham forcing himself on a woman lit a fire in me.

I looked around to orient myself, and it took several seconds for my eyes to adjust in the near-darkness. We were inside a building, pots and dead foliage littered around us. Clumps of dirt and fragments of pottery were scattered, and empty windowpanes formed the shape of a toothless smile. We were inside the greenhouse that I'd noticed when Lacy and I had explored the back of the property.

Dr. Bellingham stood with his glasses slanted across his

nose and his hair mussed, as if he'd either been in the middle of a passionate embrace or a barroom brawl.

I was on him immediately, leaping onto his back while Jemma kicked him in the stomach and Summer tackled him in the knees. He was on the ground, flailing and shouting as something fell from his hands and clattered onto the ground. Jemma sat on his chest while Summer lay across his legs. I picked up the objects he'd been holding. It was the jars of honey—the deadly ones. So, Dr. Bellingham did know about the toxic honey, and had likely planted one such jar in the Finches' apartments.

A muffled groan came from a few feet beyond us, and I turned toward it.

"Go," Jemma said, her long legs straddled across Bellingham's chest. "We've got him pinned."

I followed the sound past a row of high tables lined with an assortment of pots and brown stalks of all sizes and shapes. The hilt of a long shovel leaned against a cracked windowpane, and rope and duct tape lay on the ground. Oh God. I wanted to close my eyes against what I might find in a few steps.

The groan came from the ground near me, and I had to kneel to find the source. On her stomach, underneath one of the tables, was a groggy Katie Gilman. Her eyes, wild and frightened, looked up at me as she let out a tiny whimper, more pitiful than any scream she could've mustered.

"I'm okay, I'm okay," Katie whispered to herself again and again as she began to cry harder. "I'm okay, I'm okay, I'm okay..."

The look of her helpless body lying there and the cries coming from her reminded me too much of my own mother on her worst days at the end. I crawled under the table and wrapped my arms around her shaking frame, rocking her back and forth.

"Shhhh... I'm here," I said, not knowing what else I could

offer this woman who had obviously been through a horrifying ordeal. Somehow Dr. Bellingham had lured her out there, planning to... to do who knew what to her. It made me sick to think what might've happened if we'd arrived a few minutes later.

Suddenly, I heard Sheriff Strong's voice rising from the ground beneath us. He'd come out of the tunnel and was forcing Dr. Bellingham into a sitting position, pulling his hands behind him.

Summer and Jemma stood nearby as if ready to pounce again.

"This is none of your affair," Dr. Bellingham protested as the sheriff began to handcuff him.

"You can stop talking now, or I can make you," the sheriff said, surprising me with the disdain that replaced his usual stoicism. He despised this man as much as I did.

Dr. Bellingham let out a breath. "I want to speak with my lawyer."

"In due time," Charlie told him, his tone icy. He was angry, and Dr. Bellingham knew it.

Katie's cries quieted even though the look of terror remained. "He said... he told me..." She stopped and caught her breath.

"Take your time," I said softly.

"Jim... he said that he... he put the crown in your aunt's room... and he..." She caught her breath again. "He killed Mr. Finch."

It was the confirmation I needed. I looked at the sheriff, who nodded to signal that he'd heard.

"I know," I told her as she broke into a sob. "You're all right now."

"My guys are right behind," the sheriff said loudly enough for all of us to hear. "We'll get Bellingham down to the station and finish this thing. Good work, ladies."

It was three words, but three words that echoed both in the

greenhouse and in my mind as I kept one arm around Katie's shoulder. I had the sudden realization of what Dr. Bellingham's arrest would mean: Aunt DeeDee would be released.

I stifled a tight cry as I attempted to keep the tears at bay. My aunt would be safe and all would be right in this strange little pageant world. I let out a heavy breath I'd been holding. I hadn't heard such good news in a long time. If I could still place in this pageant, then I could keep Momma's house and restart my life. My heart might explode before the weekend was out.

It took a few minutes for the other police to arrive and twice during that time, the sheriff congratulated us on our detective skills as well as on the physical work of capturing Dr. Bellingham, who continued to request his lawyer.

While the sheriff and his deputy took Dr. Bellingham into custody, and Summer and Jemma stayed near Katie, I decided to take a quick look around this part of the property to ensure that the archives were as we'd left them that afternoon.

I hurried to the original house and to the back room where the archives were kept. The light from a flashlight I'd found shone across the boxes, and I looked over my shoulder, almost anticipating someone following me. No one was there, but one of the boxes—the one labeled *Misc.*—was overturned and empty.

SATURDAY—UPDATED SCHEDULE
THE ROSE PALACE PAGEANT SCHEDULE: DAY 4

Note: In light of recent events, the schedule for Saturday has been altered to accommodate a late start. Notably, Jemma's workout has been cancelled, and a substitute judge has been appointed for this year's show: Savilla Finch will fill in for Dr. James Bellingham.

BREAKFAST: 8 to 10 a.m. Available for pick-up at the 1940s tent.

"THROUGH THE DECADES CENTENNIAL SHOW": Noon. Gates will open for pageant attendees, contestants' families and friends, and the public to take part in the celebration of the pageant across the past century. Contestants should report to their tent fifteen minutes before their scheduled performance. Do not be tardy.

. . .

CALL TIME FOR SHOW: 6 p.m.

PAGEANT: 7 p.m. Begins with the ball gown portion before moving into the talent showcase and ending with a combination of swimsuit and interview.

Dakota's To-Do List:

1. Place.
2. Win?

THIRTY-TWO

I got only four hours of sleep that night, but when I woke around 9 a.m., a text from my aunt was waiting for me. It had been sent at 5:30 a.m.

> Dr. B confessed to framing me but won't say more yet. Out of the clink. Going to shower off the filth. I'll see you soon.

I smiled as I read the words. Dr. Bellingham was behind bars—as he should be—and I could get through this day with the knowledge that even if I didn't win the money, which I very much needed, at least I would go home tonight with Aunt DeeDee.

All is not lost, I could hear Momma saying. Granted, when she'd said those words, she'd just been referred to at-home hospice and the words had come out stilted and slow—and in no way referring to the Rose Palace Pageant. Still, the sentiment seemed fitting.

I took a deep breath. I'd done hard things before, and my resolve had always served me well. I would dress and give Aunt DeeDee a hug. Then, I would polish up my routine and try my darndest to win in the next twelve hours. If that didn't work, Aunt DeeDee and I would deal with it together.

After the night I'd had, Lacy had slept downstairs in my tiny cottage again. I'd told her every terrifying detail: the maze, the tunnel, a frightened Katie, finding the missing evidence and, most of all, Dr. Bellingham's twisted grin as the police had led him away.

I showered and left a note for Lacy on the kitchen table as she snored lightly. I decided that before I did anything else, I would make my way to what I needed most—coffee.

Outside, I passed the 1920s tent, where a huge finger rose over the entryway and the words *This Way to the Speakeasy* stood aloft in blocky gold letters. Jazz echoed out of the tent, and I could already see a couple of early birds milling about in tasseled flapper dresses. The day would be sunny and warm, a fitting last day for the pageant, and the mountains in the distance loomed over the estate as if keeping watch.

I passed a pair of Gatsby-era blue and green cars in the center of the 1920s. An info sheet next to them read that this make and model had been the grand prize in the first-ever pageant. I could almost see the contestants sprawling across the hoods for photo-ops in a few hours.

For the 1930s, I spotted two signs at opposite ends of the canopy. The first was written in a scribbled font: *Soup Kitchen.* The second sign read, *Talkies Through Here.* A miniature and enclosed *Picture Palace* had been erected, taking up almost half of the tent. The theme here seemed to be the persistence of the pageant even during the Great Depression.

When I reached the 1940s, I noticed that one half of the tent space was an open-air beauty salon with period-piece hair dryers, while the other half featured models of planes, tanks, and ships used in the fight against Germany's world domination. The national anthem blared across the speakers in a kind of patriotic tribute to beauty and war—an interesting combination.

A few contestants, bright-eyed and filled with adrenaline for the day ahead, stood around the breakfast bar, chatting.

"I wanted to thank you again," Katie Gilman said, approaching me as I took my first sip of a strong cup of coffee. She held a plate with a blueberry muffin and sliced strawberries. She'd showered, and the fear in her eyes had settled into a sort of acceptance of what had happened—or could've happened—hours earlier.

I wasn't quite sure how to respond to a thank you of this magnitude, so I dipped my head in acknowledgement and took another sip.

"I talked to the sheriff for a long time last night," she continued, checking to make sure no one was close enough to overhear us. "I felt so stupid, letting Jimmy lead me out there under false pretenses."

False pretenses? Jimmy? Had she been expecting a romantic evening? I didn't want to pry, but I mentally urged her to say more. I tossed out a casual comment that she could expand on if she wanted. "I noticed Dr. Bellingham hanging on Savilla's every word last night at dinner."

Katie nodded furiously, her cheeks heating. "That's why I directed his attentions to me. My God, the idea of him taking her out there to do his dirty work."

I tried to keep my eyes from widening and waited for her to continue.

"Not that he would be interested in an old biddy like me, but I think he realized he wasn't getting anywhere with Savilla. When I asked him if he wanted to go for a stroll in the garden, his eyes lit up. He led me into the maze and then into that terrifying tunnel. When I saw the blood and the shoe, he told me what he'd done. Said I was an accomplice now. Told me he wanted my help fixing things on the back side of the property. He shoved me in front of him and made me walk."

"We found a list of names... of pageant contestants," I said, hoping she could explain.

"He likes to keep a list of top contenders with him. Makes a new one at the end of every day based on the score card."

"But my name was scratched out at the top."

She smiled softly and lowered her voice. "Because you were his pick. For winner."

"Me?" I swallowed hard. "But I barely even spoke to him. He wouldn't have any reason to—"

She gave me a pointed look. "I know his process. It's the same one he always uses."

"What did he want you to help him fix?"

"No idea. By the time he forced me out there, I was a blubbering mess. He left me in the greenhouse for a while, but I don't know where he went or what he did. I tried to make myself go back through the tunnel, but when I thought of Mr. Finch and what had happened to him down there... I just couldn't."

That, I understood. I'd ridden back in one of the estate's golf carts with a police escort last night. I never wanted to step foot in that underground tunnel again.

Katie put a hand to her chest as if she needed to catch her breath. "I'm sorry. It's... it's a lot. Before last night I didn't think the tunnel was in use any longer. The last time I was down there, Savilla was nine and wanted to be an explorer when she grew up. She pretended to be the archeologist and made me her assistant." She smiled at the memory, but almost immediately, the terror crept back into her features. "How could he do that to Mr. Finch? To Mrs. Finch?" She studied me, remembering the personal stake I had in all of this. "And all the while, framing your poor aunt. Thank God she's out."

"Have you seen her yet?" I glanced around. "Or the sheriff?" I wanted to hug DeeDee's neck and... well, I didn't know what I wanted to do to the sheriff, but strangely I wanted to see him.

"I left the police station after I gave my official statement. I couldn't stay awake for another second. Came straight back here and collapsed into bed for a few hours."

Katie arched her shoulders and pasted a beauty queen smile on her face as she attempted to brighten our conversation again. "Your man is so very... well, so very strong. No pun intended."

"My man?" I was glad to hear her returning to some semblance of herself, though I knew the trauma of last night would linger. Still, I wasn't sure what she meant by referring to "my man."

"Sheriff Strong," she clarified.

"Oh, he's not... we're not..."

"I see." Katie patted my arm and then crossed two fingers. "We'll keep hopeful thoughts for a happy ending."

THIRTY-THREE

As I finished my second coffee, Aunt DeeDee hustled over, throwing her arms around me. "You're a sight for sore eyes, Dakota Green."

I let myself sink into her embrace, and my eyes began to fill. I blinked back the tears, and Aunt DeeDee released me. "Let me get a good look at you, sweetheart." She wiped a thumb under one of my eyes. "Now, none of that. Pull yourself together. We don't want your face puffy for the grand finale."

I laughed at the words. "I see prison didn't change you."

"It was just jail, darling," she said with a grin.

"I was afraid you wouldn't be... they wouldn't let you..." I didn't know how to finish the statement, so I kept it simple, looking her directly in the eye, trying to communicate how sorry I was for the years spent overlooking her efforts, years of forgetting the importance of her presence in my life. I didn't have my mother, but I had a close second: the woman who'd been there in the background, making cookies and chauffeuring me around town and bringing me forgotten homework. "I missed you."

Aunt DeeDee seemed to understand the depth of my feeling because she pulled me back into a long hug.

"I have so much to ask you... and tell you," I said, surprising myself at how badly I wanted to recount the past forty-eight hours. "I made friends, and the people here... there's more to them than I thought."

I'm not sure why this was the thing that felt most important to communicate. Maybe it was because I wanted to validate my aunt's life's work, or maybe because I wanted her to know I saw her and appreciated her.

"And I cannot wait to hear all about it," Aunt DeeDee told me. "But now that they have the perpetrator behind bars where he belongs, all that can wait. You've got a job to do."

She nodded toward the 1950s tent, where Summer and Jemma and my other fellow contestants were waiting for me to rehearse. Even from where I stood I could tell that Jemma's arms were crossed, and she wore impatience like a mantel. Summer had an anxious look on her face as she darted back and forth trying to be of help.

Aunt DeeDee nudged me toward them. "I'll be here when you perform, I promise. In the meantime, Savilla's acting as our substitute judge. What do you think?"

"She'll be great," I said. "Just don't let her give any speeches with big words."

By noon guests had parked in downtown Aubergine and were shuttled to the front steps of the Rose Palace. Soon after, they began streaming through the gates, eyeing the ornate architecture and making their way to the decades tents, for which Lacy had outdone herself.

"Don't be nervous," Jemma said. I could tell she was trying to be helpful, but her entire vibe was a bit left of bossy. She must've realized it because she took a deep breath and tried again. "You know your lines, so you'll be fine—great, even."

"Thanks," I said, sending her a soft smile. "I appreciate that."

She patted me twice on the arm as we took our places.

An hour after the gates had opened, there I stood in the kitchen in my polka-dotted red dress, proudly proclaiming, "Robert will tan my hide if I can't learn how to cook. And fast." I turned to Jemma and asked with my inquisitive tone, "How did you catch your cool cat?"

While she answered, I caught Aunt DeeDee and Lacy on the fringes of the crowd crammed beneath the white canvas. In front of them was Mrs. Glenda Finch, seated but present, and I almost broke character as I did a double take when Savilla strolled to her side. I wasn't surprised to see her there—at least no more surprised than I was to see her stepmother—but the look of utter ease on Savilla's face, the genuine smile she gave as she watched us perform, did catch me off guard. After all the chaos, she seemed fine. Better than fine.

Jemma held up a cookbook from the era, facing the audience as she proudly announced her lines. I was so distracted by Savilla and her stepmother looking so normal, I nearly forgot my cue.

Jemma said her line again, prompting me gently, and Summer stared at me, mouthing the words.

"Geez. That cookbook sounds like it's full of swell recipes," I said, coming back to myself and the moment at hand. "The pageant judges and Robert are gonna love the new and improved me."

Thankfully, that was my last line, so my eyes trailed back to the audience, where Miss 1962 stood on the fringes, her arms crossed at the content of our ridiculous little tableau. But when I saw her gaze dart to Savilla, her frown deepened as if she too thought her manner a bit casual.

A memory pulled me back. Years ago, Aunt DeeDee told me and Momma one night over dinner, almost casually, that the pageant had almost been canceled that year because of in-fighting. I hadn't paid enough attention to her stories back then to know who was fighting or why, but I do remember Momma asking her about it. We were seated at the café downtown, me and Momma side by side eating burgers and slurping milkshakes while facing Aunt DeeDee, who ate grilled chicken and drank unsweetened tea.

"You know," Aunt DeeDee said. "They're arguing over what fights are always about: love or money."

Love or money.

As I took the cookbook from Jemma's hands and held it up for the audience to see, I thought about these two motives, so familiar that Aunt DeeDee would toss them out as a blanket for most troubles.

I'd seen the insurance policy that Savilla had taken out on her father, and I'd seen the kind of attention that Dr. Bellingham had paid to her as soon as her parents were out of the way.

My eyes traveled back to Savilla, who cheered and applauded our efforts on the makeshift stage of the 1950s kitchen. Jemma grabbed one of my hands, and Summer held the other, and everyone in the scene took one final bow.

Dr. Bellingham was behind bars. I wanted that to be enough, but I couldn't pull my eyes away from Savilla. She hadn't returned his admiration last night at the Gilded Age dinner, but perhaps that was only because Katie, in her role as former nanny, had lured him away from her. As thoughts crowded my mind and I attempted to put them in some kind of cohesive order, the crowd dispersed to see the next show.

A line formed to greet Mrs. Finch and Savilla, who handed out hugs and quick pecks on cheeks like a trained politician, like she'd been born for this kind of spotlight.

Aunt DeeDee approached to congratulate me on the performance while Lacy was waiting, no doubt to poke fun at the ridiculous show I'd just put on, but before either of them could say a word, they saw the look on my face.

"Are you okay, dear? Are you feeling ill?" Aunt DeeDee asked, instantly reaching to feel my forehead.

"You need me to grab a water?" Lacy echoed.

I shook my head and swallowed back tears, unable to speak the questions swirling in my mind. What if Dr. Bellingham's accomplice was still on the loose, shaking hands and having a grand old time? What if the sheriff and I had gotten this—or at least a big part of this—very, very wrong?

THIRTY-FOUR

Since I didn't have any other official duties until that evening, after the guests dispersed I excused myself to grab a sandwich and a drink before heading back to my room to make a list of everything I'd discovered since I'd stepped across the threshold of The Rose.

I knew Aunt DeeDee and Lacy needed to mingle and be on call for any last-minute emergencies, so I told them I would see them soon.

"Oh, hey—on your way back to your cottage, swing by the 2000s," Lacy told me, something teasing in the suggestion.

"I arranged to have a little surprise delivered there even before all this began," Aunt DeeDee added. "Lacy said the two of you have been asking about Miss 2001, so I thought you'd find it of particular interest."

I narrowed my eyes at them, but they gave nothing away.

"You go grab lunch, and we'll see you this evening," Aunt DeeDee said, her tone much like the one she'd used to send me off to bed when Momma had worked the night shift.

I walked outside the 1950s and got my bearings before

heading to the 2000s, which featured contestants floating around displays that ranged from 9/11 to the Olsen twins.

Beyoncé's "Crazy in Love" played through the tent, and I caught sight of a small group of contestants huddled together and doing a last-minute run-through of their skit, which seemed to be an homage to the reality TV show *Survivor*, based on the skimpy island clothes they wore.

At first I didn't see anything that would warrant Lacy and Aunt DeeDee sending me in this direction, so I wandered around the edges, watching the crowd milling about, attendees grabbing sample cups of French Toast Crunch and Trix Yogurt. My mouth puckered at the combo before I saw a solitary Mrs. Finch, eye to eye with a cardboard cutout that I could only see from behind. I followed a circumference around her and watched Savilla break away from a group of guests and come to her side.

Savilla's eyes flashed with... something. Anger? Or was it shock?

I skirted behind them to view the row of cutouts they were studying, cardboard likenesses I'd recognized in the foyer on the first day as the winners from 2000 to 2009.

Savilla was rubbing reassuring circles into her stepmother's back. I followed their eyes to the sign at the bottom of the image of particular interest: *Miss 2001, Exhibit Coming Soon to the Rose Palace!*

The cutout featured two women with a man, Dr. Bellingham, between them. He smiled proudly into the camera, happy to have two beautiful women flanking him. The woman to his right was obviously a young Glenda Finch. She wore no sash but held a single rose. Her smile was toothy and didn't reach her eyes. I could envision her having only just flung the losing sash from her body before pasting on the runner-up smile for the camera. The woman to his left wore a sash that read *Miss 2001* and a crown—the one that my aunt had been accused of stealing only days ago.

This was the cutout that had been missing from the row of images greeting guests in the long entryway on my arrival. It was also an enlargement of the photo that had been cut up in the archives.

I squinted, trying to recalibrate my vision as I took in the image of the other woman in the photo with Dr. Bellingham. To the attendees who passed it without a thought, this was one of many sights, sounds, and smells assaulting their senses. They had nothing personally invested in this pageant. But for me, I couldn't stop staring at this other woman, the original winner of 2001, head and all.

The figure in the cutout in front of me had to be the elusive Cathy Peabody.

I couldn't pull my eyes away because she looked remarkably similar to the person standing in front of me: Savilla Finch. In fact, if I hadn't known that this photo had been taken more than two decades ago, I would've thought it was Savilla.

I shifted from foot to foot, realizing how uncomfortable my tight dress had become, as I pieced together what this photo meant. Could the original Miss 2001, aka Cathy Peabody, be Savilla's birth mother? Could that be why, according to the forgotten police report, she'd taken Savilla with her on the morning after she'd won the crown? Perhaps she'd never competed to win the pageant but instead to get close enough to her daughter to steal her away. But she'd been found within hours. Something had gone terribly wrong, and then... she'd disappeared.

My eyes drifted back to the man in the center of the cutout: Dr. Bellingham, the person who seemed somehow present in all of this. I moved closer to Mrs. Finch and Savilla, who spoke to her stepmother as the older woman composed herself, glancing around to ensure no one had seen her shock.

"Everyone knows you're the real Miss 2001, StepMommy," I heard Savilla say, her words tense. "This is just a nice little way to remember this... this other woman."

Savilla's voice caught on the last words, I was sure of it, but I couldn't tell whether or not she knew that this *other woman*—who had somehow disappeared off the face of the earth—was actually her mother.

THIRTY-FIVE

My feet felt like they might break off at the ankles. Somehow, as I'd been trying to grab lunch and get back to my cottage, I'd ended up being pulled in different directions: helping Lacy by rushing from a Disco-mania performance in the 1970s to an appearance of members of the cast from *Saved by the Bell* in the 1980s.

All the while, I'd been tossing around questions I wanted to ask Savilla: *Do you remember when Miss 2001 kidnapped you? Do you realize how much you resemble that woman? Do you feel any kind of animosity toward your father and stepmother for keeping you from your birth mother all these years? Would you have tried to kill either of them because of it?*

As I observed the smiling Savilla, I tried to see a crack in her armor, but she was very good at giving the visitors and contestants what they wanted: a young heiress—and now makeshift judge—ready to ascend to the pageant owner throne.

When I accepted there was no way I was getting Savilla alone, I finally excused myself during a break in the late afternoon, set aside for visitors to grab an early dinner at one of the numerous upscale food trucks parked in front of the estate and for contestants to prepare for the grand show. Hair and makeup would happen in our individual rooms, but backstage would also be lined with rows of well-lit mirrors and beauty supplies for in between the main events: the opening dance routine in our ball gowns, talent, swimsuit, interview, and presentation of the crown.

When I finally reached the sanctuary of my cottage, I peeled myself out of the Minnie Mouse dress I'd worn for the 1950s pageant-girl skit and tossed it onto the floor just as Aunt DeeDee let herself in. She was beautiful in a one-shoulder pink dress.

"Dear, you look exhausted. I thought you were going to rest." Aunt DeeDee laid out my dress and assessed her makeup tote.

"Did you know?" I asked, resting my head against the back of the couch.

"Did I know what?"

"That Miss 2001 is Savilla's biological mother?"

"I see you visited the 2000s," she said as she fluffed the bottom of the gown. "No one else said a word about that cutout. I was almost offended, going to all that trouble to bring it from the back of the property for nothing."

I waited for her to add more. When she didn't, I asked again. "Did you know?"

Aunt DeeDee plugged in the hair straightener and curling iron and motioned for me to hold out my nails for inspection. She gave me a pointed look as she gripped my hands. "I am not at liberty to say," she answered firmly. "I signed a nondisclosure agreement that I cannot violate."

"What?" I frowned. "When?"

"I am not at liberty to say. I signed an NDA."

The phrases sounded like a troubling rhyme. "Is that one of those things that lawyers train you to say?"

"I am not at liberty—"

"Okay, I get it. You can't tell me."

"You're brilliant, Dakota. It's right in front of you, all you need to do is put the pieces together." She gave me a sad smile, but I knew she believed in me. "I have no idea if Dr. Bellingham was working alone, but I do know that, in the past, some things have happened at The Rose, things that have only been speculated about in Aubergine. A missing pageant queen, a secret child..."

"Then Cathy Peabody is—"

"I am not at liberty to say," Aunt DeeDee answered again firmly. "But all of this is why Mr. Finch closed the hotel to the public more than two decades ago. He wanted to keep things quiet. He intended to reopen, but never did."

Aunt DeeDee had known something for a long time, something that she'd had to keep quiet and bury within herself in order to keep her job and her place in the pageant world. My aunt had layers I hadn't even imagined.

I took a deep breath, choosing my next words carefully enough to avoid the same trained response she'd been giving me. "But... what if I... got it wrong? It feels like there are things I still don't understand."

Aunt DeeDee tilted my chin, so our eyes met. "Then I trust you'll figure that out too. But, for now, it's time to win some money."

She was right. I wanted to know the truth, but in the next few hours, I also needed to place in the pageant. *First things first*, as Momma would say.

I sat in front of Aunt DeeDee and let her do the work of turning me into royalty, straightening my hair before pulling it into an updo with soft tendrils lining my cheeks and carefully applying all of her makeup magic to bring out my best features. Within the hour she was forcing me into some kind of torture device that was a precursor to the floofy yellow gown that would make me look like a cross between Belle from *Beauty and the Beast* and a Twinkie.

Pageant perfection.

"Hold still," Aunt DeeDee commanded as she clasped a lace-up corset around my ribs and began to tug the edges together.

"Oh my Lord," I screamed as she fastened me in. "How am I supposed to breathe in this?"

"You're not," Aunt DeeDee answered. "You can breathe after you win."

The preparations continued for another forty-five minutes until Aunt DeeDee sprayed my face with sealant.

"My eyes look all shimmery," I said, taken aback by how good I looked. I thought she'd already prepped me at the house earlier this week, but this was a whole new level. I was almost... queenly.

"You look like me on the night I won," she said, her eyes welling. "I told your momma you could do it." She sniffled and checked her watch. "I suppose people will be lining up outside the Main Ballroom any minute, so I better get going."

Aunt DeeDee wiped under her eyes and ran a hand across my off-the-shoulder sleeves before turning me toward the mirror, standing behind me like I was a bride on my very yellow wedding day.

"You're beautiful," she said, leaning her cheek against mine. "Your momma would be proud."

"I don't know about that..."

Aunt DeeDee brushed a strand of hair behind my ear. "I know she would. You've reconnected with people, you're helping bring justice, and even if you don't win the grand prize tonight, we'll figure it out."

"Thanks, Aunt DeeDee, for everything," I said.

"Anyhoo, I need to get to the ballroom." Aunt DeeDee's usual levity returned. "I'm back on as the MC, thank goodness.

Lacy might've peed her pants if she had to run the show behind the scenes *and* take center stage." She pretended to kiss my cheek but didn't touch my makeup-clad skin with her lips. I surprised myself by returning the air-kiss. "You'll be great, and I'll be rooting for you. Unofficially, of course."

I had fifteen minutes to myself before I needed to make my way to the ballroom.

I'd been musing all afternoon on the cutout of Miss 2001, of the quote about Cathy Peabody's daughter from the library book, on Savilla's strange connection to the original winner.

I'd also been listing Dr. Bellingham's potential motives for killing Mr. Finch:

1. Money, maybe, though he'd need to bypass Savilla and Glenda Finch—to reach the millions for himself.
2. Revenge. He could've been angry at Mr. Finch for whatever happened all those years ago to make Cathy Peabody disappear.
3. Love, perhaps.

I thought of his fingers laced with Cathy Peabody's in the photo we'd found on the back of the property, but I could see him holding almost any woman's hand.

That familiar feeling of missing something crept back into my gut.

In my tiny cottage I lay back on the couch as much as I could in my dress. I thought back to my arrival at the Rose Palace, being dropped at the front steps by Lacy, wandering into the mansion on that first day, chatting with Savilla, the meet and greet, the three judges ascending the stage.

Something inched its way forward. I closed my eyes, seeing

that moment in the ballroom again—before Mrs. Finch had come in and fainted and turned the entire show on its axis—when I'd waved my arms as I'd danced next to Savilla.

Her eyes had been warm with nostalgia as the pageant song had played and we'd swayed across the stage, practicing the choreography. *I grew up listening to this song over and over while Mommy and I ran errands*, she'd said, and I'd tried to imagine a childhood filled with pageant tunes. Neither the mention of *Mommy* or *running errands* rang true for how she referred to Mrs. Finch, whom she always called, rather strangely, StepMommy.

My mind scrolled back through our school days. Graduation, Junior Dance, Sophomore Social, Freshman Retreat. Backward and forward through the years, I traversed play performances, choir recitals, art shows, Valentine's Day parties, and end-of-year programs.

Mrs. Finch had been at most events and performances and achievements. Mr. Finch had come to about half. Had there been anyone else? Someone I was missing?

My mind jumped forward to Cathy Peabody's quote. I sat up and opened the book that I'd dropped onto the coffee table.

"My child will grow up in a different kind of world than even I did," Ms. Peabody said. "I'm here at this pageant to create a better world for her."

My eyes roamed back up the page to the only other mention of this woman.

At the Miss 2001 competition, I spoke with a young woman named Cathy Peabody, who grew up in the nearby mountains on a farm with her family. Instead of blue-blood, she's from a blue-collar family, but she hopes to one day work on the Parisian runways.

I organized the information in my mind:

1. Grew up near here
2. Farm
3. Blue-collar family
4. Parisian runways

Wait. That last one. That was it. She'd wanted to work in fashion, likely near home, which could mean in Aubergine. There were only two people with any sense of fashion in this town. My aunt and...

My eyes widened as I saw all of these moments again, this time conjuring kindergarten graduation. I thought of how Lacy and I had found our class photo in the file for Miss 2001 in Aunt DeeDee's office, something that hadn't made sense at the time but could be explained if somehow the winner had been in the photo, standing on the edges, watching and waiting.

That same person had hovered in the background of many of my childhood memories until Savilla had graduated from high school a decade ago and her services had no longer been needed. That's when she'd opened her own boutique. That's when she'd become a judge at the annual Rose Palace Pageant. I dropped the book as I realized that I'd known Cathy Peabody, Miss 2001, almost my entire life.

After serving Glenda Finch glass after glass of whiskey on my first night, I'd pretended to admire the paintings in the room. When I'd asked about the depiction of Miss 2001, the women had gone silent. I'd thought it was because Savilla and Katie didn't want me reminding Mrs. Finch that she'd once only been runner-up, but no, it was because all three of them knew that the actual Miss 2001 was in that very room.

THIRTY-SIX

When I entered the ballroom, three contestants stopped their conversation and stared at me, two ladies gave me finger waves, and one of the staff members paused to let me pass in front of him. The mirror hadn't lied. I looked like royalty.

After the photographer snapped a hundred or so group photos of all of us in our gowns, we were rushed backstage so the audience could enter and find their seats. As we lined up in the wings, I peered out at the crowd, at the judges' dais, at Savilla, who sat sandwiched between Miss 1962's hunched shoulders and Katie Gilman's buxom frame. Savilla wore a floor-length white gown that looked as if it was made out of whatever angels wore. The smooth satin trailed around her like rippling water.

Katie, in a silver sequined sheath dress, poured Savilla a glass of water, and the younger girl leaned forward and whispered in her ear. Katie threw back her head and laughed. The action struck me as intimate, as familiar, as far from employer to employee as one could get.

It was almost time for the show to start, and although I wanted to keep an eye on those two women, I needed to mentally prepare myself for the evening ahead. Afterward, I could think about the real Miss 2001 and why she had been hiding in plain sight—and if her hiding might mean something more sinister.

"You look amazing," Summer said when she greeted me. "That shade brings out your eyes and your highlights..." She paused and brought her fingers to her lips in a semblance of awe. "You're stunning."

Jemma reluctantly agreed, so I knew it must be true. "You look just like the photos of your aunt the year she won."

Until tonight I'd never seen the resemblance to Aunt DeeDee as quickly as everyone around me. Even Momma had called me Aunt DeeDee's Mini-Me on occasion, because our mannerisms and expressions were so similar. Still, I had trouble believing I looked half as good as Aunt DeeDee had on her big night.

As I watched the room fill, goosebumps prickled my skin. Behind me, Summer rested a hand on my shoulder before heading to the other side of the stage. "Don't worry. The show goes by super fast."

Jemma offered a rare smile from a couple of contestants behind me. "You'll blink, and it's over."

I took as deep a breath as my corset would allow.

"Places for the opening number, ladies," Lacy called backstage. "Places!"

The Rose Palace Pageant's theme song blared through the ballroom and the house lights dimmed as we made our way across the platform, waving our arms and stepping in time to the music. The lights on us felt like heat lamps, and I began to glisten. I was grateful when a single spotlight shone on my aunt at center stage.

"Welcome," Aunt DeeDee said to the room filled with people.

Resounding applause and a few cheers echoed. Every seat was filled.

"We couldn't be more thrilled to have you here with us to celebrate the one hundredth anniversary of the Rose Palace Pageant, as well as these remarkable women."

Her arms extended toward us, and I found myself proud to be among these contestants: Jemma with a hard outer shell that hid a deep love for her family, and Summer with aspirations to help every child in need. Some of them could be silly or mean or ridiculous, but most were just women with insecurities and flaws, strengths and dreams.

Next, Aunt DeeDee segued into a video of this week that had been spliced together. We exited to the dark wings of the stage, and those up first for the talent portion prepared quickly. As we waited, I caught images on the giant screen of us ladies making silly headpieces, conversing at morning tea, and rehearsing in the tents. Photos flickered across the screen, conveniently leaving out the darker side of the last few days: the murder and poisoning, the missing crown and the discovered corpse.

"And now, it's time for our first performance of the evening. Please welcome to the stage... Summer Patel."

The staff rolled a giant piano across the wooden stage, and Summer sat in front of the keys, a calm resolution on her face as she placed her hands on the ivory and began to play. I recognized the piece as "I Hope You Dance" by Lee Ann Womack, a song I would've thought cheesy except for the fact that it had been one of Momma's favorites.

She played lyrically, her fingers gliding over the notes and I couldn't tear myself away from the edge of the velvet curtain as the words came back to me, a mother's wish for her child. I felt a hand on my shoulder and caught a whiff of Aunt DeeDee's perfume.

"I miss her too," she said softly, reminding me of another

thing we had in common. Aunt DeeDee handed me a Kleenex from her cleavage, and I dabbed at my eyes.

Several acts passed quickly as women danced and mimed and played instruments.

I perched on the edge of a stool as I waited for my turn to showcase my talent. I studied the judges. Miss 1962 wore a flat expression; Savilla sat with a straight spine, taking her new job very seriously; and Katie Gilman was all smiles.

Forty-five minutes later, Jemma walked onto the stage and began singing and dancing to *Rent*'s "No Day But Today," and my breath caught. Jemma, this law-student-turned-barista who wanted to produce an off-Broadway show about her brother, was an incredible performer with a mystifying stage presence, though I had to admit that this song didn't have the same kind of soul as the one she'd sung in the tunnel when she'd been calming our fears. Still, her talent was astounding.

I was reminded that the women here contained multitudes —and I was next. I went quietly to where Lacy had left my saddle, a stand, and a brush. Then, I slipped out of my heels and stepped into my boots, grabbing my tools of the trade and pressing the leather against my hip. I set them at the edge of the curtains so I could pull my supplies onto the stage and finish as quickly as possible before making my exit.

In what seemed like mere seconds, Jemma ended the song to applause and bowed twice before hurrying off-stage.

"Good luck, cowgirl," she said, her smile playful.

I grabbed my supplies and put one foot in front of the other until I stood under the bright lights, trying to keep myself from shielding my eyes in the glare as I spoke.

"Hello. My name is Dakota Green," I said, my nerves rising to the surface. How I wished I could rope a calf or even ride a bucking bronco—anything to take the attention off of me and onto a majestic animal.

I squeezed my eyes shut for a second, and a couple of hoots

came from the audience. "I love your boots," one woman yelled from the back.

The corner of my mouth lifted in a grin. There was no need for nervousness. I had three minutes to show the judges I knew something valuable, and dammit, that was what I was going to do.

"This evening I'll be demonstrating how to properly clean and mount a leather saddle," I said, focusing on the judges seated on the raised dais: they were the people who mattered right now.

"The first thing you want to do is properly prepare everything so you don't get soap and water on any part of the saddle that could easily rust."

I began my ministrations, methodic but quick, and though at first the audience seemed confounded that this was my talent, within a few seconds, I sensed a few of them leaning forward, actually interested. The cameraman angled around so he could zoom in on my hands, and a hush settled across the room. I unbuckled and removed the saddle's fittings, chatting as I did each evening with Bella, pretending that I was bedding her down for the night.

"Horses were first domesticated in what is now known as southern Russia, but long before, they are believed to have evolved fifty-some million years ago from a creature known as *Eohippus*. But, please, don't ever call them by that name because it's hard to pronounce and they find it offensive. Oh— and never, ever call them Mister Ed. They're very sensitive about their depiction in the Golden Age of television."

A few chuckles emerged from the crowd, and I was relieved that at least some people were tracking with me.

"Another fun fact that I rarely bring up with my equine friends is the reality that their brain is actually smaller than the space taken up by their teeth."

I gave a wide, tooth-filled smile, and a few more people laughed.

"I'm often asked by the students who come to the stables whether a horse is a boy or girl, and for the really young kiddos, I don't always want to point out a horse's huge... or tiny... you know... so instead we count their teeth. The boys have forty while the girls have only thirty-six. I'm like, how cool is that? In the backwoods of Virginia, sometimes I'm lucky to find a guy with any of his real teeth."

Bigger laugh.

"Also, I'm really jealous that horses can sleep both lying down and standing up. It would make bad dates a lot more bearable if I could just force myself into a comatose state while waiting in line at the shooting range. Because that's where guys with only a few teeth take you on the first date." I paused. "Afterward, if he's still got his molars, we might grab a burger."

As I brushed the metal pieces with a wet towel and continued the kind of conversation I usually only reserved for Bella, the nameplate on the saddle glinted in the stage lights, and I couldn't help but read the words: ones I'd skimmed in the stables a couple of days earlier.

To Savilla, All This Will Be Ours. Love, Your Mom.

Now, as I read the full message on this particular saddle, the inscription carried a new meaning. I read each word carefully as I continued to clean and chatter.

"Horses have huge eyes. They can actually see three hundred and fifty degrees, and if I hadn't graduated from the Virginia public school system, I might know what that means."

More laughter.

"If the saddle... if it's especially dirty, you may need to... to redo this step several times," I said, holding up a clean sponge. This saddle hadn't been used recently. If ever. But it did hold a clue, a clue I was processing onstage in front of hundreds of pageant-goers.

I squirted more glycerin soap onto the sponge as my brain tried to dissect the engraved words, my mind forming the phrasing of the dedication into a list.

1. *Savilla*—daughter of Mr. Finch and... Katie Gilman.
2. *All this*—the estate? The pageant? Life itself?
3. *Will Be Ours*—Katie Gilman was taking something, and she was planning to share it with her daughter, Savilla.
4. *Love, Your Mom*—Also known as Savilla's nanny, Cathy Peabody, Miss 2001, Pageant Judge Katie Gilman.

Twenty seconds passed as my thoughts slammed into one another and my mouth ran on autopilot.

"Now, a... a little... um... a little conditioner goes a long way —something I've learned from my own... uh... beautification process this week." I swallowed and wiped off the soap. I dripped a nickel-sized dollop of leather conditioner onto a brush, keeping one hand on the saddle as I nearly rubbed a hole into the leather. "Do y'all know how hard it is to look like the ladies on this stage? I do. And so do my hair extensions, my fake eyelashes, and my push-up bra. As of last Monday, I was a stable hand, and I cannot seem to get rid of the dirt, so I'm a bit like Weird Barbie: I'm fancy, but I've also been played with outside for too long."

I recalled what Lacy had said in Katie Gilman's bio on the first night here: she'd worked at the estate as a maid and worked her way up to the position of Savilla's nanny. When she'd been a maid, she must've had some kind of tryst—or encounter—with Mr. Finch that had left her pregnant with Savilla.

The sharp edges of the past few days began to fit together into a seamless mosaic. It was like I could see a continuous thread running through the past, present, and near future.

"If your saddle has silver fittings, you'll want to... uh... be sure to add a bit of... of polish, not only for the... the shine, but also for long-term protection."

I saw the sheriff listening to me from the very back of the ballroom, and then I glanced at Katie Gilman, who now sat with her hands folded on the table in front of her ample bosom. I thought of my first night here, how she'd found the pinky ring in my aunt's drawer. Mr. Finch's words from the first day came back to me all at once: *It's my personal design*, he'd said. Later, Dr. Bellingham had referred to the design as a judges' ring, which presumably meant that only the judges received them.

Only the judges, which included Katie Gilman. What if it was her ring? She'd been a judge for years, so she would've had the very same design as all the other judges. What if she'd taken off her own ring, held it up to the light, and fooled me and the sheriff? How far had she gone to hide who she'd once been? Had she also worked with Dr. Bellingham in order to win the 2001 pageant, and later excised herself from the archives?

Katie Gilman had no idea that, as I performed my odd talent, I was on to her. She had no idea that she was fast becoming a primary suspect in Mr. Finch's murder, at least in my mind.

I needed to let the sheriff know about the message on the saddle immediately, but I couldn't exactly leap off the stage.

"Saddles don't really get worn down with age. In fact, once you break them in, you can enjoy them for the rest of your life. You can probably even pass them on to future generations for... for both practical and sentimental value. And"—I couldn't help myself—"if you share the same great backside, your child might be able to use the exact same saddle for years to come. After all, family sticks together. Mothers, daughters..." I rambled as I looked from the sheriff to Savilla Finch, who was watching me with an amused but puzzled expression.

I ran through potential motives again, but this time those of Katie Gilman.

1. Money, for sure.
2. Revenge against the man who'd taken her daughter from her, yeah.
3. Love for a child, definitely.

This was a crime of passion, just not the typical definition of the word. Still, a mother's love was its own kind of passion, a passion that could justify anything. Even murder.

As I finished my talent portion of the show, Aunt DeeDee came back to the stage and waved an arm in my direction. "Give it up for Dakota Green, everyone."

To my utter astonishment, people applauded and kept applauding as I packed up the saddle and cleaning gear. A few even stood up and, at one point, whoops issued from somewhere in the back as I waved to the crowd and made my way to the wings.

I couldn't believe it. Not only had I possibly solved a murder, I'd actually entertained this crowd.

THIRTY-SEVEN

I was thinking about Katie Gilman and the best way to get a message to Sheriff Strong when, backstage, a practical stranger undid my gown and helped me out of the yards of tulle. I shimmied into a red swimsuit with ruffles that Jemma had told me were intended to visually increase the size of my bust.

Summer rushed around backstage, telling each girl to bend over and flip her hair upside down before she quickly sprayed it, while Nina reminded all of us to add a bounce to our step. I was surprised to realize something I'd never seen from my seat in the audience: these women were acting like a team. Only one of us could win the crown, but we were all in the competition together.

I slipped on my shiny black heels and glanced at myself in one of the rows of mirrors, surprised to see that the ruffle-effect was working. Despite the fact I hated that showing off my body was the goal, I had to admit that I was elongated and curvier than I'd ever looked in my entire life, the stretchy fabric hugging my hips and the red hue complementing my sun-kissed skin. Almost like a beauty queen. I only hoped I sounded like one too as I mentally prepared for the interview that would take place while scantily clad.

Jemma hurried toward me and grabbed my left breast.

I yelped and she put a hand over my mouth.

"I'm just smoothing out your padding," she said, as her hand worked fast to unwrinkle the insert. "You don't want to be lopsided." She gave me one last look. "Knock 'em dead."

A few minutes later, I was standing under the bright lights, vaguely hearing the other contestants answer questions about what they'd do if they won—everything from "open an emu sanctuary" to "donate the proceeds to childhood leukemia research"; where they saw themselves in five years—"um... modeling for *Playboy*?" to "working to make solar energy afford-able"; and what had been their biggest struggle—"not being chosen for *The Bachelor*" to "facing my mental health issues head-on with intensive therapy." Like I said, containing multitudes.

When it came to my turn, the question was, "If you could make one wish for every person in the entire world, what would it be?"

I took a deep breath and began. "My one wish would be for each person to have someone in their lives to love and support them. An entire community for each person would be even better. Loneliness needn't be an affliction if we open ourselves up in transparent and authentic relationships.

"I've been surprised these past few days by how much I've connected with the contestants here. These women are strong and capable; they have dreams and plans to enact as soon as they leave tonight." I gave a nod of affirmation to the rows of women on each side of me. "What I thought might be one kind of experience has become something else entirely: a way to really see other people, a way to connect with people who are different than me, a way for me to belong."

It was true. If I had one wish for myself, it would be to

bring Momma back, but knowing that was impossible, I would go with the next best thing: having people to love and who loved me—and also some cash to keep Momma's house and start over.

As soon as the interviews ended and everyone took a brief break, I found Aunt DeeDee fixing her face before she needed to usher the ladies into the very last part of the evening: the judges' decision. The audience had a half-hour intermission while they deliberated.

"I need the master key," I told her.

Aunt DeeDee's eyes held a question we didn't have time to discuss, so instead, she pulled a key card from her cleavage and placed the warm plastic in my outstretched hand. That was one way to keep track of things. "You best be quick about it. I have a good feeling about who's gonna win."

"Thanks." I gave her a quick hug.

"What's that for?"

I didn't know exactly, but it was just so good to see her back where she belonged, all dolled up and running things. "I'll be back before we go onstage next."

She didn't remind me of the schedule. Instead, she squeezed my shoulder, trusting me.

I took the door that connected to one of the main hallways before scurrying to the elevator bank in the lobby. A few staff members milled about, their eyes wide as they watched me, the escaped bathing beauty, rushing past them.

Katie had told me on my first night that her room was on the fourth floor of the residential wing, right next to my aunt's, in the old nursery. That's where I would look.

I pressed the elevator button several times, willing the lift to come quickly. When it arrived, I rode it up to the fourth floor and hurried down the hall, watching for the décor to signal that the residential quarters were up ahead.

I passed my aunt's room and stood in front of Katie's door. I held my aunt's key card to the sensor, the lock clicked, and I stepped inside, quickly pulling the door shut behind me.

The room was not what I'd expected, more like an homage to a child who'd once lived there than a once-a-year hotel stay. I imagined that the room likely looked exactly as it had when it had been Savilla's, with a rocking chair and pink-maned rocking horse in the corner, sparkly dress-up clothes secured to pegs in the wall, and games like Hi-Ho! Cherry-O and Chutes and Ladders stacked on a bookshelf. The only thing signaling that this was no longer a nursery were the scattered dresses and beauty paraphernalia.

I noted a few hair products on the edge of her dresser, then opened a drawer of her cabinet to find a silver box that had once held an assortment of perfume bottles. Taped to the lid was the same kindergarten class photo I'd found in Miss 2001's folder in Aunt DeeDee's office, except this time two figures had hearts drawn around them: Savilla and her nanny, Katie Gilman. At the bottom was written the words *My Girl*. I untied the pink bow holding the box together and opened it to find keepsakes. A locket of fine baby hair, a child's tooth, and drawings signed by their creator in a childish scrawl. Savilla had written her name with a backward S. I was definitely on the right track.

In the closet was a row of hangers and a couple of remaining gowns. Other than that, it was bare. I couldn't see the full top shelf of the closet, so I stood on tip-toe and ran a hand along it until I felt a canvas bag. I pulled it down to find a black sack with a label that read *Dr. Jim Bellingham.*

Inside, I found a bottle of pills prescribed to him, as well as a Polaroid camera. Lining the bottom were photos of my aunt's sash. These pictures didn't have any kind of message on them, which meant they must have been extras, the ones the perpetrator hadn't needed in order to frame my aunt. The fact that Dr. Bellingham's bag was in Katie Gilman's closet meant that either he or she had likely taken the photos and deposited them in my room, which meant the two of them had been working together.

I thought about Katie Gilman dropping off beauty supplies the night that Aunt DeeDee had been taken into custody. She'd come inside to check on me, and I may have run to the bathroom while she was there. I blinked hard, trying to remember, but the lack of sleep was catching up with me. I suppose she might have deposited the photos upstairs in my bed before giving me a hug and reassuring words. What an idiot I'd been.

The message scribbled across the bottom of the photos I'd found in my bed—*SHE KILLED BOTH OF THEM*—repeated in my mind.

I'd known that was a lie from the very beginning, but now I could confirm the lie: Miss 2001 was very much alive—and it appeared that she was involved in framing my aunt. My stomach turned. I'd trusted this woman, and she'd betrayed the person closest to me.

Next, I went into Katie Gilman's bathroom. Hanging over the side of the shower was a pair of stockings, a bra, and a set of pajamas. On the vanity, a curling iron had been turned off but left plugged into the wall, and makeup, perfume, and moisturizers were scattered next to the sink.

Taped to the back of the bathroom door was a handwritten list on a piece of lined paper torn from a yellow legal pad, the letters slanted. I read the contents carefully.

Meet with Deanna for marketing review

Savilla—Meet & Greet ideas?

Ask GG to send thank you notes to sponsors

Update Rose Palace accounts

Hmmm... this didn't seem like the kind of list that a boutique owner would need to make. It looked much more like a to-do list for a man in Mr. Finch's position.

The garbage bag was filled with torn pieces of yellow paper. I bent and picked them up, placing the bin on the counter and removing the pieces on top, flattening them against the edge of the sink. The pages had been ripped and discarded, but I was able to see which edges fit where.

I made quick time to assemble them into the proper order until a message emerged.

I regret what I did to Miss 2001. I'm only getting what I deserve from the one who took her crown. To the real jewels...

Oh my God. I'd heard these words before. Out of Savilla's mouth as she'd read her father's letter to the entire ballroom. Except this letter was unfinished, and around the edges were half-formed words repeated in various iterations: *regret* with a loopy *g* and *deserve* with a swooping *d*. As if someone had been practicing to get the look of the words just right.

I pulled out the next piece of paper and the next, arranging them to find the messages not quite as finished, the letters around the edges repeated again and again.

I held up one of the strips beside the to-do list, comparing the handwriting. The script wasn't an exact match, but it was close enough. Close enough to fool me from a distance. But close enough to fool Savilla and Glenda Finch up close? I wasn't sure.

Katie Gilman had written these letters, using Mr. Finch's handwritten to-do list to get his handwriting just right.

I tore the list from the wall and grabbed the strips of paper, throwing them inside Dr. Bellingham's bag and tucking it under my arm. This, along with the Polaroid photos, was the proof I needed that Katie had been involved in the entire plot—or at least as close as I could get.

As I turned to leave, I spotted something on the ground. Beneath the edge of the door was a golden high heel with rhinestones running across nearly every inch of the fabric. This was the other half of the pair that Jemma, Summer, and I had found in the tunnel last night, the heels that Savilla had stolen from *Mommy's closet*. I could hear her saying the words on my first day here.

Mommy. Savilla Finch knew her mother was Katie Gilman, and she'd been wearing the woman's very gold, very suspicious heels.

The other shoe was about to drop.

THIRTY-EIGHT

I spotted the sheriff in the Color Gallery and ran up to him.

"Nice swimsuit," he said as he glanced at me appreciatively.

"I made it myself out of duct tape and super glue," I quipped. "I only have a minute, but I need to show you something."

He glanced back and forth and then led me behind a glass case and through a door that was visible, but just barely. We stood inside a small room with a cabinet filled with dishes and drink supplies.

"A butler's pantry," he explained. "According to the blueprints, there are two more of these on the first floor." He pointed to the objects I'd brought with me. "What's all that?"

"I found them in Katie Gilman's room," I said, as I spread everything out in front of him like a sacrifice, explaining as I went.

When I finished, he pulled out his walkie-talkie and requested the presence of two of his officers before he began snapping photos of the evidence.

"Good work," Charlie finally said, his hazel eyes fixed on

mine. I was fairly certain that he wanted to thank me properly, but that would have to wait.

I hurried to change back into my ballgown, and as I followed the other ladies onto the stage for the announcement of the Centennial Queen, I thought about Katie holding up the ring—likely her ring—and allowing the sheriff to take it as evidence against my aunt. I pictured Katie lifting her glass at the Gilded Age dinner, toasting to justice. I imagined her studying Mr. Finch's writing. I could practically see her getting rid of evidence at the back of the property. My pulse sped and my muscles tensed as I considered the magnitude of deceit that this woman had employed to fool us all.

"After difficult deliberation among the judges," Aunt DeeDee began, as she stood center stage, "we have our top three contestants in this year's Rose Palace Pageant."

Light applause. My heart beat a steady rhythm that began to increase.

"These women embody the core principles of the pageant," my aunt continued. "Confidence, comportment, and conversation—and they look great in their costumes. Each of the three women I'm about to ask to step forward will take home one of the top prizes in tonight's contest."

Applause again. My mouth went dry.

"Now, ladies, please step forward when I call your name."

All of us fanned out across the stage as music blasted through the speakers, and I tried to keep the humming in my chest at bay. A teary-eyed Summer stood with her hands clenched, and Jemma's expression seemed almost hopeful. While they thought about their prospects, my attention was split between anticipation of potentially winning and wondering how the next few minutes would play out.

The music swelled and two staff members dressed in black made a show of rolling a locked, clear box onto the stage.

Aunt DeeDee took the key from them and opened it. "Now for the moment we've been awaiting all evening." She reached a hand into the box. "Inside these envelopes are the names of the women who have stolen the hearts of the judges—and of all of you, no doubt."

A few audience members let out soft hoots of excitement and two people actually called my name.

"Our first finalist is..." An electronic drumroll sounded as Aunt DeeDee opened an envelope. Her face lit and her voice pitched up nearly an octave as she read, "Dakota Green."

Cheers broke out, and despite having worked toward this outcome the entire week, I froze. I'd scored high enough to be a finalist? I'd accomplished the Four Cs? Had Jemma and Summer been right in saying that I'd unexpectedly proven myself to the judges this week? Had Aunt DeeDee and Mr. Finch been correct when they'd said that I would be a breath of fresh air?

Apparently so. I'd fulfilled my mantra: *You just need to place.*

Music sounded and then cut out seconds later, and the girl next to me—Nina—had to push me forward. I staggered to the front and gave my best beauty queen smile, trying to hide my shock.

Aunt DeeDee reached inside the box and took out the next envelope. "Our second finalist is... Jemma Jenkins."

Another round of clapping, this a bit more robust. Music played again. Seconds passed to build anticipation.

Aunt DeeDee reached for the final envelope. "And our last finalist in tonight's competition is... Gina Kominski."

As applause sounded again and Gina walked toward us, Aunt DeeDee motioned to a staff member, who ushered the three of us front and center.

I glanced at Summer, who stood behind me, tears glistening in her eyes. She gave me a big thumbs up despite the disappointment she must have been feeling, and I realized in that moment how genuine her praise and concern for me had been. If I won first place, I would make some kind of donation to her and her fiancé's goals of working with children.

I clenched my jaw, put on a smile, and turned to Jemma, who looked like she was actually happy to be standing here next to me.

Time stalled, and for a brief flicker of the lights, each woman on that stage and on the judges' dais and in the crowd was connected in a kind of beautiful in-between. Maybe we were all aspiring queens in our own right, or maybe we were regular women trying to get through each day. Regardless, we felt a mixture of fear and anticipation and joy and sorrow because whoever won would take the crown from all the women who didn't win, but whoever won would also be the new queen of a hundred-year-old tradition.

"We have had so many fine contestants over the years, and the centennial is a celebration of that grace and beauty," Aunt DeeDee said, looking at the audience before turning to us. The pride in her eyes was evident. She'd truly believed that with a bit of polish and shine, I would have what it took to win.

"With that in mind, let's find out tonight's winner." Aunt DeeDee popped out the bottom of the box to reveal a secret compartment containing a scroll tied with a blue ribbon. She was remarkable at building suspense as she unfurled the paper and read from it. "Third place this year goes to... Jemma Jenkins!"

Music played, and Jemma took a few reluctant steps forward, hiding any disappointment behind a wide grin as the audience cheered. Jemma might not have been thrilled with her prize, but a hundred grand would be enough for an off-Broadway production—or to get other investors on board.

Besides, she was not only getting cash. She was also getting a tractor.

When the clapping died down, Aunt DeeDee beamed at the audience. "Two contestants remain and only one can be crowned queen this evening. There's no doubt that anticipation is in the air."

My eyes went to the judges' table. If Jemma was third place, then I would be first or second, which meant enough money to at least cover mine and Aunt DeeDee's debts. My heart now pounded and my stomach roiled.

"The person the judges have chosen as our Centennial Queen will represent the Rose Palace Pageant for the next year, enjoying all the privileges and fulfilling all of the responsibilities that accompany such a role." Aunt DeeDee took a deep breath. "Without further delay, this year's Rose Palace Pageant Centennial Queen is..."

Gina actually grabbed my hand, squeezing the blood from my fingers.

I glanced at the middle-aged judge who sat with her hands folded on the table in front of her, oblivious. Katie Gilman: mother, nanny, pageant winner, accomplice to murder.

A drumroll echoed from the speakers as Aunt DeeDee inhaled deeply, choking back a cough to hide her tears as she declared the winner: "Miss Dakota Green!"

The sights and sounds zoomed out and then rushed at me in a seismic wave. Aunt DeeDee had called my name.

I could almost see myself in my gown with the shimmering yellow fabric the color of a moonlight tea rose. Underneath, I was still the girl who would rather talk to horses than a crowd of people, but I'd somehow returned to myself over the course of the week, relearning how to explore, to observe, to take a chance, to have an adventure. This often-dusty, boot-wearing stable hand had turned into a pageant queen. I'd won first place and everything that came with it, and despite the mystery and the murder, relief at being able to pay the debt collectors, to keep Momma's house, and save Aunt DeeDee's finances washed over me.

I could restart my life. In my mother's wisdom, she'd somehow intuited that this pageant would be the thing I needed.

Cheers arose as the audience stood, hollering as they'd done after the talent that I'd expected to bomb but had turned out to be a crowd favorite.

Jemma nudged me from behind, reminding me that I needed to finish this thing, all of it.

After a deep breath to steady myself, I stepped forward. Aunt DeeDee placed the crown on my head and gave me a long hug. Tears formed in my eyes and I swiped them away. I whispered a quick, "I love you," before stepping back and walking to the center of the stage, where I waited for the clapping to subside.

"Ladies and gentlemen..." I put one hand on my crown and used the other to quiet the room. My Twinkie-colored gown swished at my feet.

"I am honored to accept this crown, particularly because I know the kind of women who stand beside me tonight." I looked at Jemma. "Jemma Jenkins is fierce and talented, a loyal companion determined to expose the truth." A tear shimmered in Jemma's eye, and she quickly brushed it away. "And Summer Patel is nurturing and brave, willing to do whatever it takes even if she's terrified." Summer beamed at me. "The women on this stage are beautiful and cunning, bold and resilient, as gorgeous as they are savvy. As women, we must be all of these things in a world which demands such a strange mixture of fragility and strength from women." I inhaled deeply, turning my attention to the most important matter at hand as I faced the judges' table. "There's also someone very special I'd like to dedicate this crown to tonight, someone who has made a lasting impact on this pageant."

I could sense Aunt DeeDee adjusting her dress as if preparing for a grand honor, and I realized she assumed I was talking about her. In a minute, she would be glad that I wasn't.

"I'd like to give my crown to the real winner tonight, to our very own disappearing Miss 2001, to the beauty pageant queen who thought she could get away with murder..."

Aunt DeeDee gasped, and no drumroll sounded this time.

"... to former winner and current judge, Ms. Katie Gilman."

Despite the bright lights, I could see the outline of the sheriff hurrying forward just as Katie Gilman stood, eyeing an escape route. I could almost see understanding dawn on her face. The jig was up and she'd lost.

Sheriff Strong approached with his usual steadiness and pulled out his handcuffs, clasping her hands together behind her back. He might not have trusted my instincts when he'd first met me, but we'd learned that we made a decent team.

"Katie Gilman, alias Cathy Peabody, you have the right to remain silent," the sheriff said, the microphone catching his voice and echoing through the Primrose Ballroom.

THIRTY-NINE

Except for the reporters, who were furiously scribbling into notebooks or mumbling into microphones, the crowd sat in stunned silence. Savilla's mouth hung open in disbelief as she turned to Katie Gilman. From the front row of the audience, Mrs. Finch stood.

"Sit down, Gigi," Katie hissed, her hands behind her back.

I scanned the stage, the crown in my hand, at first wondering to whom she was speaking. When the reality hit me, the last domino fell.

My eyes trailed to the banner on the far right wall, listing Mrs. Glenda Finch as the winner. I thought of the wedding announcement that I'd found in one of the storage boxes, which had also named her as Glenda Finch. Strangely, no maiden name had been used for Glenda—it was as if she'd forever and always been Mrs. Finch.

But in my first conversation with him, Mr. Finch had called his wife by the same name Katie had just used. *Gigi*. At the time, I'd assumed it was spelled *G-i-g-i*, like the classic film, but on his to-do list taped to Katie's bathroom door, he'd written that he needed to *Ask GG to send thank you notes to sponsors*. The

290

first G was for Glenda, and the second G was for... Oh Lord, how had I not seen it?

Glenda Gilman, sister to Katie Gilman. This was a family-friendly show, after all.

The women didn't look alike, not even in the enlarged cutout from 2001 when they were both younger and thinner. They didn't have similar personalities from what I'd seen, but neither had Momma and Aunt DeeDee. What both women shared was their connection to Savilla—and the deceased Mr. Finch.

"Are you two... sisters?" I stammered.

The two women, only a few years apart in age, stared at one another before turning to me.

"He got me pregnant and then stole my child from me," Katie finally said, as the crowd gasped.

"What else were we supposed to do?" Glenda followed, as if whatever they'd done had been a foregone conclusion.

Katie Gilman and Glenda Finch, née Gilman, had sat side by side on and off all week, and they'd been together in the Finches' apartment my first night there. I wanted to hit myself for not seeing it earlier: their body language, the way they communicated so much in a glance. I'd assumed it was a long-time employer–employee relationship, but this was so much more. These were sisters who'd loved—and perhaps sometimes hated—one another over the years, but they were bonded, none-theless.

Glenda looked protectively toward Katie, and the intensity of the look passing between the two women told me I'd guessed correctly.

"This isn't her fault," Glenda shouted across the aisle and to the audience at large.

Katie staggered slightly upon hearing her sister's words.

"It's mine," Glenda insisted.

Katie's eyes widened and she called, "Hush your mouth and

sit down, Glenda. The police already have the culprit." She looked at Charlie. "The person you want is Dr. Bellingham, and you already have him in custody."

"We know he wasn't working alone," the sheriff said. "Now I'm wondering if he was even involved as much as I first thought."

A universal shock went through the room.

Glenda almost seemed to bask in the surprise before continuing. "My name is Glenda Gilman Finch, and Dr. Bellingham and I are guilty of my husband's murder." She stared at the sheriff. "You can release Katie."

"I'm afraid that's not how this works," Sheriff Strong said as he motioned for one of his men to approach Glenda as well.

Katie squared her shoulders, despite the handcuffs, making her appear more like the confident Miss 2001 she'd once been. Her eyes moved to her sister, and she spoke as if they were the only two in the room. "You don't need to take the fall for me. You've... you've done enough."

"It could never be enough," Glenda countered. "After Frederick took everything from you. After he kicked you out of the estate. After he stole your child. He deserved what came to him."

"Why?" I stepped forward, genuinely wanting to know what Mr. Finch had done to deserve death. Yes, he'd somehow tried to keep Savilla from Katie Gilman, but it obviously hadn't worked, at least not completely.

Katie sniffled as she reopened her past. "I was trying to get a job and start a life when I took a position here as a maid. I was young and dumb and believed it when Fred said he loved me."

"You weren't the problem," Glenda gently corrected before turning to the sheriff. "My sister couldn't sue for custody. She had nothing, and Fred had everything. So we made another plan: she would compete and win the money in the 2001 pageant under a pseudonym."

"He let me win, was baiting me, but I couldn't be that close to Savilla..." Katie turned to look at her now-grown daughter. "I was impulsive. When Fred said I'd never be with her, even if I won all the money in the world, I took her and ran."

"But you didn't get far," I added.

"I had a backup plan," Glenda broke in. "I would marry him and hire Katie as the nanny. Then I would divorce him and take half of everything." She sighed. "Unfortunately, he was one step ahead with a watertight prenup."

"But when I told him I would go to the tabloids, tell them everything, he did allow me to return as Savilla's nanny," Katie said, her voice quiet, as if to show her own weakness. "For that I'm grateful."

Sheriff Strong couldn't keep from asking the question that was on all of our minds. "How could you kill the father of your own child?"

"It wasn't hard," Katie answered, looking at him as if he was an imbecile for not realizing such a thing. "It was time. I knew that according to his will, Savilla would be free to inherit at twenty-five. It just took me a few years longer than I'd expected to figure out how to do it without getting caught."

"And how'd that work out for you?" the sheriff asked.

"It would've worked if—"

"Mother," Savilla said, extending a hand in Katie's direction. "That's enough. You don't need to discriminate yourself."

I had no time or energy to address that one. None of us did, and besides, maybe *discriminate* was exactly what she'd meant.

Sheriff Strong turned toward Savilla now, and I could see he was trying to discern whether he needed to take another member of this family into custody. His voice was heavy with authority as he asked, "Savilla Finch, do you have anything to say about these recent confessions?"

Glenda spoke for her. "Leave her out of this. She only found out that Katie is her biological mother a few months ago."

"Before or after Savilla took out a life insurance policy on him?" the sheriff asked.

Kudos to him. I wondered if he'd also been poking around the Finches' liquor cabinet to find this detail—but he likely had more official means of gathering intel.

"I was a witness to that," Aunt DeeDee said, bravely stepping forward. Even though my instincts were to tell her to keep quiet, I was proud of her for being willing to help after all she'd been through. "Despite how it might look, the policy was a simple practicality."

"That's right. Daddy said it never hurt to have more money. I signed the policy, but I had no idea they were planning to kill..." Savilla was shame-faced and vulnerable, like the child I'd grown up with.

Her expression and Aunt DeeDee's testimony were convincing. I'd been wrong about Savilla's involvement in all of this. She hadn't killed her father, and she couldn't control her mother or stepmother. Her only fault was trying to live up to all of their expectations.

Savilla turned to Katie. "You never said anything about"— her arms flailed wildly in the air as if the gesture could encompass the events of the past few days—"any of *this*."

"You must understand. Your father wasn't a person," Katie calmly told her before turning to the audience. She wanted all of us to feel her justification. "He was a monster, a baby stealer, a narcissist that everyone loved because he had money and power."

"And... what about StepMommy?" Savilla asked. "Why would you want to... to poison her?"

"Oh, baby. I would never... That was all Jim's doing," Katie said. "I had no idea. We asked him to help ensure everything ran smoothly, but apparently, the money we'd promised him wasn't enough. He wanted a chance at killing Glenda and seducing you for the entire inheritance."

Glenda stared at Savilla as if willing her to believe them. "What happened to me had nothing to do with your mother, and after I came to, I was afraid that you might be next."

So, Dr. Bellingham's greed had gotten the best of him, and he'd gone rogue, sneaking those toxic honey jars into the Finches' liquor cabinet to get rid of either or both of them.

Katie's eyes filled with tears as she looked from her sister to her daughter. "Savilla, we just... we just wanted you to have the family and the resources you deserve. The three of us, together."

As I thought about my own mother, about what she would've done to stay with me, tears sprang to my eyes, and that's when a photographer snapped a picture that would appear on front pages of newspapers everywhere the next morning. The ugly cry of the beautiful new queen.

"Now I've lost Daddy and both of you..." Savilla's voice trailed off as she choked out the words. "All because you wanted to be filchy rich."

"*Filthy*, darling," Glenda corrected, almost sounding like the kind of uppity woman I'd assumed she was for most of the show.

"No," Savilla blurted. "You tried to *filch* everything, to steal, to take it all for yourself."

"The money wasn't the *thing* for us," Katie cut in. "Savilla, you have to believe that we did all of this because we wanted you—and we wanted you to have it all."

Emotions ran across Savilla's face: confusion, hope, longing. All of it was on display, and I knew it would take a long time for her to unpack what her family had become.

Aunt DeeDee stepped forward, her brows drawn together as if she was in physical pain. I ached for the betrayal she must have been feeling. "But we've known one another for years... We've worked together; we were room moms together; we've been at every pageant together. Why would you frame *me*?"

Katie's eyes widened, the hint of tears as she was confronted with the extent of what she'd done. "I'm so sorry. I didn't know what to do, and Jim suggested you as the perfect decoy. I panicked." She swallowed. "The police were supposed to take you in and question you for theft, not murder." She bent forward at the waist as if she wanted to plead for forgiveness despite the sheriff's handcuffs. "The letter wasn't supposed to implicate you, but then Jimmy got it into his head that you could take the fall for everything. He's the one who took the Polaroids and put them in Dakota's room before she even arrived. I swear I didn't know he was planning to do that until after..."

Aunt DeeDee's eyes darted to me. She hadn't known about the photos with the implicating message under my duvet and, for a moment, the idea of Dr. Bellingham being in my room was more concerning to her than anything else.

"I'm good," I told her. "Nothing happened."

"Please, forgive me," Katie said to Aunt DeeDee, her eyes pleading. "I... I knew they would eventually let you go."

That wasn't true. It couldn't be. No one could know that.

As silence settled again, I stepped forward. I couldn't keep quiet. I needed to know one more thing.

I looked directly at Katie and asked my question. "Mr. Finch died in the middle of the night, so where was he during the evening before his death? And how did you hide his body in the 1950s tent?"

"He was with me," Katie answered, showing all her cards now that it was too late to refuse to play the game. "We'd reached a truce years ago, but he was still nervous that I would blow his cover, let the world know what kind of man he really was: one who had slept with a maid and then stolen her child. That kind of reputation could ruin his beloved pageant. I'd told him that with Savilla now grown, I wanted to talk to him about me leaving Aubergine for good, and to meet me at the back of the property during the meet and greet one last time to discuss a final payout. Stupid man. He waited and waited for me, spending time with his bees and his honey while I planted the note in his apartment and the crown in DeeDee's room." Katie looked sheepish for the first time, but she continued. "I told Fred to leave his phone, his keys, everything. I said I didn't want us to be interrupted, that if he would do this one thing, he would never hear from me again after this week. He did everything I asked—that's how much he still despised me. When I got to the back of the property late that night, Fred and I took a walk." Katie swallowed. "I talked about his plans to build a museum memorializing the pageant. He joked about making an exhibit that would honor me. He thanked me for my service, for giving him our daughter—as if I'd had a choice. He thought he was actually getting rid of me as we started back through the tunnel in the early morning hours. He had no idea what was coming."

Glenda spoke now. "I helped move his body sometime after two a.m."

"That's right," Katie added. "In the dark of the night, she and I hauled him up the stairs and onto a rusty old cart. We did what we had to do, and Dr. Bellingham met us in the 1950s tent and helped shove him into the kitchen cabinets."

My eyebrows rose clear to my brow line and another photo snapped. I considered the image of the three of them working collectively to hide Mr. Finch's body. I wondered, only for a moment, why they would hide him there, in a place where he would be found in such a public way. But then I looked at them and understood: it was poetic justice.

The sisters wanted the man who had controlled and dictated their lives to be discovered in the most domestic part of the home in the most housewifely era. The Gilman sisters also needed him to be found. If he'd simply disappeared—like Miss 2001, aka Cathy Peabody, had done so many years ago—then his estate and his money would be in limbo for what could be years. Katie and Glenda had wanted everything finished as soon as possible. They'd waited long enough for what was due to them and Savilla.

I tried to blink away the image of the two women hauling him up from the underground tunnel and through the opening in the heart of the fake rose-hedge maze, but the thought of these two sisters working together one last time stuck in my mind. The evening had been full of reveals, but this was my primary takeaway: Dead bodies were heavy, but angry women got things done.

FORTY

Once upon a time, a maid rose in rank to catch the eye of a millionaire. She gave him her greatest pride and joy: a daughter. Out of misogyny or sheer power-mongering, he discarded her, using his resources to keep their child from her, but the maid had a surprise ally, a sister who would sacrifice anything for her happiness, a sister who would marry a man for his riches and find a way to reunite true daughter with true mother once again. So the sisters went to work, tricking and cajoling and manipulating the man. The four of them—millionaire, sisters, and daughter—lived fitfully ever after at the royal palace until one night, when one of them stabbed Mr. Finch through the eye. They achieved their goal, but not their freedom. The End.

This is the story that would be told again and again among Aubergine residents in coming years, but for now, we were living it in real time.

"I did it for my daughter," Katie Gilman yelled to a handful of reporters as she was led away in handcuffs by Sheriff Charlie Strong, whose name would become nationally known in coming days. "No matter what they tell you, I did it for her!"

Savilla, meanwhile, stared on from the ballroom stage in her family mansion as her mother and stepmother disappeared through the grand doors. The sisters would soon be united again, and I could only imagine the two of them sharing a cell.

So many audience members held their phones aloft that it looked like a concert rather than a pageant. Maybe for the first time ever, Aunt DeeDee was stunned into silence, but she soon did her best to recover the show, asking everyone to applaud for this year's winners. Even so, by the end of the final song, as I stood with the crown on my head, DeeDee gave up and set the microphone on the podium. As soon as the last refrain echoed through the speakers, the seats emptied fast.

The show had gone on, but it had concluded with a bang—thankfully, only figuratively—from which it might never recover. The centennial pageant may have been the last for the Rose Palace.

Lacy came backstage, her headset hanging around her neck. "Are you okay?" She pulled me into a hug. "What an insane way to win."

"Right, but... I mean..." I took the crown from my head in disbelief. "After all of this, I'm having a hard time believing that I actually won."

Aunt DeeDee joined us, eyeing the crown. "You won fair and square, sweetheart. I just looked at the tally sheets. The judges—even Dr. Bellingham before they took him away—were particularly impressed with your confidence and comportment, especially being such a new contestant. They tracked you from the first moment you stepped foot into the ballroom for the bonding session, and their notes said you were a natural. You scored one more point than the second place winner."

My heart nearly skipped a beat. I'd won this thing. Legitimately, like Aunt DeeDee before me, like Momma knew I could.

"So the money?"

"It's yours." Aunt DeeDee smiled. "The prizes will be

distributed just as they were awarded this evening. It's all held in a separate account from the Finches' personal assets. I'll meet with the board first thing Monday morning and see to everything. The winnings don't come overnight, but you'll get it all."

"That means I can go back to school. Maybe for the fall?"

Aunt DeeDee and Lacy both wrapped me in their arms at the same time, making us look like some kind of beauty pageant sculpture, arms entwined and heads together.

Despite my best efforts, I began to cry, my face buried in Aunt DeeDee's hair. "You know I did this for you and Momma."

My aunt rubbed a finger at the mascara under my eyes, and Lacy kept a hand on my shoulder.

"I know, baby girl." Aunt DeeDee took a long look at me, her eyes filling now. "She knew we would need the money—but more than that, she hoped finding your footing might help you get unstuck."

"I bet neither of y'all expected a murder to be involved," Lacy said, her eyes now watery but her voice tinged with sarcasm.

"True," Aunt DeeDee conceded. "Even I might not have let you compete if I'd known *that* was on the agenda."

"Thank you," I told her as I pulled her into a hug. "For everything."

"Of course, darlin'." She relaxed into my embrace. "Oh, and one more thing. Your friend Summer Patel won the title of Miss Rosie by a landslide, but don't tell her yet. We'll announce it and have a little toast with all the contestants after law enforcement clears out."

"Good. She deserves it," I said, happy for my friend, for Aunt DeeDee, for myself. "But if you ever want me to enter a pageant again, please make sure nobody dies."

My aunt wiped at her own eyes and grinned at me. "Deal."

We let Lacy get back to work. Tear-down was scheduled for first thing tomorrow.

The two of us Green girls—me and Aunt DeeDee—grabbed our things and walked back through the ballroom doors, ready to face whatever came next. This time and every time after, we would face it together.

EPILOGUE
MOMMA'S LETTER, MONTH TWELVE

Honeybee,

I know it's likely been quite the month for you, competing (and winning?) this year's Rose Palace Pageant. Regardless of your status in the show's rankings, please know I'm so proud of you. Whatever's in store for you, I'm rooting for you from my perch in heaven, hoping you'll find all the happiness you deserve.

When you were young, I took you to the pageant to support your aunt's passion for the hoopla, for the dresses and whimsy, for the snacks and silly nonsense of it all. But I'm finally ready to admit as I near the end, there was another reason as well. I wanted one person in particular to see that you existed, to get past their narcissistic lens, to behold you in all your wondrous beauty. I stuck my hand as close to the flame as I dared.

Which brings me, one year after my death, to a final order of business, a bit of news I wish I'd had the courage to share with you while I was still on your side of life and death. Alas, your mother was something of a coward when it came to sharing information that would change your life. I apologize, but I know I can't shirk the responsibility any longer.

Dearest, my Dakota, my Honeybee, as a child you asked about your father, and I always made up fairy tales to hide the truth. I wanted to wait as long as possible, maybe forever, and I thought the news could keep at least until you could handle the idea of your mother committing an indiscretion, a one-night stand at the end of a drunken soiree celebrating the conclusion of the 1996 pageant. I wanted you to stay out of that family's shadow. Because, you see, on that fateful night that brought you to me, I slept with Mr. Frederick Finch, owner of the Rose Palace Pageant.

The act was one of passion, though I'm sure you'd rather me not go into the details. Afterward I regretted it, that is until I realized that the night gave me you.

No one knew about what Frederick and I had done. Well, of course he knew we'd been together, but I don't think he ever paid enough attention to realize you were born about nine months after that night. By the time you made an appearance, he'd closed the hotel at The Rose and announced the birth of Savilla.

Though it was tempting to ask him for financial help over the years, frankly, I didn't want him involved in our lives. Living in Aubergine, I've watched the way the Finches operate as if they are somehow one of us and above us at the same time. I didn't want to owe him, I didn't want him making decisions on your behalf, and I certainly didn't want him luring you, an impressionable child, into his extravagant lifestyle. It is true that he could've provided ample child support, but we had plenty—until we didn't and, at that point, after so many years, I couldn't bring myself to tell you the truth. I'm sorry, but please know I only acted out of the intense love I felt the first time your tiny foot gave me a little kick.

Now it's your turn to decide what to do with this information. You could be wealthy. You could be co-owner of a giant mansion and a silly pageant. Heck, you could have a sister. Whatever you decide, I know it will be a grand adventure. Forgive me for not telling you sooner, and be the amazing Dakota I know you are.

Love,
Momma

P.S. If you have a chance, tell Frederick thank you for that night long ago. I don't regret it one bit because I got the real prize: you.

A LETTER FROM THE AUTHOR

Thank you for reading *A Beauty Queen's Guide to Murder and Mayhem*. I hope you enjoyed Dakota Green's first of many adventures. If you'd like to hear about my new and upcoming releases, you can sign up for my author newsletter.

www.stormpublishing.co/kristen-bird

If you enjoyed *A Beauty Queen's Guide to Murder and Mayhem* and could spare a moment to leave a review, that would be hugely appreciated. Even a short review can make all the difference in encouraging a reader to discover my books for the first time. Thank you so much!

I set my mysteries in the southeast region of the United States, the place where my family has lived for generations. When I began envisioning Dakota's roots, I was particularly drawn to the setting of the Blue Ridge Mountains with their hazy beauty. The Rose Palace is inspired by the sprawling Biltmore Estate in Asheville, North Carolina, and my search history is filled with photos, quirky facts, and blueprints for this breathtaking estate.

Though I'm neither a beauty pageant contestant nor a cowgirl, I live right outside of Houston, Texas, where pageants are rampant and the rodeo is the main event every spring. In fact, in high school, I cheered on one of my best friends in the Miss Houston competition, and years later, as a mom to young kids, I often took them just down the road from our house to a working cattle ranch that gives daily tours. In other words, to be Texan is to have basic knowledge of beauty products and our equine friends.

Dakota and company are an incredibly fun cast of characters to write, and I hope you enjoyed reading about them just as much as I've loved imagining them and their world.

Kristen

www.kristenbird.com

facebook.com/kristen.bird.writes

x.com/kbirdwrites

instagram.com/kristenbirdwrites

linkedin.com/in/kristen-bird-b28233224

ACKNOWLEDGMENTS

Thanks to my agent Jill Marsal for first believing that *Beauty Queen* should be out in the reading world. You are fast, efficient, and communicative, and I so enjoy working with you.

Thanks to my editor Claire Bord for seeing Dakota's heart so clearly. Your notes are excellent, and you make her character sparkle and shine.

Thanks to my mom, Kathy Brock, and my friend, Gina Johnson, for reading multiple versions of this book and giving tons of feedback to help the story flow. Thanks to Katie for reading things in one weekend whenever I ask.

Thanks to my writing group for reading early pages and for providing emotional support through all the highs and lows of writing. Olivia Day Wallace, Allison Buccola, Jennifer Fawcett, and Jenna Satterthwaite have been hugely influential in helping shape my approach to this weird thing we call publishing.

Thanks to Jessica Lee for reading this book in one day on a road trip with three kiddos who were likely incessantly asking for snacks from the backseats. I love that you'll tune out the noise for me. Now, give them their Skittles and Cheetos.

Thanks to Dr. Tara McDonald Johnson, Dr. Jenny Howell, and Dr. Robin Riehl. Y'all are the kind of doctors I want to be when I grow up. I'm so glad to know that you'll be there whenever I fall apart.

Thanks to Sarah Dean, whose friendship and humor are all over this book. Thanks to Brandi Lucher and Christie Green for the many prayers. Thanks to Dr. Marilyn Copeland, who first read my writing twenty years ago and said it was good even though it was not.

Thanks to Macie, Sadie, and Ruby, who teach me something new about love and kindness every day. You three are amazing humans, and I'm so proud to be your mom. And, finally, thanks to Tim, who does dishes and folds laundry and makes dinner so I can write. You are the best partner and friend that I could imagine, and I would do a thousand lifetimes with you. I love you for far more than your cooking skills, but they do help.